FIC     Gough, William.

The last white man
in Panama

$16.95

| DATE | | |
|---|---|---|
| | | |
| | | |
| | | |
| | | |
| | | |
| | | |
| | | |
| | | |
| | | |
| | | |
| | | |
| | | |
| | | |

# — THE LAST —
# WHITE MAN
# IN PANAMA

WILLIAM GOUGH

VIKING

# VIKING

Penguin Books Canada Ltd., 2801 John Street,
Markham, Ontario, Canada L3R 1B4
Penguin Books, Harmondsworth, Middlesex, England
Viking Penguin Inc., 40 West 23rd Street,
New York, New York 10010 U.S.A.
Penguin Books Australia Ltd., Ringwood,
Victoria, Australia
Penguin Books (N.Z.) Ltd., 182-190 Wairau Road,
Auckland 10, New Zealand

First published by Penguin Books Canada Ltd., 1987

F|c

R00623 52594

Printed in Canada

**Canadian Cataloguing in Publication Data**

Gough, William
  The last white man in Panama

ISBN 0-670-81659-0

I. Title.

PS8563.08396L38 1987    C813'.54    C87-093529-1
PR9199.3.G68L38 1987

*To Anna Sandor*

# —THE LAST— WHITE MAN IN PANAMA

## 1

Azucar slept late the day she was killed.

The morning began with children's cries squeezing in through the slatted blinds along with the car horns and police sirens. It was a Tuesday, the tail end of the rainy season. Rangoo the cockatoo screamed and perched on the window ledge while Maria the ocelot emerged from under the bed. She arched her claws disdainfully and fell asleep again.

Red had been up for about an hour, moving carefully so he wouldn't wake Azucar. Today was her holiday. No working the casinos, no looking for rich tourists, no men for her except him. And he was also taking the day off. No third-rate con games, no helping sailors find a map to paradise, no rolling drunks. He stretched back on a faded green armchair, staring up at the ceiling fan. It hadn't turned for more than a year and this wasn't the morning to fix it. Rangoo flew from the window, landed on his bare shoulder and began to take small, stroking bites along his earlobe, never closing her beak enough to hurt him.

Azucar stirred and reached towards the empty side of the bed. Other people might wake up with small moans and groans, eyes blinking out the sun. She woke up talking.

"Red, I have a plan. A plan for when I stop the life. Do you want to hear?"

She sat up quickly, breasts swinging, as she reached for her pack of Camels and scraped a kitchen match across the cluttered nightside table. Sucking in the smoke, she grinned at Red.

"Sure I want to listen. I'm too tired to do any talking."

"The other girls, they like jewels..."

"I like jewels. If it's time to skip town they're easy to carry."

"You do the listening, I do the talking. Are you paying attention?"

"I always pay attention. That's what accounts for my success in life."

"Good. Go let in the day."

Red tried opening the blinds at the same time he was pulling up the pants of his famous wrinkled white suit. Azucar dragged contentedly on her cigarette, cradling her knees to her breasts as she talked.

"The other girls do not plan right. They all want America, they all want an apartment, a house."

Light spilled in as Red finally opened the blinds. Blinking, he turned away and squinted as he moved into the shadows.

"Don't you want a house?"

"I want a home, Red. With no walls, no bed, no floor, no roof."

"You'll get wet when it rains."

Azucar didn't laugh. Instead she lit another Camel off the butt of the first and studied him silently. His face was Irish rough and jowly, shaved close. His eyes were sharp blue and, unlike her, it only took him one glance to size people up. When other eyes stared, his own would cloud over and hide like milk had been poured through them.

"Don't make jokes, just listen, because someday you may discover I'm gone."

"I'm sorry. From now on I'll be real serious. I promise. How about going back to bed?"

She gave him one of her smiles. The one that men noticed even before they saw her body. The one that got them checking their wallets and hoping.

"After I make enough money to buy my mother a proper house, stuffed with food and chocolates, then I will go away to live in the jungle where only you can find me. The ocelot will bring me food, small warm animals. She and your Azucar will eat them raw in the night and purr. The cockatoo will bring me gossip from the city, we will laugh and talk as the stars twinkle on her beak. I will need a parrot for my confessor, and I will need you for love. You don't laugh?"

"Why should I laugh? Makes sense to me, as long as I can visit. Now, what I want is some breakfast. Do you want breakfast?"

"All I want is another smoke, but you must eat much food, because I love you fat, I love you pale. Today we will stay in the shade and eat."

In the marketplace the rain had stopped, making the air smell ripe. A bloated sheep had washed into the road and a condor had buried its head in the carcass. The bird dipped up when Red and

Azucar went by, as if to say, "Don't come near. I got this one staked out."

A flood of water spattered them from a bus that swayed by, covered with vivid paintings of orange and yellow. It nearly ran over a child who was playing in the street, naked except for a shiny disposable diaper that gleamed in the sun like a snowbank.

The bus's radiator sent a small cloud rising in front of the sunset painted above the window. Red had always liked buses, even in Boston, where the exhaust pipe spilled clouds across the snow towards his six-year-old eyes. In those days he would hang around the bus terminal listening to the loudspeaker rattle off destinations. He'd think of his Daddy who was just a postcard by then and wonder if the Boston bus, with its New England snow melting, could get to Bogota, to Santa Cruz to Rio Bamba or Isla de Sangallan rocking through the jungle.

His plans in those days were simple. He would hide in the big suitcase, the one with the coat of stickers showing warm and steamy places. Would lie as quiet as a lizard until the bus had bounced into the jungle. Then, when the suitcase was opened, he'd jump into the arms of his father, who would put down a machete, unsling a gunbelt and spin Red like a ball in the sun.

But in the terminal in Boston the loudspeaker never called out the names of any exotic places. It only talked about New England, and he didn't think his father was anywhere there.

Red forgot about Boston and stared at another bus that squeaked, splashed and swerved to a stop right in front of them. Azucar swore at the driver, expertly and in three languages.

A family of Indians got off. Their hair was oiled and clean, and their young daughter had gold bracelets tight against the deep brown of her arms, burning sunshine into her flesh. The Indians unfolded the vivid cloth-cut *mola* with its purple cats on red trees, and glanced briefly at Red, while their eyes blowdarted towards Azucar. One of the *molas* showed American and Panamanian flags growing out of the jungle. Another showed a cat with its claws becoming a tree. The oldest of the Indians reached past these to one unopened piece of cloth. Never looking away from Azucar, he pulled it out of the shadows and quickly into the sunlight, where light caught the small black figure of a naked woman. She was surrounded by the jungle, and through the thick green cloth peered feline eyes, cut like machete marks. It made Red shiver, but Azucar walked towards it and held it up.

"Buy me this, Red."

"Goddamn it, you know I've only got enough cash for the casino."

"Ah, an American lover. The other girls all tell me I'm crazy. They say I should not go out with Red Williams because he is fat, he is pale, he's broke all the time..."

The Indians now grew interested in him. They all nodded and grinned when Azucar continued to go through her list of his faults. Finally the old Indian stood up and, bowing, presented the *mola* to Azucar, insisting it was a gift. She planted a kiss directly and wetly on his wrinkled lips and sambaed into the traffic wearing the jungle cloth over her shoulder. Red grabbed her out of the path of another bus, and they kissed.

"Hey, you still do that real good. Perhaps I should keep you, even though you're a Yank and never buy me anything?"

"The *mola* gives me the creeps."

"I love it. It smells of the jungle and danger."

Even though she laughed, the feeling of chill that Red had when he first saw the picture wouldn't go away. He felt like someone was watching them, swallowed in the noise and insect color of the marketplace. But when he looked around, everything was normal. The street was jammed with large Yankee cars, rusted and out of date, all V8 engines and missing mufflers. Pomegranates were resting on platforms of plank, smells of deep-fried chicken drifted out of Deli Pollo, and from inside the Restaurante Labrador came the clink of glasses. Red forgot about the feeling of being followed and started towards that sweet sound of glass on glass.

"Azucar, let's get breakfast. We can drink it together."

"One minute. If I receive a gift, I must give a gift."

"Live like that and you'll never have any money."

She laughed, loud and deep, the kind of laugh that made anyone near join in. Red suddenly felt better, linked arms with her and turned the corner. He licked his lips and thought of the morning's first drink, but he was content to wait.

In the dark of the alley, there was a door that led inside to a small shrine. The outside odors of the marketplace mixed with the scent of burning candles as hot wax dripped down and rippled in still wings upon the sand. Azucar crossed herself and slipped a balboa into the box near the fresh candles. She placed the candle in the sand at the feet of the virgin and lit it with another of her kitchen matches. She crossed herself once more before kneeling down.

Red looked up at the face of the statue. He'd lost his faith a long time ago in the smell of incense sparking on charcoal in a Boston church, but he always liked to look at this virgin. She was set in marble and around her ran the words *Oh, Maria Sin Pecado Concebiga Rogad Por Nosotros Que Recurrimos A Vos.* Red didn't really have to translate. He heard the words in the original Latin, they spun across the ocean from Massachusetts, and he thought of his own mother, Mary. The reason he liked this plaster statue was because she reminded him of her.

In the back of the shrine, tucked into the shadows at the edge of the door, were two men. One was lean and sharp like a knife blade, the other man was large with eyes that glowed like a cat's. They watched Red and Azucar, and waited for the night.

# 2

In Boston, Karen Chapman decided to give up hope.

She decided this somewhere between the time she began misting her orchids and the moment when her husband, Scott Chapman, announced that he was leaving her again.

The last time he'd told Karen they were through, she'd screamed, cried and pleaded. She'd even, months after the separation, phoned him up and asked him out for a drink. The drink had led to Borachi's, their favorite restaurant, and the dinner had led him back to their apartment and that had led to his moving in again.

They managed to stay together for a few months after that. Karen had tried to swing better shifts at her job in the television station, so she could be in the apartment whenever Scott came home from the law firm. She'd ended up losing the kind of story she'd always liked to report; the seamy, the gritty and the down and dirty. But she kept telling herself that there'd never been a divorce in her family and she'd done her best to make sure there never would be.

She and her husband had stayed together until now. "Now" being the time that Scott had looked up at work and seen a new woman. Her name, he told Karen, was Brooke, she was articling and she was assertive, aggressive and ambitious. Those were all qualities that Scott had seemed to dislike in Karen, qualities that she'd been trying to fix. She began to spray the plants with more force. If she concentrated, she could hardly hear Scott over the sound of mist on the leaves.

"This time it's final. Better for both of us. Even if this were not as good an action as it might be, in ethical terms, it is, for all parties concerned, the best of, if I may say it, possible worlds."

There was more along the same line, all delivered from his fit and sun-lamped face as it looked up at her while she watered the assortment of her plants that were outlined against the latest Boston blizzard.

Karen tuned Scott out, and looked at the lushness of a deep purple orchid as she sprayed it. The mist rose warm and moist around her and as she sniffed, it seemed for a moment that she could smell a better place, a more dangerous place, a land of dreams. However, the wind spit snow at the panes, the mist cooled and when Karen looked down, Scott was still talking. A record of Bartók, his favorite, continued playing at the exactly correct level as he stood, earnest and neat, suitcase and squash racquet in his hands. Karen smiled at him, aimed the plant misting device and squirted it directly in his eyes.

"Goddamn it, Karen, do you consider that the act of a mature woman?"

Karen didn't reply. Instead she stepped down the ladder and continued to squirt him as he retreated towards the door.

"Half of everything is mine. Half. I'll be back for it."

"Why don't you start with the Bartók?"

And she grabbed it from the turntable, with a scratch and scrape, and frisbeed it towards the fleeing Scott. It reached the door just after him and shattered against the portal. There was a nice clatter on the perfectly refinished pine floors. Karen then went to the record cabinet and began tossing a large collection of treasured records around the apartment. She was careful to let none of them go sailing towards her plants.

Then she picked out an old album, her own signed Elvis Presley record, which Scott had claimed would fetch a pretty penny and should be sold. She turned the volume up to a totally unacceptable level and made herself a rum punch. As Elvis sang "Love Me Tender," she sipped her drink and returned to spraying her flowers. They still smelled of dreams and the mist felt as hot as the tropics.

## 3

In the middle of Panama there was a small white clapboard house. Jungle light spattered faded boards and dappled the backs of lazy lizards that hung like drunken sailors from every warp of the wood. Despite the heat a wood fire was burning in the house and clouds of damp smoke lifted slightly from the chimney, rolled down the roof and caught near the folds of moss at the edges.

Animals and birds, tree frogs and huge insects stopped their creeping crawling buzzing snapping and crunching as the sounds of Freddy Fender twanged around the tree trunks.

"If he brings you happiness..."

And the frogs joined in.

"Then I wish you both the best..."

Fuzzy spiders rubbed their legs and checked the epicenters of their webs.

> ...It's your happiness that matters most of all.
> But if he ever breaks your heart,
> If the teardrops ever start,
> I'll be there before the next teardrop falls.

The lizards wiggled in time to the music as the record joined the jungle sounds and from inside the hut a damp baritone sang along and even the trees seemed to sing as the evening rain suddenly crashed down and vibraphoned the leaves.

Inside his little house Jack smiled and drank tequila. He was old, scrawny, tanned the color of deep oak, and he hardly shuddered as the tequila slipped down his throat. Rain hit the roof in great tin buckets of sound and Freddy's voice quavered from the record when the old Victrola slowed down.

Jack reached over and gave it a quick couple of turns as he admired the sheer wonder of the singing. Hidden in the vibrato were the echoes of jail cells and the clinking of guards' keys, things Jack was also familiar with. A lot of sorrow—a lot of life. It was either Fender or Caruso in the evening concerts and this time Freddy had won out.

Despite the jungle and its cries, despite the smell of a rainforest in a downpour, despite the parrot's creak and jaw from a nearby tree, the inside of the hut gave a lingering sense of being somewhere a couple of compass points off New England. The rocker had been shaped by crazed Massachusetts hands. An easy chair smelled of the ocean, and so did an old blue sea chest in the corner.

Smoke drifted up from the open hearth. The back was made of solid firebrick, and around the front ran a handcarved mantel showing scenes of sea battles. Galleon attacked galleon while a windjammer rounded the corner of the mantel to a half-finished port where the carver ran out of patience.

There were no photos along the walls, but a special enclosed series of shelves ran down one side of the hut, filled with records of operas and country-and-western music. There were some old cylinders black and coiled with music from a simpler age.

Jack smiled. Rain trickled through the roof and down his collar. He didn't worry. Tomorrow was the time to buy his weapons and go look for work. Money would be good, the old familiar tingle of danger would return and he could get a rare pressing of *La Bohème* that would make the toucan sing.

Panama City was waiting.

## 4

The Hotel El Panama had decided that Christmas should come early this year—a genuine evergreen tree glittered against the golden tiles. Perhaps it was the glitter that changed Red and Azucar's plans. Instead of making their way towards the loving click of the roulette wheel at the casino next door, they stopped. They could hear the dice, the clatter of the chips, the snap of cards on cushion but Red chose to pay a visit to the Christmas tree. Like two defective wise men they made their way towards the glow of a purple neon star.

The tree was covered in metal garlands, emblazoned with red and green sparks, and laden with candy canes. Like a demented elf at harvest time, Red began gathering armfuls of the candy. Azucar whooped, the kind of whoop that can only be properly done after a day of drinking at the Restaurante Labrador, and joined in.

Red sang "I'm Dreaming of a White Christmas" while the sweat rolled off his brow and tourists looked at him from the outdoor bar. Azucar sang along in Spanish, and picked up the many canes that Red kept dropping. The doorman frowned and went to get the security guard.

Finally the tree was stripped, and Red and Azucar sat down under it and began munching contentedly. Azucar leaned over to lick off some splinters of peppermint from Red's lips just as the lights of the tree were obscured by the arrival of the hotel's security guard.

Neither Red nor Azucar looked up, but Red did stop chewing long enough to speak.

"It must be Juan Chinchilla. There is no need to look, I can tell by the pungent bouquet of your unique cigar."

"No one likes my cigar. They say it is foul, that it stinks like the sewer at the Pacific beach."

"They also say it smells better than you," added Azucar.

Juan laughed and sat down with a thump next to them. He chose a candy cane from the group that Red offered to him.

"In many ways it does. That is, to tell you the truth, the only reason I can stomach smoking such a thing."

And he laughed even more. The lights of the Christmas tree glistened off him, his oily dark poorly shaved face shook and wobbled.

"I am supposed to throw you two out of this area. They say you are a disruption to the tourists. I say, because I enjoy continuing to be paid as a security guard, that I will go and make you vamoose. So now, I must do my reluctant duty. Vamoose."

"But Red wants to gamble and we are on holiday."

"How much do you have to gamble with, my friend?"

Red set down the candy canes and extracted an old wallet with someone else's initials monogrammed upon it.

"Twenty dollars."

"That isn't enough."

Azucar reached down the cleavage of her dress to extract a wad of money.

"He has three hundred dollars."

Red took the money, stared at it and back again at Azucar.

"You can't have that much. You haven't turned a trick all day. We're poor!"

Azucar winked at him.

"I have some secrets, Red."

"I don't want to gamble. Let's get a bottle and go back to your place."

"Sorry, but my vacation is over."

Juan had delicately turned his back on this section of the conversation and busied himself hanging candy canes back on the tree. Even the half-eaten ones were returned to the branches. He whistled *La Cucaracha*, until it seemed Red and Azucar had stopped arguing. Then he spoke.

"There is another reason for you to come back from vacation. Two men are asking for your services. I told them I do not normally find women, but..."

Red knew the vacation was over. He wandered away, counting the money while he walked, and discovered that he had three hundred and twenty-five dollars. Whatever the hotel had requested, the casino didn't seem to mind that Red had come to gamble. He fanned himself with the cash as he walked in through the doors.

By the time Azucar came in through the same doors, Red had managed to lose all but his original twenty-five dollars. He turned to go towards her but she touched her finger briefly to her nose, and he changed course. She was working and he knew enough to stay clear. This day that had started with such promise had turned bleak again. In despair he cashed in his last chip, the twenty-dollar one, for some sparkling silver dollars and moved towards the slot machines. It had come to that.

He saw that Azucar was talking with two men: Americans. She had leaned towards them so they could look down the front of her dress.

She was now touching them and glancing from crotch to crotch. She leaned closer and closer until it seemed they were touching each other through her, the tall lean one, and the fat one, both blending into a single figure.

Red started to feel angry, knew he shouldn't, and turned his attentions to the slot machine. He picked the one called "El Grande" so he could burn through his money as fast as possible. He stuffed ten silver dollars into it and pulled the huge handle. It clicked like a cement mixer as it moved inexorably towards three totally different symbols. While the machine did its futile spin, Red looked at his love. For one moment the two men had turned aside from her and were busy checking their wallets and talking to each other. In that instant Azucar smiled across the room at him, the same smile that he'd seen in her vacation that morning, and she blew a kiss towards him. The machine stopped its whirring, and for one second all the sound in the casino stopped. He blew her a kiss, and was going to cross over and run away with her far from the casino, but it was too late. The men had turned back. Azucar was now leaving with them and the ten silver dollars felt small and hot as sound returned to the casino. Red slammed in the last ten silver dollars and pulled the handle again. He strained to hear what Azucar and the men were saying. Just as they vanished, a little bit of their conversation floated back to him. Both men were speaking Spanish and this startled him, because he could have sworn these guys wouldn't know a word of the lingo. Something was wrong and Red was about to warn Azucar when he hit the jackpot.

Bells rang and money spilled from "El Grande" into the plastic container and then over its edges in a mound of silver that started to fill the carpet around his feet. Hundreds of silver dollars rolled and bounced and made tracks in the scarlet plush, pinging against each other as they fell. Red was on a roll and he knew it. For a moment he thought of Azucar, but figured she'd be gone by now, and perhaps he was wrong anyway, and the money kept pinging and bouncing and if he followed the roll, chased luck, she would never have to work again and they could go away and live in the jungle. He started gathering up the silver dollars, and looked around the casino, knowing it was waiting to give him more money.

## 5

The last night of Azucar's life was also the longest.

It began with great promise when the men from the casino turned out to have plenty of money. She'd named a price double what she usually asked. It had been a chance but if she'd lost then, what the hell, she would have been back on vacation. She was actually disappointed when they'd agreed to the cost.

When she suggested they get a taxi cab, the fat man only smiled while the thin one went away into the shadows. There was a click of metal and a sleek, expensive car pulled out of the shadows. Its headlights were off, and only the gleam of reflected Christmas tree bulbs pulled along its bumper.

Azucar and the fat man climbed inside the car and she stroked the smooth leather of the seats. She looked at the hotel doorway as Juan Chinchilla emerged and looked around. Azucar wound down the window and was about to wave to him, but the fat man put his hand over her mouth so she couldn't call out. She jerked her head towards him, but, with a gesture and a grin, he managed to turn his action into a joke. When she looked at the doorway again, Juan had vanished.

The *mola* that she'd tucked over her shoulder was still rakishly in place, but now it seemed to cut into her skin, so she loosened the cloth and it fell into her lap. The car picked up speed and passed the brightness of the casino entrance. Light fell on the small black figure in the *mola*, and shone on the cat's eyes in the jungle. When Azucar looked at the fat man his eyes were the same.

The car slipped into a network of alleyways and crossed the city without going near any of the main streets.

"You have been here before?"

"Once," purred the fat man. "Once with my boss."

"And you?" she asked the thin man.

"My first visit, and my last."

"You never know that. Perhaps if I make this time as good as you hope, it will not be the last?"

The thin man laughed, but when Azucar asked the meaning of the joke he said nothing. The fat man chuckled a little. She felt that something might be very wrong, and knew it for certain when the car pulled up outside her apartment. She reached for the doorhandle, but there wasn't one, and as she smashed her hand towards the window, the fat man caught her fist. Then there was a sound of steel against steel and the thin man turned around. His knife edge caught the glow of the dashboard light.

"Azucar, I will kill you in this car if you make the faintest noise. If you try to call out you are dead. No matter how scared you are do not say one word. Understand?"

She nodded. There was a click and the car door opened. The fat man stepped outside and extended his hand. She flinched until she realized that he was only offering to help her out. Her legs wobbled and she had to hold tightly to his arm.

As they moved down the hallway towards her room every step seemed to take an hour and each breath she took echoed in her ears. Her heartbeat filled the hallway and she blinked rapidly like she was trying to get rid of a bad dream. What she hoped was a nightmare wouldn't go away and the long slow walk to her room continued.

The door was already open and the lights were on. The cockatoo's cage had a blanket pulled over it, and there was no sign of the ocelot. The bed was unmade from her last night with Red, and lying on the sheets was a man whose face she remembered. He was holding a package in his hand, and he opened it as she entered the room.

The door closed just as Azucar realized there was nowhere in the world for her to run.

## 6

It was the middle of the next morning when Red's luck changed.

Until that time he'd been on a roll and he knew it. That feeling had slipped a little when he'd made his way to the roulette wheel where he noticed a slight tip in fate and moved instead to the kidney-shaped poker table. He waited until an Albertan dropped out of the game—a big loser. Red had ordered a stack of chips and then helped the other players get rid of their money. He'd talked and talked at the quiet shrine of the table until he'd spun tales of love and death and the days of revolution and adventure in the Americas.

The other players had not noticed how much money they were losing to such a wonderful stranger; they just felt glad to be at a table of danger and adventure. One player was a movie producer who told Red that he should become a writer and who once in a while called for a phone to try to track down Brando in Colombia. The producer had a doctor's bag that was filled with money until he joined the game. The money went while Red talked about life. He had always maintained that you didn't have to cheat to win at poker, it was necessary only to be a good storyteller.

When the sun rose he felt tired, his jaw hurt from so much conversation, and he felt that little turn of the wheel that means *now* is the moment to get out of the game. So, for the first time in his life he did. It was because of Azucar and the way her eyes would light up when she saw the cash, when she found out that any dream she had could be real. He craved a drink, but wanted to see her even more, so he was out of the casino before anyone knew he was going.

He spent the afternoon doing some complicated banking, realizing that he was a rich man. He salted away his money as well as it could be salted before closing time. As a crook, Red had a great fondness for banks, their marble floors, solid steel vaults, cool air and sense of security. They sensed his love today and were glad to see and to help him. Putting ten thousand into his money belt as a gift for Azucar, he headed towards her place, figuring that with daylight the two guys would be gone, their cash spent, perhaps feeling a little embarrassed with each other.

When he neared her apartment he saw a small boy pedaling towards old Panama. The boy had a bright yellow cart with a block of ice tied down upon it. In front of this block of ice was a group of bottles with different syrups as bright as a new box of crayons. Red took out a twenty and waved it. The cart stopped instantly, and the boy's knife plowed little drifts of snow across the surface of the ice. Quick as a blink the snow was scraped into paper cones and, when Red nodded, lime was spilled across one, and orange across the other. He

gave the boy the whole twenty and strolled towards Azucar's apartment.

He passed the old woman who lived next door to
her and shouted in Spanish as he went by.

"I'd bring her flowers, but they don't taste as
good."

The old woman laughed

"They don't melt down your arm either."

And Red looked at the red and green ice melting and running down his sleeve. He didn't care,
he could buy a hundred new suits, he could throw
them away for each day of the week until he and
Azucar went to live in the jungle.

The door wasn't locked, and he opened it very
quietly. The syrup on his fingers stuck to the door-
knob.

Inside, the lights were on and the blinds half
closed. The cockatoo had its cage covered, the ocelot was nowhere to be seen. The overhead fan
turned and caught the sun's rays as they sloped between the blinds. All around the room there were
feathers from ripped and slashed pillows. The
walls had been cut open, the rug ripped apart, and
at the center of a blood-soaked, torn mattress, with
her throat slashed, was Azucar, his love who
would never know of their fortune.

He felt sick and ran to the small washroom off
the bedroom. Tiles were peeled off the walls and
the medicine cabinet torn down. He could see
shards of smashed porcelain all around the room.

When he went back, he found fragments of the
bedsheets and spread them so as to cover Azucar's
face. The overhead fan was reflected in her staring
eyes. He took the blanket from Rangoo's cage, and
heard him swear. The swearing stopped when the

cage door opened and the cockatoo fluttered to perch on his shoulder.

The ocelot crept from under the bed and tried to look fierce.

"You're no more than a bloody housecat. Why didn't you slice the bastards who did this? What did you do, purr?"

The ocelot rubbed along his ankles and Rangoo said very distinctly, "Bitch." Red scooped up Maria, curling her into the crook of his arm. He let Rangoo stay balanced on his shoulder and headed towards the door. Just after opening it, he thought a moment, took out a large dotted handkerchief and wiped the knob. Then he headed along the hallway and down a creaking set of steps. With the record he had, the petty crimes he'd committed, there was no way he could report the murder. He also knew just how interested the *policía* would be in the case. For them it would not be the death of Azucar his love, it would be the killing of some cheap whore.

He was fat, out of shape and a physical coward, but he was also the only person who could do any avenging for Azucar. Before he did that there was a visit that he had to make. There were a hundred awful ways that her mother could find out about the murder, so telling her was the first thing he had to do. After that he would find the two men who went away with Azucar.

He moved towards the marketplace and Rangoo screamed at a passing bus. The ocelot slept in his arms.

Red peered inside the Restaurante Labrador, but didn't see the man he was looking for. Even in the shadows Alberto would have stood out, his shirts provided their own illumination. He went over to a battered light blue Falcon which was parked next to the Restaurante, opened the door and got in. The windows had been left down and the seats were soaking wet from the rain, but he didn't care. Rangoo yelled "bitch," while Maria snored.

He sat as still as the small breeze that drifted through the market. A rainbow of a bus tossed a flock of hens into the air, lost its brakes, coasted up a hill, paused, and then crashed through a fruit stand. People began yelling at each other, and Miguel, the owner of the small cantina next to the Restaurante, leaned out.

"Red! Come inside into the cool, don't let your brains boil over."

"There aren't any left to boil."

Rangoo yelled "si," and everyone in the cantina laughed. Alberto appeared from the fish market. He was wearing a lime-green shirt and smelled of wine and tuna.

"If you want to steal my car, old friend, you should begin by sitting in the front seat."

"I need a ride, Alberto."

"No deal. You never have any money. You don't even have enough money to clean your suit."

Red looked down at his sleeves. They were still stained from the ice cones, and beneath the orange stain was a small spot of congealed blood. He felt like crying and couldn't move his lips to say anything else. Instead he held a hundred-dollar bill out the window. Alberto was in the car before Rangoo could screech one more time. They started up, bouncing over a few remaining coconuts from the smashed stand, and passed the bus driver who was busy trying to prove the entire accident was the fault of the fruit vendor.

What Red didn't see, as Alberto sped through too small a space between a couple of huge, antiquated trucks, were the two men who were watching him. The fat man's eyes still shone like a cat's, as the lean sharpened man started up their car. They tried to follow Red, but couldn't because of the havoc created when Alberto scraped the fenders off both trucks at the same time. His own bumper was tugged away and spun clanging like a balboa on pavement. The trucks collided and the street was blocked.

Red ignored this because his mind was filled with thoughts of Azucar. The first time he'd seen her was at the Blue Goose, where the smoke draped her with a shawl and she looked at him and winked. He had gone into the joint looking for booze. The wallet he'd lifted had only thirty bucks U.S. left and he didn't want to invest it anywhere but in a bottle or two. That's the way he tried to think, but Azucar's look made him unbutton his jacket and smile at her.

She was kind and he was fine, so afterwards they felt like talking, while the clock ticked away into what was supposed to be the time of the next customer and they laughed until there was a drunken sailor opening the bedroom door and demanding that his turn start now. Red told Azucar that she'd better leave because the sailor wanted a turn with him, and she laughed but the sailor didn't and the fight started and...But he couldn't dare start to remember or he would cry again, so he looked at the ocelot and at the cockatoo.

Alberto drove towards the airport, through a section where the jungle tangled its way past some huts towards the road.

"Stop here."

"No sweat. You've only used up twenty bucks. You can go anywhere you want for another two hours."

"Four hours!"

And Red opened the door. Rangoo jumped back onto his shoulder from her most recent perch on the front dash. Maria stretched and purred. Red got out and walked to the very edge of the jungle where he let Maria go and tried to get Rangoo to leave his shoulder. The ocelot looked like she was being asked to swim in cold water, but after a few encouraging words from Rangoo, caught the scent of something small and furry, and slipped into the foliage after it. Rangoo didn't want to leave Red's shoulder so he had to hold her by the legs and throw her towards the sun. Rangoo was arching her feathers to return when she suddenly realized that she was flying higher than ever before. She caught a thermal and was startled, pinwheeling into shadow. "Bitch" floated from the jungle, as other birds began to complain.

Red turned back towards the car. First he was going to tell Azucar's mother about her daughter's death. Then he would return to the city, go to the casino and find his friend's murderers. After that he was going to kill them.

## 7

On the same morning, Jack had awakened before the jungle. He could hear the sound of sleeping animals and the chill of vampire bats coming home. Lighting no lamps, he shifted from bed as secure as an old blind man. He walked in the dark towards the stove and remembered, just before crashing into it, where he'd left the rocking chair the night before. This was a game he'd always played, even as a child, this moving around in the dark by memory. It had saved his life a few times, but no doubt about it—he was getting older.

He cooked breakfast in the dark and then ate by the first light. In his own house he didn't keep any weapons except for his throwing knife. He'd always figured if anyone was waiting for him it was better if they brought their own guns. His throwing knife was always secure in the small sheath just a neck scratch away from his collar. He touched his neck and quick as light let the knife arc across the room where it quivered in the door. It was a fraction of an inch off from the center of the boards. Jack sipped his coffee and shook his head.

Getting up, he retrieved the knife and then cleaned the dishes. From under the floorboards he took out a small kit that held his battle fatigues along with some other odds and ends. He slipped it over his shoulder.

He let a toucan loose and it fanned its way to a nearby tree where it settled and teetered. Jack always thought it was going to fall over following its huge beak to the ground. But it didn't, just stared at him with its Buster Keaton sad eyes. Then he set his security devices. From a small cage nearby he shook two tarantulas into his house and then closed the door behind him.

He drifted along a path that no one else, besides the animals, would have known was a path. He crossed a river that smoked and swirled as he made his way along a narrow log slippery with green slime. Stopping for a moment, he listened to the bellbird's clear loud call and watched a scarlet macaw, white beak like bone, red and blue feathers like blood and sky.

Then he followed a path that knifed its way in a thin edge along the cliffs, and he was on his way to catch the bus. The afternoon was steamy and the sun licked through his shirt to his back. It felt like a perfect day.

## ❧ 8 ❧

Red would have welcomed a storm with rain and ripping, tearing winds. Instead, the sun returned and the water dried, and small children came out to play.

As the Falcon bounced its way up the dirt road towards a hut, children fell into line, running and trying to tag the fenders. One small boy grabbed the edges of metal that used to hold the bumper and skidded along over the muddy road. His little callused feet left twin tracks dead center of the car's tire prints. Alberto slowly applied the brakes so the boy wouldn't flip over the trunk. Then he flung open the door and started chasing him. Red sat inside the car for a while, but Alberto didn't return. The engine was left running. Blue plumes of smoke poured out of the Falcon, and a breeze carried the fumes into a few small huts, making more children come running out to see what was happening. The car backfired twice and then cut out, giving out two final greasy clouds of smoke. When it had stopped, Red left the car and was surrounded by more children than he could count. A young black teenager flashed a smile and then held hands over her head in a karate-chop pose.

"Are you from the movies?"

"No, kid. I'm from the city."

"Do you have money?"

Red gave her a dollar and all the other children held out their hands. A big boy with ears like jug handles took the next dollar and skipped back into the darkness of his hut. A chicken, scared, fluttered out into the road. Some toddlers chased after the bird, making it hop every time it attempted the dignity of a landing. Red gave out all of his dollars, and then turned his pockets inside out. When they saw there was no more they all left, except for one little girl who was dressed in a blue swim suit. She was about seven years old, her hair was wet from the rain and pulled back with plastic barrettes in the form of ducks. When she smiled all her upper teeth were missing. Her smile was so broad and so crinkled that Red grinned back.

"You look familiar."

"I know who you are. Christina described you to me many times. You are Red."

"Then you must be her sister, but I called her Azucar."

He looked away before speaking again.

"I called her that because she was like sugar."

The little girl grinned.

"That is because you are her boyfriend. We call her Christina, and I am Angelina. All of us, the girls, our names they end in *a*. My brothers, Mama was too tired to do anything special. Why did you give away all your money?"

"Because they asked for it."

"Christina is your sweetie, your dollars should go to us."

And she turned and walked towards a nearby hut. Red followed, as eyes looked out from doorways and around the edges of galvanized tin sheets to see where he was going. There was the spinning sound of a hubcap leaving Alberto's car and splashing in the road, and then Red was inside the hut.

A fat woman was breastfeeding a small brown baby. She was in a corner next to a window that had been cut into the wall, and the light was so bright as it streamed in behind her that Red could not see her face. She'd been eating an orange, and the peels were scattered on the dirt floor, near her bare feet.

When Red glanced into the shadows of the nearest corner, his breath stopped, he thought he was looking at Azucar as she'd appeared when he first met her. But as she stepped into the light, carrying a battered blue kitchen chair, Red could see that this was someone different.

"You must be Red, I am Juanita, Azucar's sister. You can tell us apart easy. I am more beautiful."

And she left the hut, laughing. Azucar's mother took a closer look at Red. He sat on the kitchen chair. One leg sank slightly into the dirt floor. He sat straight and still.

"You do not come with good news."

"My name is..."

"I know who you are, but if you are here without Christina, there is much trouble. I am her mother, and she is my darling, my little girl. They are all my little girls, Angelina, Juanita, Maria, Christina, all of them, no matter how old they are. Look behind me."

Red stood up and went to the wall where a group of Polaroid photos were pinned. The heat and sun had faded them, but all the daughters smiled out at the world. Azucar, or Christina as she was known to her mother, smiled from the snapshot closest to him. The sunlight bounced off her photo and Red felt his eyes filling up so he moved away. Azucar's mother passed the baby over to Angelina who took it outside to play.

Red had come to comfort the mother, but he found that she was the one who offered strength as she touched his shoulder.

"I knew her life would someday go. She was too lucky as a little girl. Now she pays for the luck of babies."

"She..."

"I do not want to know how it happened..."

"She was murdered."

"Because of the life. I told her not to do that, and all she said was, 'What else can I do?' She didn't listen, ever."

And Azucar's mother took down the Polaroid of her daughter and brought it towards the only work of art in the house. There was a cheap reproduction of a print showing the Sacred Heart of Jesus. Around it ran an even cheaper plastic frame, tinted gold. She tucked the photo into the frame. Red reached into his back pocket for some money.

"Azucar, Christina I mean, would have wanted me..."

"Will you pay for her funeral?"

"Yes, and more besides."

"That is all I can take from you. I will light candles for her, she will have a proper funeral and then I will come back here and look after my babies."

"I'll find her killers."

"Be careful. She cared a great deal for you. Now, go. I will not cry in front of strangers."

And she stayed by the print of Jesus. Red walked out into the bright sun where Alberto was back in the car and already quite drunk. Another cloud of blue smoke poured out into the road as the car started. Red managed to get inside and slam the door, just before they bounced towards the city. At the edge of the road, Angelina and Juanita were playing with the baby. They had small sticks and were drawing in the dirt. The black girl who had pretended to karate-chop him now waved goodbye.

He looked straight ahead, towards Panama City.

## 9

Karen Chapman hadn't seen Scott since their last fight. And she'd spent most of that time trying to put an "ex" in front of "husband" whenever she thought of him. She had received one letter that explained patiently what items in the apartment were his, and why she must arrange to deliver them at once. She'd sent a carton full of shattered records as the first installment, and was expecting to hear from Scott any day now. She was beginning to enjoy being on her own. Now she had only one big problem, Kirk Jr, the anchorman of Channel Five's newscast.

Since Scott left and she had begun working her old hours again, Karen had returned to reporting the proper kind of story. Tonight was her most important report, one on homeless women in Boston's winter streets.

She waited through story after story, through what seemed like hours of Kirk's mellifluous tones as he beamed at the cameras and still there was no sign of the item. Finally as the closing theme began Karen realized that the report she'd most recently invested her life in had been dropped.

The second the show was over she stormed towards Kirk Jr. Even though the camera was off, he was still smiling. He probably smiled in his sleep.

She stood on tiptoe, which brought her almost up to the bottom of his chin. Kirk looked like he was about to pat her on the head before she spoke.

"Junior, what happened to my story?"

"Now, Karen, honey, you've got to admit it was a downer."

"Of course it was! Women freezing to death in our streets is a downer."

"Just because it's happening isn't enough reason to say that it's happening."

"Right, Kirk. You ever stop to think why we have the worst newscast in Boston?"

"Watch what you're saying, sweetie. Dad and I are in complete agreement on this."

"Of course you're both in agreement. You're both assholes!"

That wasn't exactly what Karen had planned to say. Like the time she sprayed Scott instead of the plants, it just seemed to happen and, once it did, felt great.

There was a moment's silence before the cameramen burst into loud applause, but Karen knew this was going to be a hollow victory. The real power on the show was Kirk Jr. He was prettier, he had a deeper voice, and he was the son of the station manager.

"Well, Karen, perhaps Dad might like to hear about this outburst."

When his grin intensified she knew that her career as a reporter, at this station anyway, had about ten minutes left. Given the influence of Kirk

Sr her career as a reporter anywhere in Boston wasn't looking too good either.

She went to her desk. Some of the other reporters came up and slapped her back, while others looked with rapt attention at their keyboards and pretended she'd never been there.

Clearing out her desk, she headed for the door, possessions crammed into her briefcase. Near the door she hesitated before tossing the case into a large wastebin that leaned against the teletype machines.

When she stepped outside a cold wind ripped across Kenmore Square, direct from the Charles River to her. Karen was pushed away from Fenway Park towards the Prudential Center. She turned around to fight the snow and get to the nearest bus stop, until the small flakes drilled into her eyes. About that time Karen suddenly decided to go with the wind instead of fighting it. It was easier that way; traffic was a mess, and, as another consideration, her favorite bar lay leeside of Boylston Street.

The wind, snow and Karen blew into Dooley's bar in pretty much that order. The owner himself welcomed Karen with a big hug while giving the kiss-off to winter with an almighty slam of his frosted door.

"Saints preserve us, 'tis the beauteous Karen."

"Save it for the tourists, Vilmos."

This didn't go over too well. He liked pretending he was Irish, he enjoyed running a bar, but most of all he loved being called Dooley instead of his real name, Vilmos. That's why he'd bought the bar, name and all, one rainy Boston night.

"Call me Dooley and I'll buy you a drink."

"Make it Laphroaig."

"No, Karen, there's only a wee drap in the bottom of the precious bottle, and..."

"Vilmos!"

"...you're welcome to it."

"Thank you, Dooley."

As he poured out the single malt he watched it warm the bottom of the thick cut glass. Karen pulled some change out of her purse and made her way towards the old pay phone that rested chipped and jet black in a warm wooden booth in the corner. There was no door to be closed because Vilmos liked to hear what his customers had to say. She talked with Information in Gloucester so she could get her mother's number, while Vilmos gave her a tut-tut. In Hungary, just like Ireland, a child would always know a mother's number by heart. He was going to tell Karen this, but she turned her back towards him.

She usually enjoyed talking to her mother for the first few seconds. After that, it was a problem fielding Em Chapman's two million questions, because there were never any answers. That's why she couldn't bring herself to remember her mother's phone number.

Em answered on the first ring and shouted a suspicious "Hello" into the phone.

"Hi, Em."

"What's wrong?"

"What do you mean, 'what's wrong'? I was just calling."

"You never just call. Don't tell me that you and Scott the fool are back together?"

"No."

"Good. When are you going to visit?"

She had begun the call with a half-formed plan to go see her mother, but the last question ended that. So the rest of the time was spent in gossip about neighbors Karen could only remember from when she was a teenager fifteen years ago. Their conversation ended with three more questions about what was wrong, and assurances from Karen that nothing was. She hung up feeling very gloomy.

As she walked over to the bar the wind gritted the corners of the building, while snow rattled the windows. The glass of single malt looked warm and cozy. Karen sipped it, enjoying the scent of peat moss and the odd taste of iodine. Once you got past the distinct impression that this drink might do you in, the taste of the ocean was worth the shudder. Vilmos had poured himself a stiff drink from a similar bottle that had miraculously appeared. He winked and toasted her.

"*Égészsegedre.*"

"That's Hungarian, Vilmos..."

"Dooley."

"I caught you speaking Hungarian."

"Only to cheer you up, my Celtic princess. Think of it as Gaelic and then you can call me Dooley again."

For a while they said nothing. As the storm grew and then lessened they kept drinking. Vilmos sensed that whatever her troubles were, she didn't want to discuss them.

By the time the storm had diminished, so had the bottle. That was just before some other regular customers, an odd assortment of Hungarians and Celts, came by for their various drinks. An old Irishman near her, who was drinking Tokay, burst into a chorus of "Tipperary's My Dream," and Karen decided it was time to leave. She gave Vilmos a kiss, her thanks, and goodbye, while moving towards the door.

"If you ever decide to marry again, would you glance my way, sweet Karen?"

"Phone my mother, maybe you can strike a deal."

When the door closed behind her it shut out a feeble voice that continued singing of days in the "ould country." She looked at a Boston digging out of a late winter storm. A lone snowplow, its blue light flashing, was scraping along. She walked towards the bus stop and stood there as the solitary echo of the departing snowplow bounced off the deserted office buildings. There wasn't another sound to be heard. A strange glow lit her face, drawing her attention to the translite poster that illuminated the inside of the bus shelter. She was looking at the picture of a young couple lying soaking up the sun. A vast beach curved along a sparkling ocean, and under some graffiti that said quite plainly "Fuck the Sistem," there was the name of this magic land where everyone looked warm—"BERMUDA."

## ⚜ 10 ⚜

A shadow leaned against a tree and watched Red pass by on his way up the hill to the casino. It was a steep climb and the sound of many cigarettes and lots of cigars rattled through Red's windpipe. The skinny man who watched him had smooth and steady breathing. His knife was all oil and silence and he greased the blade open and shut it in a beat that hinted of the samba. His black jacket soaked up the remaining night heat but it didn't bother him. A lone hooker thought there was a puma beneath the tree and shied away until she saw it was only a man. She started moving towards him. Moonlight spilled on the angles of his face in small sharp pools, like sea water caught at the bottom of a cliff. The hooker shivered and backed away.

There were a few more whores by the casino, trying their unsuccessful best to look like international jet setters. One of the older women gave a huge smile as she saw Red.

"My friend! Take me inside and I will bring you luck."

"Is it my imagination, Linda, or have you heard about my winnings?"

"You have won something, my friend?"

And he shook his head.

"I have lost something."

In the hotel lobby there was a desk that proclaimed "Tourist Information." The sign had faded, like the man behind it.

Juan Chinchilla rarely seemed glad to see anyone—however, when Red appeared he smiled and offered a cigar.

"My friend, my wealthy friend, may St Jude lift your hand and spill money from it into mine."

"Juan, why did you tell those two men about Azucar?"

"What two men? Why speak of two men when we can talk of money?"

Red leaned close and pulled the smoldering cigar from Juan's mouth.

"Azucar is dead. The two men killed her. You're the person who picked her for their tastes. I want to know why."

"You are sure?"

"I've been to her place. She has her throat cut..."

"Mother of God, I had nothing to do with that. I was the friend of Azucar, we were..."

"If you were her friend tell me about the two men."

"You have not called the police?"

"Why would they listen to me? As soon as someone finds her, then they will listen, and they will come looking for me. So I don't have a lot of time. Are you going to help?"

"The men checked in here two days ago. They described Azucar and wanted to know where they might find her."

"They knew what she looked like? You're sure?"

Juan nodded. He was beginning to sweat.

"Why the hell didn't you tell me last night?"

"It didn't seem important."

"Are they still here?"

"Room 225. I would take care, my friend. These men have dead eyes."

Red was already moving across the lobby towards the small elevator. It rocked its way slowly to the second floor and the doors creaked open. When he moved along the corridor his heels clicked on the marble tile.

He was forty, overweight and out of breath, but he was not without his resources. In a worn corner of his wallet there was a small kit of delicate instruments, of metal so well crafted that it still sparkled. In a moment the steel whispered into the lock and a series of tiny clicks echoed down the hall.

The room was empty. A lamp had been left on and its light lay in the center of the long room. In the outer area there was a clothes closet, then the room went down one step to a sitting room that led out on to a balcony. Red wondered what the hell he was doing here. If he was in one of the movies that used to make Saturday afternoon come alive when he was a kid, then he'd take time to drag on a cigarette, look around and find the important clue. He couldn't find a clue, important or otherwise, so he settled for a cigarette. He went over to the armchair that was angled at the window to look out on the night air. There was a bottle of tequila next to a cluttered wicker table. He swept a bible, some old *Saturday Evening Posts* and a mirror, along with a stack of dirty postcards—the kind the Blue Goose sold to its departing clients—off the table. Then Red sat down and opened the stranger's booze.

He looked out the window and he remembered Azucar. Just as he was taking the first slug, he felt a small pinprick of pain at the side of his neck. He reached back to kill the bug and felt instead the cold sharp edge of steel. He looked up and saw the two men who had killed Azucar. One was smiling, the other wasn't. The guy with the smile was holding a knife against his neck. Red tried to get up, but the smiler twisted it just a little, making a fine trickle of blood run down his collar.

He stopped pressing when Red slid back in the chair.

"Good, Mr Williams. We don't want to slit your throat and I sense that you may feel the same way."

"You killed my friend."

"So?"

"You admit it?"

"Nothing to admit. There was a job to be done ... someone had to do it."

This made the smiler grin even more.

"Now we've got another job to do. We can kill you here and make it painful and messy, or we can do the job somewhere else if you come quietly. That death, I can promise, will be clean and without pain."

"Like the dentist."

"I feel comfortable being in the company of a man with a well-tuned sense of humor. Why don't we go and fill a cavity? No smile? Ah well, my best jokes never get a laugh. One thing more, if you make the slightest move to attract attention, do the faintest thing out of the ordinary, I'll slit you like a mackerel's belly."

The knife pricked at him again and he moved towards the door. As he looked at the killers he remembered what Juan had said about their dead eyes.

## ❧ 11 ❧

Red was sweating. The car bounced its way into daylight and followed a winding road close to the coast as early morning light scraped green from the jungle. Parrots screeched at the day and near a cliff in the distance hang-gliders were bobbing in the early morning updrafts. As Red watched, a tiny figure got into trouble when cross drafts hit the glider. Under the kite the small pupa of a figure swayed from side to side. For a while it seemed he would drop and Red held his breath. Finally, after a shuddering sideways sweep the glider tilted back and forth to a level uprise and the small creature seemed safe. The smiler stared out the window as a beach hove into sight; the fat man was perspiring right along with Red.

"I don't understand why you killed her."

The smiler looked at Red.

"No reason you should. Now, if you would like to try and save your life, perhaps you could answer one of our questions."

The Mercedes stopped next to a fishing boat. For some reason the boat was still tied up, even though the fleet had been long out trailing their nets through the Atlantic and the Pacific. A man in

47

very dirty whites slouched towards the car. Two naked children busied themselves inspecting the hubcaps, while their father examined the handful of money that the fat man gave him. Red watched the fat man and thought that he would never forget those eyes, cool and smoky, as dangerous as a cat's claw. The owner of the boat pocketed the money and vanished in the direction of the undergrowth just as his offspring began to touch the car. The smiler took out his knife and flashed sunlight in a cut towards the children. They followed their father into the jungle leaving a dent in the light. The foliage rushed back to fill it as parrots were rolled into the air, and when Red looked towards the boat its painter was untied and the two men motioned towards it. He climbed in.

"What question do you want me to answer?"

Instead of saying anything, the skinny man made a thorough and quick frisking of Red. He tossed some pocket lint, candy and chewing gum over the edge of the boat, ignoring the money belt after he saw it contained only cash.

"Did this woman give you something to keep for her?"

"She didn't have anything, except her pets. I set them free."

"Very kind of you."

"Perhaps you could do the same for me?"

This time the fat man laughed.

"So you have no keepsake? Nothing special that she asked you to safeguard?"

Red shook his head and looked around the boat. The stench of fish was strongest where a thin blue sheen of scales had glued itself to the gunwales. When the motor started a smell of oil and gasoline fumes mixed with the sea and the ripeness of the morning. Soon the beach was a crescent of lemon peel. The sea caught all the green in the world and bounced it off the blue of the water. The boat heaved and dropped as the smiler opened his shirt collar after flashing his teeth at the morning.

There was a greasy brown paper package that had been left on the deck. Inside were strings of fish entrails, and a pig's bladder filled with blood. Red felt his arms being pinned so he could not move. The smiler took the bladder and hurled it directly at Red, splashing clotted blood all over his shirt. Next he hurled the fish guts at him. Then the two men moved forward and flung him in a short arc towards the sea. He bounced once on the gunwales and his whole back numbed until he found himself choking in the salty water.

The ocean tasted like blood and the boat struck him as it pulled away. The undertow tugged Red beneath the surface of the sea, making his eyes hurt and his nostrils sting while he coughed and swallowed more water.

He flailed around until he struggled to the surface again. Clearing his eyes, he saw the whole circle of sky and water was empty except for him.

The sun was high and his hair felt like it was made of wire. It was so hot that every time he bobbed up after dipping his face in the tepid sea he could feel the salt caking along his face and gritting rime on his brows. He licked his lips and tasted salt. He felt something push against his leg and realized why the smiler had spattered him with blood. He kicked in panic and the pushing stopped. As he looked down he could see pink clouds mixing with the water, and a large shadow stub away.

Red did the most logical thing he could. He undressed, leaving on only his money belt. It took longer than he thought it would, because every time he tried to tug something off he started to sink. Again the shadow slid beneath him and he kicked, missing it, but as his clothes floated away, leaving a cloud of blood, the shark followed.

Finally Red bobbed wet and naked, a pale salted thing at the edge of the ocean. He wasn't sure where land might be but he'd always been a gambler, so in his mind he flipped a coin. He shrugged as much as a naked man in the ocean could shrug and began swimming towards what he thought—even odds—was the shore.

## ≈❧≈ 12 ≈❧≈

Jack was drunk, making his way towards the El
Panama casino and finding it heavy going.
Consuelo, or that's what he thought her name was,
it sounded like Consuelo, was also drunk. They
tilted their way up the incline as they held hands.
Both looked at the way their fingers laced together,
leaning like they were holding a transparent
cane. The hookers of the hill moved to either side
of them as, blessed by a miracle, Jack and Consuelo managed to follow a straight line dead center of
the sidewalk.

It had been a good day. He had found out about a
little covert action that was going down in El Salva-
dor and figured if that was the case he could then
offer his services to the rebels. He knew enough
about governments to usually be on the side of the
people who were opposing them and this time was
no exception. Besides, the money was fine. He'd
made contact and by tomorrow should be getting
the upfront money; after that an issue of arms
would be waiting for him when he reached El Sal-
vador. Already he was feeling more like the old
soldier of fortune again and was celebrating in the

accepted manner. Maybe he wasn't all that old. The evening breeze slid along his face; Consuelo squeezed his hand harder when light grinned at them from the casino. He grinned right back.

"Got a hunch that the wheel's going to spin just right for the two of us."

"When you win, we will share the money?"

"I like that. You said when, you didn't say if, so I sure as hell will split the money. Fifty-fifty, my little sweet."

Just inside the door was a sucker wheel. Jack bought some blue chips and laid a bunch on the 40-to-1 square. The wheel spun and quivered on the wire that said 40 to 1, but when he turned and kissed Consuelo to celebrate, the pointer quivered past the big payoff. That's the time when luck started to leave, just before it arrived. Towards two in the morning it seemed to come around again so Jack took all the chips he had and rushed over to the roulette table. When he got there he found that good fortune had departed and taken Consuelo along.

Finding himself pretty much sober, totally broke, and with nowhere to stay, he figured he might as well go and look in on his son. Jack always went through this on every visit to Panama City. Once he'd gotten so far as starting to climb the stairs that led to Red's small flat, but had stopped short. The way Jack had figured it, maybe the kid wouldn't want to see him because of the way he'd vanished and all. He had dealt with a lot of disappointments in his life, but this would be one that could break him. It was enough for him to know that his son had enough savvy to keep ahead of the cops, just like his old man. Other ways he didn't seem to take after him at all. Like the red hair, for instance—that was right from Red's mother and the whole Irish side of the family. Jack had stark Welsh black hair that now was hidden, like coal beneath snow, by the passing years. He was small and wiry where Red was large and looked soft of body. Maybe the real reason that he'd never gone to see his son was because he didn't want to remember Red's mother, Mary, and the way the firelight had once played its fingers through her hair.

Then, one night, thousands of miles and a lot of years away from Boston, a strange thing happened. Jack had spent the evening nursing a drink or two in the Blue Goose. He was close to the corner, back turned towards the wall, and looking around to see if any old enemies or people who might turn out to be new ones were in the joint. He noticed a big man in a crumpled white suit. The big guy was laughing and joking, and when things got quiet he even burst into song. The tune was one that Jack hadn't heard since his days with Mary. The man's flaming red hair caught the light as he leaned back and sang loud enough to shake glasses on the table. When he stopped singing even the sailors burst into applause. The bartender whistled and called out, "Give us another one, Red." But the big man stopped and turned to some serious drinking. By then everything had stopped for Jack as he realized why the singer had looked so familiar, why his voice had held the echoes of Mary's voice. The world stayed still as he saw the imprint of his wife's face on his son's.

Once when Jack had been shot—this time in the side—and the fever came and took him and threw

him around the hut, he could have sworn that his
son had come into the room and sponged his face
with melted Boston snow. The feeling was so real
that when the fever broke he still called out Red's
real name—"Michael! Michael!" But his son
wouldn't answer.

And now, here at the Blue Goose, he'd found his
son again. But he didn't dare speak. Jack wasn't
scared of many things, but one fear haunted
him—what if his son turned away?

After that it got to be a habit, his looking around
to see what Red was up to. He found excuses to
come to Panama City, even though there were better places to make the contacts that he had to make
to go and fight. Every time he'd get drunk and start
off to say hello to his son something would stop
him before he actually got there. It would have
killed him if Red had thrown him out when he
came to say hello. The more he thought about the
chances of Red rejecting him the more he felt like
looking for trouble. A good fight would help take
the mood away. Three drunken sailors spotted
what looked to them like a little old man and began heading towards him. Jack started to scratch
his neck, next to the throwing knife.

"Come on, you sons-a-bitches, why don't you
take this little old man's money?"

It turned out the sailors might be drunk but they
weren't crazy. Something in the way he carried
himself made them cross the street before they
reached him. His smile left.

When he reached Red's building there was no
light in the apartment window. That might seem
like a small thing to most people. It wasn't for Jack.
Every time he'd gone to look before, he'd always

seen the reflection of a small lamp that remained
on all night. Jack had a memory of his son being
scared of the dark, of a night when he'd taken all
the lights out of the room so the kid would get used
to the darkness. He'd listened to the boy cry into
the early hours and he still wouldn't go in to see
him. Even when Mary had pleaded with him to
let her go and see if anything was wrong with
Red he'd said "no" because he'd wanted the boy to
grow up tough and used to the dark.

Jack had found out enough about life since then
to know that men can be scared of anything, especially the dark. He'd also found out that change
meant danger. He was still alive because of the
way he paid attention to things that altered. His
view of the world was that, at bottom, it was a pretty
orderly place. It seemed to have been put together
in a way that would keep it running unless someone really screwed up. Whenever an element of
the planet was out of place it meant that something
was wrong or had been arranged to go wrong. A
tree gone where it always used to be; an animal
that wasn't at the water-hole at the usual time; a
bird that screamed when it was usually quiet. Now
something had changed in Red's apartment.

The door was easy to open, kind of embarras-
sing really because it was so simple. If Jack hadn't
been in a hurry, he would have gone outside and
broken in again just to preserve his good name.

On his way in he kept a weather eye open for tarantulas, just in case. As far as he was concerned,
if a good idea had occurred to him it might have
done so for anyone else.

There were no tarantulas, only a total mess. The
place had been tossed, and not very well, by people

who didn't figure anyone who'd care was going to come around and see what they had done. There was a litter of unpaid bills next to faded newspapers that told of races run long ago and far away. Jack picked up one racing form to see which horses Red had picked. He nodded his head in approval while he kept glancing around the room. From the way things were thrown around, he figured that the search had been done by two people, probably men, one short and one tall. "Eat your heart out, Sherlock Holmes!" he thought.

Then he began his own search. At first he thought Red might be missing because of natural causes—the chance that a drunk had fought back while being rolled; an arrest and a night in the drunk tank; or being in the wrong place when a beer bottle was launched in a bar fight. But a second discovery told him that something more serious was going on. Under a desk drawer, slipped into the wood veneer, was a new passbook for a bank. The code number wasn't with it, so it wasn't of much use to Jack. But the balance showed that a huge deposit had been made two days ago.

There wasn't much else to discover except a half-empty bottle of tequila with most of the worm dissolved. He sat in an old armchair and lit up a dry cigar while he worked away at the bottle. Scattered over the floor, where the men had thrown them, were dozens of faded postcards. Jack picked them up at random and was surprised at how familiar they looked. He flipped over scenes of Bogota, Santa Cruz, Rio Bamba and Isla de Sangallan to look at his own writing. He drank some more, and read postcards that he had sent more than thirty years ago. When he piled them up later they made a stack almost half a foot high. They all stopped after a certain date. The time, best as Jack could recall, that he had been shot real bad. The time he thought he had seen his son bringing ice water, the time he was out of his head for a month or two, the time he'd thought he was going to die. After that he'd drifted without the memory of an address to slow him down. Crazy days and crazy chances until he forgot.

The sun was rising and Jack had the most important task of his life ahead of him. To find his son.

## 🪷 13 🪷

The waves were about halfway between tides on the sandy beach when Red came to, with no idea of where he was or even who he was. Until the pain started. It was in his leg and then suddenly it bit his back and then was crawling down his leg again until he yelled out and coughed and choked as the sea water splashed into his mouth and blood salt went down his throat. His eyes were raw and he couldn't close them because of fish scales glued to his lids and baked there by the sun. When he reached his hand to rub his face the skin felt like sandpaper. The waves splashed higher and Red wondered how he could move, knowing that if the tide was coming in he would drown. He tried to crawl but when he did the pain bounced between his leg and back and he heard the sea ring in his ears and all the beach was a wide space of dots of sand and they were spreading and the dots and the ringing were one.

He thought that he was in bed—the same bed he'd slept in as a little boy. Its metal foot of white fluted tin curved in semi-circle near his own feet and his bedside table was made of sand that drifted. Some-one had tied him to the bed and every time he blinked the wind blew into his eyes.

He woke with a scream, to find he was still lying on the beach, but out of the water. A tough-looking Indian dressed all in white was standing over him. The man wore a Panama hat and the shad-ow shielded Red's eyes. The Indian was talking to him in Spanish, but he couldn't understand a word that the man was saying, all he had left was a mix of English and French words and none of them worked. The man moved back from the sun and he was the sun and the sky caught on fire.

Red began singing. He was hot and the Boston night lay down over him. He was sweating and no one would give him water. All the street sounds rode the heat right into his bedroom and he woke up crying. The corner of the room looked like the jungle where some man who was counting mon-ey looked at him. When Red moved so did the man's rifle. The man faded and he was back in Boston and there was singing, if he listened he could make out the words. It was the song his fa-ther always sang to get him to go to sleep, all about a little buckaroo, whatever the hell that was. He tried to see the face but he couldn't; instead the world went into little black dots that swam away from him and his father started to pull apart.

The next time Red came to, it was dark and he was lying on a cot. His leg still hurt but it was swathed in dark green long leaves strapped to his flesh with dirty strips of cloth. The man smoked a pipe and looked at him, a rifle leaned against the wall. The money belt had been removed and all the money was hanging on a makeshift clothesline. The wind blew it back and forth, while a lamp threw shadows of money on the wall.

Red slept and the night slipped by.

## ☙ 14 ☙

Jack's search was helped by the cowardice of Juan Chinchilla. At first Juan had sneered at the little man and refused to tell him anything. Then, later that night, on his way home, when a palm tree moved and he felt a knife at his throat, he had talked.

That took Jack to the hotel room, where there were no signs of the two men. But luck moved along. He met the chambermaid who did the room every day. At first she had not wanted to say anything. It took another day before she discovered that she was falling in love with the little man who spoke Spanish better than she did and who knew both how to talk and how to listen. She shared with him her secret of the two men who had wanted to know the name of a fisherman they could hire. After talking of her brother and his boat, she made love with the little man. In the first daylight she reached out and his side of the bed was cool. She went to the window but there was no sign of Jack, no sign he had ever been there. Hugging herself, she stood naked behind the torn curtains.

Jack had no trouble finding her brother. This
time he didn't need a knife. Carlos talked, he
would have sung, he would have danced, all for a
suck at the bottle of tequila that Jack carried.

From there it took another day of wandering
until he heard in one small village of an Indian
fisherman who bragged he had found the biggest
catch of all. Then in a small valley, where a few
huts were gathered, he got more directions and
heard more about the crazy Indian who now had
money. From there it was a couple of hours of slow
night walking before he was outside a small Quonset hut. It had both ends open to the night, and to
keep out the insects of the evening cheesecloth
billowed in front of lamplight. Jack crept around it
listening. Inside there was one voice that sang, off-
key. Another voice was counting in Spanish. It
reached eight thousand, hesitated, swore, and began again, "Uno, dos, tres..."

He looked in and saw a crazy man who was
counting his way through a pile of money, a rifle
leaning against the wall next to him. There was a
faded army cot across from him and on it was
Jack's son.

Red's leg was covered in leaves and he was tossing around in fever, singing and swaying his
head back and forth as he sang.

So go to sleep, my little buckaroo,
While the Western skies are shining
Down on you...

The singing stopped, and Jack scratched his
neck, feeling the edge of the throwing knife. He
figured it was time.

With one hand he scooped up a rock and lobbed it over the roof of the Quonset hut. As it hit the far edge the man inside swept his rifle towards the sound and squeezed off a few rounds. That was just fine with Jack because it covered his move towards the hut. He cut through the cheesecloth, and turned the knife to hold it by the point. That was just as he realized why the man didn't seem worried about counting all that money in full view. A log trap crashed down from the roof. Jack had heard it leave the notch a second before the log fell so he managed to twist to one side. It caught a glancing blow on the tip of his shoulder, and he fell to the floor. The man turned and cocked the rifle again. He was pulling the trigger when Jack threw his knife in a quick sideways throw. It sank into the neck so clean and tight that there was no bleeding. The man toppled forward as his rifle went off, blowing another hole in the side of the Quonset hut.

Red began to sing again. Jack covered him in a blanket and then turned towards the man he had killed. Using the lamp to guide him, he dragged the body outside as his eyes probed the darkness at the edge of the light. Finally he found what he was looking for—a cone-like nest. He placed the body in a natural indentation next to it, knowing the ants would do their work, aided by the small creatures of the night, and everything would be stripped to the bones by morning. No one would ever be able to tell what happened. He said a soldier's prayer over the body. Any man who had set such a good log trap deserved it.

Back at the hut he stitched together the cheesecloth and, using sap from lianas, he glued ten-dollar bills over the bullet holes in the wall. Before the pain of his own shoulder took over he began to concentrate on what he was going to have to do to help his son. He spread out the contents of his first-aid kit—pouches of sulfa powders, needles with lots of penicillin and tablets of painkillers.

Ever since the time that Jack had almost bought the farm, he took care to travel with his own dispensing kit. From what he could see he was going to need everything he had in it. He pulled the covers off his son and, as Red began to shake uncontrollably, placed the blankets where they were needed, around the neck close to the head.

The leg had been covered with various kinds of leaves and he began to remove them. Some had crusted into a layer of scab and pus that also held small imbedded insects. He selected a needle, injected a local anesthetic around the wound, and waited a few moments for the xylocaine to kick in.

By now the leg didn't jerk around when touched, so he slipped on a pair of disposable plastic gloves and using tweezers cleansed in the lamp flame began picking out all the debris. He dusted with sulfa powder and then opened the wound again. The pus spurted and dripped over the leg. He spent a good deal more time cleaning, then shot in some more anesthetic and cleaned around the edge of the bite.

It was morning. He gave Red an injection of penicillin and figured it was time to get some rest. Closing his eyes against the sun, he slept a dreamless sleep.

## ❦ 15 ❦

Jack was awakened by the sound of movement. He opened his eyes slowly and watched Red straining to reach the propped-up rifle. It was obviously taking every ounce of his strength.

"Keep doing that and the cot's goin' to collapse."

"Who the hell are you?"

For a moment he almost told him. Then the old fear set in.

"I'm the guy what set your leg and took care of your money for you. Think of me as a good Samaritan."

"You look more like Jack the Ripper."

Jack burst out into loud peals of laughter.

"You must be a mind reader. That's my name. The Jack part, not the Ripper! What do I call you, young man?"

"Red."

"Red. Not very original but easy to remember. Red, I'm Jack, how d'you do?"

He reached out and, after a brief hesitation, they shook hands.

"That's more like it. Now why don't we make sure we haven't stolen each other's watches, and then we can have a conversation."

"Nothing to talk about."

Jack started poking around the hut.

"Here's just the two of us in someone else's hut, you the victim of a very unlucky shark who tried for a main course and only got an hors d'oeuvre. I wake up—after fixing your leg, I might add—to find you trying to get your hands on a rifle. Seems to me we got lots to talk about."

Red laughed and stopped as suddenly as he had begun, clutching at his leg.

"Oh shit!"

"Exactly, sonny. Now maybe we could have that discussion."

"You fixed my leg?"

"Sure did."

"Who are you? The leg fairy?"

"I'm a party with a vested interest. I found you here, half out of your head with ten thousand smackers on one side, and some guy sitting there watching you die."

"I didn't dream that? He was hanging my money up to dry?"

"When I got here he was getting set to hang you up to dry."

Jack pointed to the tenspots holding back the bugs from the bullet hole.

"It was either him or you and I picked you."

"Why?"

"You ask more questions than anyone I ever met in my life. I picked you 'cause you seemed to be the rightful owner of the money. I'm a big fan of money."

"Why not kill me and take it?"

"Code of the West. I only shoot people who can

fight back. You can't, yet."

"I gotta get out of here."

"Me too, but we can't do that till I steal you some clothes and you're ready to travel."

"We?"

"I told you, you ask too many questions. Now why don't you just lie there while I check your leg."

It hurt just as much as it did last night but this time he was awake and knew how to handle the pain. Jack watched the way his son dealt with the surges coming from the ache whenever his leg was moved. For a con man he was amazing. After the wound was dressed Red didn't ask any more questions. Looking tired and pale, he rolled over and fell asleep.

By the time he woke again it was dark and he was starved. Jack brought over a steaming bowl of soup that smelled of the sea.

"Got the crabmeat from the trees over there. Crabs like to live in the water where the leaves catch the rain. Scooped up whatever else was in there too."

Red kept wolfing down the soup. He glanced in the corner where the money had been divided into two stacks. Jack noticed the look.

"Reason I split it up, kid, is because my line of work might fit in with yours."

"I always work alone."

"Sure you do. It was pretty impressive the way you was working everything out real fine when I come along. That's the joy of going it alone. I figure 'cause you talk a bit when you're in fever you need help to track down whoever did this to you and the woman."

"Her name's Azucar."

"You didn't say her name."

"How do I know you're not with them?"

"You're still alive, that's how."

"How are you supposed to help me?"

"I track people, I kill people, I can help out. Also, if I give my word, you're able to believe whatever I say. And I'm giving my word."

"You're kinda old."

"Better than the alternative. What you got to lose, kid?"

And Jack went outside. He checked his traps and found a small capybara. He killed it quickly, started a fire, and while he was waiting for the coals to glow white-hot, gutted and skinned it. He used some salt from a small pouch and spitted the animal. Soon the smell of cooking meat filled the camp. When he was putting it on the plates he'd fashioned from some wide leaves, he added fried plantains.

While he and Red ate they talked about how they could work together. It came down to the simple fact that there was no one else to trust. Night drifted around the hut and the lamplight folded them inside its warm beams while they talked. Red laid out everything that he knew, which wasn't much. Jack just listened—he was good at that.

Only one thing Red insisted on. When they tracked down the men and had them in their sights, he wanted to be the one who dealt with them.

Jack told him no.

"Then, old man, I guess you might as well go now, because that's the way it's going to be, or we don't work together. It was Azucar they murdered and I owe her, not you. You can be back-up, you can help me find them, but when it comes down to the moment this is something I have to do for myself. Anyway, how the hell do I know you'll find them?"

"You got money, we'll find them. Money always finds money."

"Who says those guys had money?"

"Didn't take yours, did they? See, you're not the only one that can ask questions."

Red looked at him, trying to read Jack's thoughts, but only lamplight and shadows moved across his face.

"So what do you say, about taking them myself?"

"One condition. We stay here long enough for me to teach you how to do just that."

"Don't you worry about what I can do."

"If I don't, I could be dead too, and I'm partial to this old skin of mine. If you had to take these guys with words, I'd say go ahead, but they may not be good listeners."

"Don't underestimate the power of words."

"I don't. You'll need the words to get to them, way I figure it, you're also gonna need a disguise that nature's gonna provide. But once you're right up to them you'll need what I teach you."

Red started to nod, and the nod turned into his eyes closing as he wandered into sleep. Jack sat back and looked at his son. He thought of all the things he should have taught Red over the years. He remembered all the broken promises, all the tricks he could have passed on to the kid. He didn't see how he could make up for everything in one lifetime, but he was beginning to see how he might be able to start.

## 16

The first job was getting Red's leg healed and teaching him how to walk around on homemade crutches. After his son was up and hopping Jack decided on something else, to train him like any recruit.

Red moved from the crutches to canes, until he was able, with Jack's help, to shuffle along. A few days later he was walking, and each morning and evening he went through all the elaborate exercises that had been worked out for him. Combined with the good food, this was starting to give him a strength that he'd never experienced before. Jack decided it was time to move to the next stage.

The sun was still hidden behind the wet trees when he let out a whoop that spilled all sorts of creatures out of the branches. He yelled and tipped the cot as Red rolled on to the floor to feel a knife edge touch his neck.

"First thing you gotta learn, kid, is to stay awake. Then once you're awake, we're gonna speak— mind to mind."

"What the hell are you talking about?"

"Aikido."

"Sounds like a con to me."

"Yeah? So why don't you try and hit me?"

"No way. I've seen too many movies for that. I try to punch you and you throw me way into those bushes, or against a tree."

"No, I won't. I promise. I'll even close my eyes and turn my back towards you. Then you hit me, hard as you like with anything you want."

Nearby there was a rusty old shovel that seemed to have become part of the earth. Leaves and small dark waxy flowers had made their own path up the handle. Red pried it from the earth, feeling it tug and release when small tendrils of roots dipped and snapped away from the edge.

"Turn around, Jack."

"How about if I just close my eyes?"

"Turn around, or I won't try to hit you."

"Seeing as you put it that way."

Red sucked in a breath and lifted the shovel high. He didn't want to kill the old man, just teach him a good lesson. Deciding to aim for the shoulder and not the head, he stood on tiptoe and leaned into the blow. But when the shovel arrived, the shoulder wasn't there. Red found himself tipping forward and then spinning ass-over-teakettle into the bushes where he shivered through the branches of a small tree as he crashed to the ground.

"You promised not to throw me."

"Promises are shit, unless you pay for them. And I didn't throw you, you did it yourself. That's the way it works, mind to mind."

"I've used that Eastern crap in two thousand cons, so don't feed me any Zen lines, you old bastard."

"Forget the Zen. Here, take my knife. Stick it in my guts, can't you do that? I'm only an old man. I'll close my eyes again."

This time Red didn't hold back. He took the knife and shifted it hand to hand and then, in what looked like a sudden move, lunged for Jack's gut—only to land in the same group of bushes. This time he crashed through some rotted wood.

"Did you feel me throw you?"

"No. But if you didn't, then who did?"

"The circle. Aikido. You don't bother doing anything till they attack you, and all you do is help them out. They want to stick a knife in you, well, why not help them make the thrust? Just make real sure you get out of the way a little bit. They want to kick you, help their foot along, they'll follow."

"What about if they want to shoot me?"

"Put a bullet in their teeth first. That's not aikido, that's straight from me."

"Maybe I should just learn how to shoot."

"Not yet. First thing I want to teach you is the right way to fall down. How's your back?"

"Hurts like hell."

"Shouldn't. Time I get through with you it'll feel like you was landing in your little cot."

So Red learned how to fall. The jungle shook like Jello and the ground shifted as he flew up into the air again and again—and crashed to earth, again and again. The key to understanding the whole thing meant landing like a cross between a drunk and a wet cloth. That was the way Jack described it and that was the way it worked.

Every morning for the next week, Red was awakened as Jack spilled him out of the cot. He tried to stay awake so it wouldn't happen, he tried to wake up early so it wouldn't happen. But, no matter how he planned it, every morning he was tipped out of the cot with a solid crash. The day would start and Red would once more practice the falling. He knew he had it right at last when he could lie in his cot without feeling like it was made of sharp stones.

From then on he figured how to help every attack. He helped the knife move towards the jungle and Jack went right along with it. Red found ways of taking a blow and turning it into an upside-down flight towards bigger and bigger trees. He copied movements and throws again and again, and as the days passed, his strength and skill growing, Jack told him that he shouldn't have to think about any of his actions. Each move should be a reflex, meaning that every possible attack was repeated as often as raindrops. At the end of each day Jack would keep running in a circle and he would keep throwing him. The more he threw the more a sense of power and strength sent circles through his arms.

One night Jack told him that what he was feeling was called *ki*: the building of power and balance. To demonstrate, he asked his son to lift him. An easy task, Red smiled. The old man stood in the center of the jungle, next to their campfire. Red went over and lifted, but nothing happened. He threw all his new-found strength into the lift and Jack didn't budge. He pushed, he pulled, and still nothing happened.

"See, it's not my body. You could lift that easy enough. It's my mind."

This time Red didn't scoff.

Early the next morning Jack moved softly towards the cot. But Red was waiting, and the old man found himself flying through the air, smiling as he landed. His son was ready.

## 17

Karen Chapman stood on the sand below the Elbow Beach Hotel. She tried to tell herself that she was having a good time, but the wind was on the beach and the ocean whipped up a fine spray that was blowing all over her. Despite the gales, she would have gone swimming, just to feel the suck and challenge of the waves, but the sea was full of nasty, slimy purple jellyfish of some sort that periodically rolled in quivering sandy mounds towards her feet. She wondered if she could manage to swim and still dodge them and decided not.

There was another two hours until lunch and she dreaded it. She'd been seated with a honeymooning couple from New Orleans who rejected all the hotel food as not spicy enough and spent hours praising Popeye Fried Chicken. They told her the way to make a fortune was to bring the franchise to Bermuda. Karen had better things to do with her time. Precisely what those better things were she wasn't sure.

Turning back from the beach she hopscotched her way over the mortal remains of various members of the Portuguese man-of-war family and headed past tropical blooms towards the hotel. A few weeks ago she'd have traded her life savings to be in the middle of such flowers, plants and sweet brush; now she walked past them without looking.

An old couple were making their way slowly down the beach. He was wearing a vivid pair of swimming drawers (the word trunks didn't apply to such a voluminous garment) and the old woman was in some form of geriatric bikini.

"Better not go near the water, there's jellyfish in the ocean."

Karen felt better now that she'd roused herself enough to initiate a conversation. The aged couple looked at her suspiciously and went by quickly. The old man pretended he hadn't heard.

"Bert doesn't swim, so it makes no difference," offered the woman.

"Nothing does," replied Karen, but the wind took her words, blowing them past Bert and Mrs Bert and over the jellyfish out to the ocean.

That night she decided she would have fun. After all, she'd emptied her bank account, including Scott's half, had arranged to have her plants watered and misted at the right intervals, and said goodbye to her old life. If she couldn't say hello to the right sort of new life, she had no one to blame but herself. How to go about having fun she wasn't sure, so she decided to do what a man might do under similar circumstances. She looked at the row of cabs parked in front of the hotel and waited until the one with the most disreputable driver pulled up. She elbowed past a nattily attired couple into the cab. The driver turned and smiled an evil smile. Karen was up to it.

"Take me someplace where I'm going to have a good time!"

That's how she ended up at the Hotel Inverurie nightclub. The room was dim and smoke filled. But it was the kind of smoke that smouldered in old men's pipes. The scent of tropical flowers came from perfumed lace handkerchiefs of blue-rinsed ladies in long white gloves. An Irish folk singer was doing her best to give life to "Danny Boy" accompanied by the oldest steel drum band on the island. The drinks, at least, were good, but tonight her hangover was developing as she was drinking.

Karen was ready for adventure, but it didn't seem to be anywhere in sight.

## ☙ 18 ❧

For the first time in his life, Panama City looked strange to Red. After the jungle training, after mornings of having the old bastard roll him out of the cot, after days of walking past heavy undergrowth and suddenly finding a knife next to his throat, the city looked like he had never seen it before.

Then again, Red looked strange to Panama City. He'd gone away pale and fat, and come back brown and lean. He also looked ten years younger. Before this time he would have strolled down the street with his nose on the sniff for an afternoon drink. Now he walked looking straight ahead. He used his side vision to warn him of anything out of the ordinary and he held each image in his mind like a snapshot that he could examine later when he felt like it.

He rounded the corner of the market and headed towards home. Just past the fish market he came across a tailor shop that was set up on the street. Water and fish scales lay in small pools as they trickled into the midday heat and began to congeal near the bare feet of the tailor. That didn't stop Red, what did bring him to a halt was a full-length mirror that quivered in the heat. He noticed it as the looking glass caught the sun and beamed it into his eyes in a fish flash of light. Dazed he moved to one side, with the world gone blue and the people fading. He shielded his eyes from a total stranger, skin tree brown and tight as bark on the face, hair disguised in a dark stain from the betel nut. He saw a lean dangerous-looking man in a suit three sizes too big for him. He was about to step back when he realized the person in the mirror was himself.

Before he could leave, a tailor was at his side, tutting and holding great handfuls of the suit. When it tore the man smiled.

"You might ask why I'm smiling, I smile for good luck which has your old terrible suit rip, just when Panama's best tailor is nearby."

He began measuring Red and shouting out the results to a small woman hunched over a sewing machine. She nodded as her foot kept rocking back and forth on the filigreed metal pedal.

This hadn't been part of any plan, but it felt very good, one element of the new life that he wanted to build. He thought about what Azucar would have said if she could see him, of how she would have laughed, and taken him into the shade to feed him sweet things, filled him with papaya juice and made him eat cream until he purred. She would also have known who he was right away, no matter how tanned and lean he was, would have looked into his eyes and winked at the strange new mask he was wearing.

In the middle of yelling out commands, the tailor went to the side and picked up bolts of pure white cloth. He sat down and his wife shouted the figures back at him as he snipped and cut and pinned. His wife finished with the shouting, looked at the sewing machine and touched the bobbin with her thumb, making a small adjustment to the tension of the thread, bending until the sun put her face in shadow.

When Red came back in a couple of hours, his new suit was ready. No one expected him to be modest and he wasn't, changing in the middle of the marketplace.

"You are a good tailor."

"I am not good, I am great. You will come back for many more suits. Pay my wife, I have nothing to do with money."

After counting out too much cash Red moved towards the cantina next to Restaurante Labrador and went inside. The place was crowded and an old peasant woman had just finished drinking the juice of the papaya from a battered metal dipper. He spun a full balboa on the table to ring out noontime before he drank three dipperfuls of the juice. The owner stared at him as if there was something familiar about this stranger. He shook his head, decided there wasn't and then slid Red the change. As Red had been dropping into the cantina every morning for the last ten years, if Miguel didn't recognize him there was a real good chance that no one else would. He stepped into the noontime buzz and heat.

The day moved into siesta time and all of Panama City coasted into a nap. Shades were drawn, shutters were closed, baths were filled and sweat ran down the necks of those young and foolish enough to make love. Red's white suit was close to his body and cool in its pallor against the day. He moved towards his apartment.

When he saw the building he knew it was time to be very careful. Jack had warned him that if anyone had the slightest idea he could be alive there would be one place they would watch and this was it. So what he did, instead of looking at his apartment, was see if anyone else might be watching it. So much time had passed since his toss into the big drink that it was unlikely either of the killers would still be in Panama City, but Jack had taught him one important lesson—plan for the worst. He'd also pointed out that the killers thought Red might have something Azucar had hidden. She had been murdered because of it, people had tossed his apartment looking for it, and then had tried to kill him when it was obvious he had nothing. Whatever the secret was, it was important enough to kill for, and might also be important enough to keep them searching.

On Red's first survey around the neighborhood everything looked normal, so he was about to start towards his apartment. Then he decided to take a second look because of a feeling that something across the street was out of place. It took ten minutes before he could figure out what was wrong. Every window, except one, was shut firmly against the heat and the insects that lazed their way through the midday hours. That window was directly across the street from his apartment. He slipped back against an adobe building, his white suit melting into the dazzle, as he began to hear the odd noise of a battery-operated fan. It wasn't a sound heard very often in the middle of poverty, because even if someone who lived in this area

had stolen the fan they would have sold it instead
of using it. Red was almost up to the window before he realized if he came any closer he might be
reflected in the glass panes across the street. He
was supposed to check in with Jack, but didn't want
to go away. He figured if the old man had anything to tell him he'd show up.

Red curled up in the shade of a courtyard gate
and did what any sensible animal would do at
siesta time. He slept. Since losing weight he could
nap as clean and fast as a cat, and like a cat he
woke with no sound.

Once Panama City was awake, he decided that
when darkness fell there would be no way he
could stay in the area without his white suit being
noticed. So he spent his time in the marketplace
getting another suit made, a dark one. The tailor
smiled.

"I told you that you'd want another. A second
purchase gets you a discount. Five percent."

When night returned, Red, dressed in a well-
fitting dark suit, leaned against the building. He
tried to figure out what Azucar might have owned
that was so important, but couldn't come up with
any answers.

He stayed outside until three in the morning,
and that was long enough. The one lesson that
Jack had never been able to teach him was patience. He made the move quickly towards his old
building and his old apartment, jumping when a
cat fight spat out of a nearby alley.

He entered the old apartment smoothly, expecting to find someone else in it. The fact it hadn't
been taken over by another tenant was his first
puzzle. The second puzzle was where everything

that he owned had gone. The apartment had been totally gutted. Gutted and cleaned. It sparkled, even the cockroaches gleamed. Red stood there in the dark and listened until he heard a creak near the door.

He waited, but nothing else happened. Perhaps he'd imagined the sound. He tried to do what he knew he should, empty his mind of all thought, making it as still as a pool of jungle water in a rotted stump. But he couldn't. Memories of Azucar filled his mind. Mornings when she'd come in to see him and have breakfast after her night's work was done. Nights when she'd looked at him, pale in the moonlight, and told him he was the last white man in Panama, the last of those faded explorers who had come to look at the jungle because the vines had grown into their hearts. There were nights when she said nothing and lay in his arms trying to escape whatever the night terrors were that haunted her. Red stopped his thoughts as much as he could and looked out the window. He felt a slight change in the air around him, a sense that something was moving sharp and swift towards his back. He didn't think, instead he helped the attack and found he was assisting the thin man with the knife to go over his shoulder and thud upside down against the wall.

Now Red was scared. Reacting on automatic was one thing, what the hell to do when a killer got up and looked at you was another. But the thin man didn't get up. He lay crumpled against the wall, balanced on a twisted neck. Slowly, as Red watched, the body tipped and folded to the floor.

He had killed a man, almost by accident, without struggle, without thought. In a way, that was the most terrifying thing that could have happened. Moving towards the dead man, he reached inside a jacket pocket. The way the thin man had fallen his pocket was exposed and Red didn't have to touch the corpse. But his hand chilled and the hairs on it stood as if he'd touched the dead flesh. He removed from the inside pocket an old-fashioned billfold. It was crammed with hundred-dollar bills and held one airline ticket in the name of Wayne Murray. There was also a sheet of paper from a travel agency. It gave details of the dead man's itinerary. Under the reservations section it showed the Elbow Beach Hotel in Bermuda.

When Red looked at the body he felt no hate, not even the sense of a deed well done. Slipping the wallet into his own pocket, he left the apartment, figuring there was no way he could clatter a corpse down the steps of this building without having the whole street watch him. Besides, whatever he did the cops were going to link him up with this, so he decided against wearing himself out by trying to hide a body in city streets.

He heard the sound of a distant siren and figured it was time to get out of Panama.

## 19

Jack smiled and raised one lazy finger. The stewardess grinned and refilled his champagne glass.

"You must have hollow legs, sir."

"Name's Jack, and what I got is an armor-plated liver. Here, don't move away so fast. Fill that up another time."

"Why don't I just leave a few bottles."

"What a clever idea."

And Jack resumed smiling. He'd been doing a lot of that on this flight. A few seats ahead of him sat the fat man, whom his noble son had described in detail. Jack had spotted him at the El Panama and had stayed on his tail without losing him, which wasn't easy because the fat man was a guy who got around town. He didn't have time to reach Red and tell him of his good fortune, he hardly had time to get to the crapper or find a moment to grab lunch. As soon as he did raise his sandwich he had to put it down again. The fat man was off to a second-hand store where he bought a beat-up old briefcase which he took to a shoemaker.

Jack followed his quarry from the shoemaker's on a Cook's tour of banks. The fat man was carrying a cheap plastic shopping bag which he gradually filled with money all destined for the false bottom that Jack knew was being installed in the briefcase. As the heat intensified, a plan began to shimmer its way from the heat towards Jack.

The fat man made only one unscheduled stop, and that was near midday. Fat people could really feel the midday heat ("Them and mad dogs," thought Jack), so just as the fat man climbed the slope that led to the shoemaker's shop, like a miracle, there was a sno-cone operation.

The fat man mopped his brow and went to the stand. Just as he did a cloud of children descended on the icewagon. One of them cut a slit in the bottom of the plastic bag and picked up the money from inside, while another replaced it with folded newspaper. The fat man didn't notice, he was too busy fighting his way past the kids to get himself an orange-flavor ice, which he slurped on as he moved towards the shoemaker's store. Jack was disappointed. He would have sworn the fat man would have gone for raspberry. However, that was of small consequence as everything else had gone as he'd arranged.

A small boy holding a raspberry sno-cone came over to Jack. In his hand he held a huge wad of American money.

"We did like you said, senor. I could have run off with this. You know that."

"What I know is you took a real good look at me, kid. No chance of you running off with the money."

"Maybe not now, maybe in two, three years."

"Two, three years, you wouldn't be the kid I'd ask. Right now why don't you take this for your trouble."

The little boy smiled. Then he ran. His friends, suddenly realizing that he was taking all the money with him, spun around, dropped their cones and ran after him. By the time they were running, the fat man had noticed the money was gone. He looked like he wanted to cut their throats but they were too far away for that.

He headed towards the banks again. Jack followed, counting the money as he went. Not bad, almost fifteen thousand dollars.

The rest of the day was spent in mundane fashion. The fat man visited more banks so the money supply could be replenished. Jack decided not to steal this lot, but that did take some self-discipline. Then they visited a barber, went to a tailor, gambled a little in the evening, and spent a peaceful night at the Blue Goose. The next morning the fat man kept checking his watch while making frequent phone calls. Jack got close enough to the booth to hear him leaving messages around town for his brother. Then he made a credit-card call to the Elbow Beach Hotel in Bermuda and left a message there. So besides having a Bell credit-card number, Jack now knew who he was following, someone called Harry Murray.

They each took a cab to the airport, and as the money was still intact, Jack decided to follow the good example being set by the man he was tailing and also book on first class. He wondered about Red and figured he'd reach him somehow after he tidied up loose ends. Perhaps the kid might figure out that everyone was going to Bermuda, it would be a simple matter of checking at the hotel. He smiled as he imagined himself and Red strolling along the beach as he told the kid how to enjoy life. Not a bad picture, and even if it didn't come true it made him feel like he really was carrying out Red's wishes. He knew he'd made a promise to his son that he could be the one in on the final session, but *"que será será,"* as Doris Day might remark.

As soon as the plane was airborne and the seatbelt sign turned off, he wandered past the fat man who was eating candied almonds while leafing through a brochure for the Elbow Beach Hotel. Jack ambled back to his seat, pleased that he was going to be staying in what looked like a good place.

Drinks were cleared up, the tables put in upright position, and announcements made as the plane tilted over on its approach to Bermuda. He had never been there before, as there wasn't any call for mercenaries in that island, so he daydreamed about the hotel where he and the fat man would be staying.

The only thing that marred the approach to Bermuda was the racket from a plump and pale young man sitting beside him. It was a rasping sleep, which continued up to landing time. As the plane approached the runway, Jack noticed that the young man's jacket had come open revealing a large, full wallet. Obviously this guy didn't pay any attention to Karl Malden's commercials for American Express. The wallet was full of good old American cash. Now, it was true that Jack had thousands of dollars in his pocket already, but this was a moral question. The young man needed a lesson. The plane began its touchdown and he waited for the first real jolt so he could lift the wallet.

The pilot must have been trained to help pick-pockets, because the plane hit with a wallop that sent it back into the air at once. Jack removed the wallet and stripped out its cash, which he folded into his own pocket. Then he moved the wallet in position to replace it in the young man's jacket. The plane bounced a second time, waking the young man. He stared at Jack, who stared back, still holding his neighbor's thin, pale wallet in his hands.

Jack looked embarrassed when his seatmate shouted, "Thief! Thief!" This was not one of his better moments.

## 20

Red looked through the *Bermuda Herald* for the seventh time that morning. The paper didn't get any better. One disadvantage with being the most peaceful holiday resort in creation was that it also made for a peaceful newspaper. The wars of other lands, the threats of bombings and distant violent deaths somehow became dusty and proper in the Bermuda paper. There had been an election on the island recently, but by all accounts it was conducted fairly and there were neither angry demands for recounts nor any cries of passion on the part of loser or winner. At first he'd thought this island of peace would help him rest. Instead he found that the old impatience was returning and he was longing for something that he had spent his life avoiding—action.

His chair was comfortable, and the view from the sparkling picture window was magnificent. However, despite the sight of a polished blue sky and light blue ocean with a perfect beach in between, he was bored. He couldn't leave his chair and go to the warm sand, because he might miss the arrival of the fat man. The longer he waited the more his doubts grew. What if only one of the killers had stayed behind in Panama? The fat one could be to hell and gone by now, leaving him to sit guarding a hotel lobby for the rest of his life. There was no going back to Panama City, and there was nowhere else in the world for him to go. He was gradually beginning to assume the false identity of Wayne Murray, despite the fact that Wayne was a name he had always hated with the pure undriven hatred of a seven-year-old. He remembered a spring day long ago in Boston, when the annual rock-throwing fights had started. They'd begun at the same time every year. And every year Red had tried to avoid them. He'd haunted back alleys and crossed in the middle of traffic to avoid the boys who always carried rocks in their hands, as loose as a sling, ready to throw them at each other. Red could slip away from every boy, except for one dark-haired pale skinny wrath of God named Wayne, who—if the world was fair—had ended up in either the major leagues or jail.

Despite his aversion to the name, he had recently trained himself to look around whenever he heard it and to answer to it without fail. Sometimes he would look in a mirror and say, "You're looking pretty good today, Wayne." Then he would grimace, and leave for the lobby.

This morning he was trying his best to keep his eyes open as he watched the line-up of a very neat church group that seemed to have been sprayed, full grown, from cans of deodorant. In front of this patient throng was a young woman complaining about something to a very polite desk clerk. Red couldn't hear what was being said, it was obscured by the excited chatter of the religious group. But he liked the look of the young woman. He found that he was watching the way the sunlight lit her face as she leaned in towards the desk clerk. She wasn't very tall, so she was lifting herself on strong tanned legs to talk with him. This was the first time since Azucar had died that Red had found himself noticing another woman. He looked away and stared out the door at the sun and breeze of paradise and tried to think other thoughts. But he found he had to look back.

## ✿ 21 ✿

The desk clerk was still smiling away and slowly shaking his head at Karen Chapman. He looked very patient and reasonable, the sort of man she wished she could kick in the crotch, just on principle.

She had listened to the ninth variation on the same theme from him. He was explaining why, at this hotel, there could not be a cockroach, and adding in greater detail the sorts of reasons that could lie behind her mistake. At first Karen had listened patiently, the same way she'd spent her life listening to various jerks. Throughout the clerk's explanations she kept hearing something familiar in his voice. She listened harder and harder, but couldn't place it.

"So you see, Miss, there is no possible way, at this moment in time, there could be a cockroach in your room. You couldn't have seen one."

Karen suddenly knew what the familiar sound was, it was an echo of Scott. The clerk, finished with her, now pretended that she wasn't there anymore and turned towards a polyestered, scrubbed, round-faced man behind her. That's when Karen blew.

"I know a cockroach when I see one, you ass-hole, so either give me a cage for it or get me a new room!"

The church group in the lineup stopped talking and began to make a low-volume tsk-tsk noise like restless locusts. The clerk tried to hush Karen, but with no luck.

"Miss Chapman..."

"Ms Chapman..."

"There are no more rooms. All we have left is one suite."

"Does it have cockroaches?"

"Of course not! But it's reserved and it's beyond your price range."

"You've got one minute to make the switch-over, at the same price that I'm paying for my room right now. Because if you don't, I might do some-thing really stupid. Like capture all the cock-roaches in my room and bring them along with me for dinner. I'll pretend they're my pets and put them all on leads."

"Perhaps, there is something that could be arranged..."

"Thirty seconds!"

The desk clerk now looked sweaty and rum-pled, even the Harvard crest on his spotless blazer started to wilt and wrinkle. In one quick gesture he passed her the key to the suite.

Karen finally smiled. She passed back the key. "Have them move my luggage to the suite, and tell them to leave the cockroaches for one of these nice people."

When Karen strode away the looks of disap-proval from the church group changed to appre-hension as they surged towards the hapless clerk.

The man in the white suit looked at her and applauded.

She winked happily in his direction. There was something dangerous looking about him. Normally she was cautious about dangerous-looking men, otherwise some late night over beer and popcorn you were likely to hear unexpected things about their marital status. But this guy didn't look married, he didn't even look divorced.

Standing by the elevator she glanced back at him. He seemed stuck in the same lobby chair that she'd noticed him in before. For a moment she wondered if something was wrong with his legs. That would explain why he never seemed to budge from the seat. She turned away as the elevator arrived.

"I've got some bad news for you."

Karen looked behind her and there was the man she'd winked at. He was smiling and looked even better close up. The elevator doors closed again before she could climb on.

"My name's Wayne Murray," he said with great sincerity. "I've got a suite and it's got cockroaches."

"How come you didn't complain?"

"A less refined upbringing?"

"Yeah, from the look of you I'd say that's a definite possibility!"

And they laughed together. Then they went towards the outdoor bar. The breeze that came off the ocean was clean and cool and smelled like washed sand. The man blinked and, pulling out a chair, sat down. Karen scraped back her chair and joined him.

"How come you didn't pull out a chair for me?"

"You don't appear injured."

"I used to be married to a man who, I now believe, hated me..."

"He must be a jerk."

"You know him? He always pulled back chairs for me, let me enter the room before him and opened the car door for me, even if I was driving."

"What are you going to drink, Ms Chapman?"

"Karen. I'm going to have something cool, tall and loaded with alcohol. Something dangerous. What are you going to have, Wayne?"

"Why don't you call me Red?"

"How come? You've got black hair and you're tanned like a tea bag."

"I'm going to drink dark rum and Coca-Cola, with a twist of lime."

After ordering, they settled back in their seats and for a long time neither spoke. The drinks arrived and they clinked glasses, but that was it for a while. Karen looked all around her as if she was seeing Bermuda for the first time. She wasn't certain about what to do next.

"You know, Wayne, you don't have a name that I'm very fond of. I can see why you call yourself Red."

"I don't like the name much either, Karen. As a matter of fact I think it just may be the stupidest name there is."

"Scott. That's the stupidest name there is. Wayne comes in second. How come your mother called you Wayne?"

Red looked at her and felt something very weird happening to him. He felt like telling the truth. And that startled him. No matter what the occasion, no matter who the person, he slipped into a lie as easily as into a *National Geographic* magazine. He felt like an acrobat losing his balance in front of a new crowd and without a net. He also decided to fall.

"She didn't call me Wayne. No one has ever called me Wayne, except the desk clerk. I was christened Michael Denis Williams in Boston forty years ago. My nickname is and always will be 'Red.'"

"No shit? So why did you tell me you were called Wayne?"

"Because I tell a lot of lies and because I'm here using Wayne Murray's name, his suite and some of his money."

There was an even longer silence. Then Karen spoke.

"Red, I have a strange feeling that we may get along."

## 🌿 22 🌿

When Karen and Red came out of the bar they blinked. Without a word, the desk clerk passed her the key to her suite, and she and Red walked towards the elevator. They'd spent most of the afternoon talking, and Karen found herself telling him a lot about what it was like growing up in Gloucester. After finding out she was most recently from Boston, he kept asking her questions about how it had changed in twenty years. She wanted to know why he hadn't been there in all that time, and he ended up telling her about the last highly unsuccessful scam he'd tried. It had involved a shoe manufacturer from Revere and the story of an Oak Island fortune. It had also involved police a week too soon and a hasty departure from a winter as chilly as the Charles. Karen didn't disapprove. She found she was at a point in her life where she was more interested in what people did than in what people should do.

They drank, they laughed, and for the first time in a long while Red stopped thinking about Azucar. Karen had even stopped worrying about what she was going to do in three and a half days when her money ran out.

But now as they stood outside the elevator and waited for it to arrive, they had run out of things to say. She looked at her key number as did Red. He was the first to speak.

"That's my floor too."

"Is that good or bad?"

"What do you think?"

"You go first."

Red paused, and the elevator door opened. For a moment he held back. He thought of Azucar and knew he should keep watching the hotel lobby for the arrival of the fat man.

For Karen a hesitation was all that was needed for her to step inside the elevator and push the button for her floor. She looked at Red as the doors closed and she didn't smile. He wondered if he should run up the stairs, and then he looked back in the lobby. When he did, he saw the fat man, saw him as vivid and as clear as memory. Even before he turned around, Red could remember those cat's eyes and the way they had flashed just before he'd hit the water.

The fat man felt that he was being stared at, so he did a quick scan of the entire lobby. He looked in Red's direction, but only for a moment. Seeing what appeared to him to be a stranger, his eyes looked into other corners. Red started working his way closer. He needed to know the room number the killer would be assigned, and perhaps he'd even learn his name. He stood behind two born-again teachers who were deep in a discussion of what was wrong with the theory of evolution. It was going to be a long wait. Leaning against the side of the entrance, he looked outside as if he were waiting for a cab. The door opened and closed and the air that drifted in was hot and moist. One cab drove into another with a mighty smack and the drivers got out. He expected that they would shout at each other and wave their fists. Instead they both looked sadly at the dents and shook their heads.

He was musing about this when he became aware of that strange cicada-like buzz that moved once more through the lineup. The fat man had pushed his way past everyone and was talking with the desk clerk. Red leaned closer.

"Yes, Mr Murray, your brother has checked in already."

"What room is he in?"

"Three twenty-four, but actually, he's right there in the lobby. He always sits in that ... Funny, he was there a couple of minutes ago."

"Where?"

Red decided it was time to get the hell out of the lobby. The one thing that he should have anticipated, he hadn't. The killer was going to go to Wayne's room.

Red rushed around to the side entrance, up three flights of stairs, down the hall, and into his room. So far he was lucky, the fat man wasn't there yet. First thing to do was retrieve what was left of his money. He lifted the makeshift flotation bag he'd fashioned from shower caps and took it from the cistern. After pocketing the cash, he picked out a change of clothes. Then he grabbed his passport, and was just about to take some more clothing when he heard a key in the lock. As fast as he could, he climbed over the balcony and onto the ledge, closing the window behind him.

Red edged around the corner of the building. He carried his fresh suit on a hanger, crisp and black it flapped in the breeze. The money belt was over his shoulder like a bandoleer, and the money fluttered in the hot wind as he tried to stuff the cash into his pocket. He kept trembling his way along the ledge until there was a pause in the wind and he heard his room window creak open again so he knew the fat man was about to join him. In front of Red there was another window. It was open and the drapes were sucked out towards the ledge in a balloon shape.

In one step he was inside, but he hadn't anticipated a sofa being directly under the ledge, so he lost his footing and took a tumble, spilling his suit, money and money belt in all directions. He staggered up to see a naked woman standing in front of him.

"And I didn't think you wanted to see me again," said Karen Chapman.

## 23

Jack wasn't in the mood to escape from jail until they brought in the one-legged Newfoundlander.

Up to that time he'd settled back to enjoy a bit of a rest. The food was amazing, better than any jail he'd ever been in. Not only was everything tasty, but it was served with a certain élan and the help here was as polite as you could expect on a good day at a decent restaurant. The head jailer would have drawn an encouraging nod from the maitre d' at "21." Here, no one seemed to think any less of Jack for his being a pickpocket. They had politely taken away all his money as evidence, without breathing so much as a word about guilt. A nice jail.

Jack swore that he would retire to Bermuda. From the look of the houses he'd passed on the way to the hoosegow, he suspected that he'd need mucho bucks to make the retirement work out. But he still had an optimistic feeling that this caper, in addition to reuniting him with his son, was going to lead to more money than he'd ever seen in his life before.

With that thought in mind he relaxed and waited for dinner. Nothing was going to surprise him here. Perhaps baked Brie might be on the menu, or Camembert fritters, perhaps a tropical surprise, something with mangos and rum; he didn't ask for much, just enough to add flavor. His mouth watered and he wondered what Red might be having for supper. Next Jack speculated on what his son might be actually doing at that moment, or, indeed, where he might be. He suspected that he might be back in Panama City. On the other hand, Red might have followed the same trail. Then he did what he swore he would never do—worry about his son. That startled him. After all, the kid was an adult, and now knew everything a human being needed to know about defense under attack. However, the guys that Red had encountered enjoyed hurting—he knew that from what had been done to Azucar. But, when blood made you smile and lick your lips for salt it also made you weak, able to be picked off like a fly by someone who was detached.

For a while when Red had started training, Jack had thought that was what made him tick. As the training progressed he saw that things were more complex than first appeared. True, Red had begun his quest in the first place to avenge Azucar. But as the weeks had gone by Jack saw that he wanted to do the killing because, in some obscure way, he felt guilty for Azucar's death.

When Red was just a kid, Jack had never worried, never cared, because in a strange way the child had never seemed entirely real, more like a dream he'd had on a pleasant morning. He'd dandled the little boy on his knee, sung songs to him in five languages, watched the way the sunlight shone on his curls. He'd looked in on him at night and felt his own heart jump when he had cried out. But all it had taken to move these thoughts away were some weeks on the road. Tension, excitement, even the look of a new country, or the sound of nearby battle would move home as far away as a goodbye from a speeding train.

The light that edged its way in from the heat of midday turned cold and blue. Like the Boston winter when Red, at six years of age, had stood watching his father leave just as the snow had suddenly shifted and the air cleared and the space in front of his son was as even as a snowflake. Jack was going to stop the taxi and run back, perhaps not to stay, just to say goodbye in the right way. But the snow blew back again and time moved, and then his mind had strayed past the heap of words towards South America, and his dreams heated with the jungle undergrowth. The little boy had faded away behind the snow squall.

Now, in the Bermuda jail, Red became real again and, like so many nights lately, the memory of how a six-year-old boy looked took over Jack's every thought, until the voices came back and he was aware that he wasn't alone.

That's when he saw the one-legged Newfoundlander, and knew that trouble had arrived. He had a talker as a cellmate—and what a talker! As the door opened, the Newfoundlander started.

"Ever see *The Best Years of Our Lives*, I saw that at the old Paramount on Harvey Road. What a picture! That could have been me up on the screen, I thought then, instead of Harold Russell, that great actor with no hands, I mean. If the guy in the

movie had a leg gone *instead* of his hands, then
where would life be? Where would it have turned,
tell me that? I'd be in Hollywood now, with some
starlet carving little hearts on my wooden leg. I'm
George Walsh, who are you? Pleased to meet you,
ah, the quiet sort, eh, well don't you worry about
the talking, I does enough for the whole place, as
Mother used to say."

Still in full conversation, he leaned back, and
with a practiced twist, did something to his artificial leg so it chirped and squeaked and suddenly
was leaning against the wall as if it had a life of its
own. A couple of times it tipped over with an almighty rattle, but then gave up on that and seemed
crouched in the corner of the cell, while its owner,
("Pegleg you can call me, like in Bates, the one-
legged dancer, if you recalls?") dug deep into his
treasure house of memories.

Jack looked down the corridor towards the entrance. Framed in the doorway, under a moon-
stone gate he could see the guard, who was talking
up a storm with a very attractive woman standing
next to her disabled moped. The guard began tin-
kering with the engine while the woman
watched. Both had their backs to the door. Jack decided that this was the time to act and, though Pegleg was still talking, managed to interrupt him.

"I wonder if I might borrow your artificial pin?"

"Sure thing." Pegleg passed it over and his
words continued. They didn't stop even when
Jack's clever hands reached inside the leg. A long
section of metal emerged. Still, the talking went
on. Jack slipped the curved rod into the lock, apply-
ing slow pressure until there was a click and the
door sprang open.

"Want to come along, Pegleg?"

"With me leg took apart? No way, but I'll make sure I keeps talking so nothing seems to change. Now my Uncle Ern was the perfect person for an inventor. Let me tell you what he was able to do with two beach rocks and a broody hen..."

Jack began moving towards the door. As he walked, despite the babble from Pegleg, the place still seemed very quiet. Every step made a clink and all the cellbars seemed to sing as he passed them. Pegleg roused himself to new limits of speech and his voice covered any extra noises.

Jack peeked at the open door. The guard was kissing the woman with the moped. In a moment Jack was around the corner.

He moved farther and farther away from the jail, and started to hum. When he entered some underbrush that led to the ocean he burst into a Freddy Fender song. The waves crashed in tune, he was free.

## ❧ 24 ❧

Karen was sleeping when the last rays of sunset buckled around the edge of the drapes and shone directly on her face. She shifted as they did, resting her head on Red's chest.

He hadn't figured on anything like this ever happening again. For one thing, whenever he thought of love or of gentleness, an image of Azucar in her death would spring at him. For another thing he had lived a life where he was used to her being the only person who ever bothered to look at him. The fatter, paler and more wrinkled he'd become, the happier she'd been. She had told him once that he was the only sort of man she could have loved—he kept her mind off work. Red wondered what she'd think of him now. He still thought of himself as carrying an extra fifty pounds and often when he got up from a chair he would find himself springing across a room because of the force he'd used to lift those missing pounds. Other times he'd glance in the mirror and think that a stranger was in the room. Karen shifted again and slid until her head was nestled in the crook of his arm.

Red was glad that it was dark in the Bermuda hotel room. He remembered Azucar and how he had failed her. His cover was gone. The way the fat man's eyes had passed over him in the lobby, he'd be remembered. And because the fat man wasn't stupid he would have deduced that his brother was dead. Now, he would not get close enough to the killer to pay him back for the stopping of Azucar's dreams. His thoughts slowed as he moved towards sleep and he tried to stay awake because he felt his problem contained his solution. Before the answer was there he was asleep.

And he was on a beach where he was tied to Azucar as they stood and rocked by the edge of the sea. And even though he couldn't see her, he knew that she was alive. He was content to stand there, leaning against her, bound to her, feeling the warm air, seeing the ocean ripen under a new moon, until he noticed they were sinking slowly in the sand. Even that didn't scare him—nor did the water that rose to his chin. Then the sea covered his eyes, and as it did the bonds that held him to Azucar swayed and stretched like rubber. She managed to turn around and look at him, but when she did her throat gaped open and a fish swam out of the wound. Red screamed and water and small fish filled his mouth when he tried to swim.

He woke to find himself with his head out the window, yelling into the night air. A light clicked on behind him and he turned around, still feeling like he was swimming, still feeling like he was strung to Azucar. He wasn't sure of who he was, of what he was, of where he was. A strong woman with beautiful hands held them out to him and stared. The covers fell off her breasts and she sat looking at him.

"Come back to bed. Let me help."

Red looked out the window into the terraced gardens that stepped to the sea, slowly becoming aware of people in evening dress looking up at him from their moonlight stroll. He took his time closing the drapes, and moved towards Karen.

"Karen..."

"I don't mind your hopping around the room, starkers, I don't even mind your screaming out the window and waving your thing at the tourists. What I do mind is that something's still wrong. Tell me what it is."

And despite himself, Red did.

Karen was a good listener. She looked at him, and held his hand while she listened. She touched his scars as he lay naked in the ocean, she stroked his head as he had fever in the Quonset hut, she felt his muscles as he trained, and she listened as he told her of the old man who had trained him, and nodded as he told her of the man he had to kill because of Azucar. As he talked of his dead love and how she had called him the last white man in Panama, he felt the tears start again like they had never ended. When he reached for the light Karen stopped him, and, as tear drops rolled down his cheeks, she licked them off and eased him flat on his back. Soon his tears turned to kisses and like candy she ate them. Leaving the light on, they made sweet love.

They held each other and slept. A peaceful sleep. And Red neither leapt up nor screamed out the window. He and Karen lay still on the bed, caught in folds of sheets and in the warmth of the light that dripped from a new morning.

He was careful not to wake her when he got up. But, coming back to the bedroom after an ice-cold blast of water, he discovered that a wonderful breakfast of scrambled eggs, kippers and champagne had been set out on drift white linen.

Karen and Red didn't talk much for a while after that. They were content to munch crisp toast as they sipped dry champagne to wash down mouthfuls of delicious eggs and kippers. From outside they could hear the enthusiastic voices of holiday-makers, while the sound from a distant jet iced past their window. Someone in another room had opened a window, letting the sound of a guitar string across the courtyard. Horns beeped while the sun bent shadows over the rug. Karen watched him eat.

"I used one of your hundred-dollar bills to pay for breakfast. Do you mind?"

"That's what it's for."

"I tipped our waiter all of the change."

"Good. He deserved it."

"That's the first time I ever spent so much money on breakfast. I was curious to see what it was like, doing something like that, even if it wasn't my cash. I just wanted the feeling."

"And...?"

"And it was all I could do to keep from running down the hall after him to get it back."

"Karen, I've got a problem."

"I knew it, you're married."

"Never been."

"Okay. Then we've got no problem that we can't solve. Shoot."

As they finished off the champagne, Red explained that because of the fat man it was going to be dangerous for him to show his face around the hotel.

"Then you haven't got a worry, because this guy doesn't know who I am or what I look like. I'll track him and as long as he doesn't see us together there shouldn't be any sweat."

"Are you kidding? I can't let you put your life in danger."

"We'd better get something straight if you want this to go any further than a one-night stand. It isn't a question of 'letting' me do anything."

"It's a question of you maybe getting killed."

"All my life people have told me what I should do. Scott was very good at knowing what I could do, he was good at not 'letting' me do other things. Now, I want to take some chances. God knows what there is about you, but it's enough for me." And she smiled.

Then Red understood that this was his big win, even more than the jackpot at the El Panama. And it was Karen's turn to tell more of her story. The champagne was gone, but the coffee was still hot, and she could spin a tale with the best of them.

Red laughed himself to the floor when she recounted the day she told off the anchorman. He listened quietly when she explained how all the anger she'd built up in the place just exploded, he approved of Dooley's Bar, and he applauded when she described seeing the picture of Bermuda and just going for it.

They were interrupted by the cleaning staff, and Red beat a hasty retreat to the washroom while the rest of the suite was being finished. Karen took her shower, until steam billowed around her when she emerged cocooned in towels.

One of the chambermaids was singing something about being lost between the moon and New York City. Red didn't know the song but Karen did and taught him the words. They danced as she sang to him. For a while Red felt so good that he thought perhaps he might have been killed, drowned in the ocean, died and gone where the good con men go. They danced over the towels that soaked up the condensation, and past the mirror where Karen swept a path through the mist so they could watch themselves. The chambermaid left the other room, but Red and Karen stayed in the bathroom to finish the song. They bowed towards the mirror and she kissed him lightly.

"Red, I will smuggle you caviar and wine, I will sing Peter Allen songs for you, but most of all I will do some spying."

And they danced until the steam left the mirror and the towels were cold and wet on the floor.

## ⚘ 25 ⚘

The fat man sat in the very seat that Red had used in his surveillance of the lobby, watching every person who arrived and departed. Every few minutes he'd pace over to the door.

In the afternoon he strolled all the way down to the beach because he was worn out with waiting. He did not look at the hibiscus that spilled into the path; he did not look at the beach club crowded with people with new sunburns and full rum punches; he did not look at the white sand. Instead he stood beside the ocean while checking the date on his watch and looking at the sky. No plane appeared and there weren't even any clouds. This seemed to satisfy him so he turned and began his ponderous climb back to the hotel.

If he could have seen what was happening while he was out of the lobby he would have walked faster. The desk clerk had received a strange and complicated call which originated in Miss Chapman's suite, but was from a man and in Spanish. That was one of the few languages that the desk clerk didn't speak well. He pleaded to be allowed to seek assistance, but the man on the phone somehow found a scattered word or so in English to help him along.

It seemed the man was a Spanish diplomat who had wandered into the wrong room of the wrong hotel. He refused to get off the phone until he was told how to find an elevator, while demanding to be informed of the reasons why he was not in the Hamilton Princess. He even made a crude joke about that request, or so the desk clerk thought, but didn't dare laugh in case he was wrong. Every time he seemed about to be rid of this man, the talk took a new twist.

While Red kept the desk clerk in the assistant manager's office occupied with that call, Karen walked across the lobby with a purposeful stride. She went directly to the guest register and discovered that the killer had not registered as "The Fat Man." He was listed as Harry Murray, address c/o the Standard Building, Boston. This intrigued Karen, because that building was home to the fastest growing television network in America and, despite leaning a little to the right, wasn't known as a home of hit men. As the register didn't give up enough information, Karen decided to go inside the counter and read the registration card on good old Harry, a.k.a. the fat man.

The desk clerk was saying something about Cervantes as he sweated over the telephone. Karen smiled and admired Red's talent. She opened the gray filing box that held the arrival cards. Yesterday's lot was still in place. When she checked the card she discovered something that surprised even her. The fat man was vice-president of the Standard Telecasting Corporation. Karen replaced the card and went back to the lobby.

She absent-mindedly went to sit in the lobby chair while she watched the door for signs of the fat man, only to find that he had returned and she was about to sit in his lap. She stopped herself just in time, and with a gasp sprang away from the chair and its occupant.

"Just when I thought you were going to make my day!"

"Funny, you don't look like Clint Eastwood."

"I've been thinking of dieting. How come you look familiar?"

"Perhaps I remind you of someone you knew, or that your daughter went to school with."

"I've got it. You're Karen Chapman, 'NewsCheck' from Boston!"

"A fan."

"Don't push your luck. Though you are good, pretty good. Too good for Channel Five."

"That's the way they saw it."

"Got the ax?"

"Yep. Are you from Boston too? Or do you get the station here on your fillings?"

"No, I'm beantown."

"Which part?"

"I get around, I work, my name's Harry Murray....You don't know the name?"

"Afraid not."

"You know about my boss...Timothy Shepherd."

"You're kidding? You work for *the* Timothy Shepherd? Mister Clean?"

"I prefer to think that I work with him."

"Is he here with you?"

"He never leaves Boston when there's snow on the ground. Likes the look of the Charles in winter with the scum frozen. That's why he sent me here, in the heat. There's a station on the island that he wants me to look at."

"Know if they need a reporter?"

"What would you do here? Report on how many waves come in each hour. I've seen you in action. You're best figuring out the tough stories. You should be working back home."

"That's what I tried to tell them at Channel Five."

"Don't give up. Things are easy, you want a job, you got one."

"Says who?"

"Me. I hire for Standard, so if you want to work, that's what I'm offering."

"Now?"

"Say yes and you're aboard. Hesitate and maybe I'm wrong about you."

Karen stared at the fat man—Harry—she must learn to think of him as Harry—while trying to get a grip on what was left of the moment. This was the first time she'd been offered a job by a killer and what surprised her was how close she was to saying "yes." She suspected that events weren't turning out the way Red had hoped they would. On the other hand, he seemed to have no clear idea about what the motive for Azucar's killing could be, and here was a chance to be able to stay close to the guy who was one of the killers. On the negative side, the fat man had killed at least one other woman, and who's to say that he couldn't get the notion to do so again.

Harry kept watching and Karen wondered if she'd already hesitated too long. She didn't see how he could link her to Red, and to tell the truth, she would love to be able to show up back in Boston

again, this time with the station that was beating
the ratings out of Channel Five. She looked the fat
man right in the eyes before she nodded.

"Good decision. Now your first assignment is to
evaluate the station I was going to look at. That way
I can sit around the lobby."

"Listen, Harry, I don't mind checking out the
station, but I've got one question. How come you're
going to stay in the lobby, when you could be out
in the sun, lying on the beach, swimming in the
ocean?"

"I don't like the outdoors."

Then he proceeded to give Karen a rundown on
the Bermuda station. He had no notes, but he impressed her with the amount he already knew
about the place, giving her the details as casually
as, at the age of twelve, she could rhyme off baseball scores. He knew how many listeners the station had, he also knew the demographics, of just
what age group listened to what and at exactly
what time, he knew the role of the station, and its
history. Harry was also able to sketch for Karen the
social, historical and political background of the island, and what would have to be done to make the
station more of a part of everyday life in Bermuda.
When he finally paused to take a breath, Karen
told him she'd head out right after she headed
upstairs to freshen up.

But before she could start off for her room Harry
had opened the front door, pushed her into a cab,
paid the driver and sent her away. There was no
chance to let Red know the news. She thought
he'd be interested in learning that she was working for the killer.

## ❧ 26 ❧

Jack decided that he liked the Elbow Beach Hotel. It was correct that the attic wasn't supposed to be the best location, but he was there of his own choice, and there were no jailers. He was also in quarters based in a luxury hotel. True, it was the most remote and most cobweb-encrusted part of the attic but there now was a ladder for easy access. Jack had rigged a piece of rope to it, and he could pull it up after him as he vanished through the distant roof of a linen closet. That way no one could follow him. His own private entrance! Why he was better off than if he was renting the penthouse suite.

As for food, all it took was excellent timing, because there were plenty of leavings from room service, no need to alert anyone by stealing the meals before they were delivered. Amazing what people left on their trays when it was late at night or early in the morning. Whenever he found himself in the position of living off what the western world called garbage he gained a greater understanding of the ways that revolutions started.

It was true that the heat in the hotel was all gathered into a warm wet ball and then rolled nightly into Jack's section of the attic, but heat never bothered him a great deal, anyway. Besides, this older section of the hotel didn't have any fiberglass insulation, so he could hop around in the nude and not worry about itching to death. Many hours he lay there, stark naked, wiggling his toes and making friends with the lizards who also liked this section of the attic. He became good chums with them and charmed them with Freddy Fender songs.

Some of the hotel guests were puzzled by this period in Jack's life. They seemed to hear, in certain sections of the corridors, a ghostly twang of country-and-western music, sung by a rusty old voice. It was faint and so difficult to place that anyone who heard it decided not to mention anything about the music to other people. Some of the more imaginative started keeping away from the hallway over the east wing, and in later life would wonder about the haunting of their corridor. For the lizards it was quite an exciting change in their daily routine and beat hell out of turning the color of wood.

But not all was diversion for Jack. He spent the late evening and nighttime, through sunrise, creeping around the ledges of the hotel, ledge by painted ledge until he could find out who was in each room. He knew that the fat man had checked in. Jack had slipped in and out of the lobby through the roof vent one early morning, so he could check the hotel register, which looked well thumbed. It showed him that a man known as Harry Murray had indeed registered, but the room number didn't show in the book. He knew that sooner or later he would find the correct room, as he had only one section of the third floor left to check, and that wouldn't take him long.

This particular night he could begin his work early. A storm was moving in and dark clouds rolled across the pink sky. As flowers began to lose their petals in a small blizzard of spinning color, Jack prepared to begin his hunt.

He'd found the storage area where all the cleaning agents, plaster and paint were stored and found the color for the outside of the building. It was in powder form, the sort that you mixed up with water and applied to stucco. Jack did mix it up, and found a wonderful, exact shade to match the outside of the building. Daubing it over his naked body, he then dipped a hotel towel to soak up the remaining mixture. He fashioned a loin cloth from the towel and squatted a moment waiting for it to begin drying before he started on his journey. The lizards watched all this with a professional curiosity.

Jack unlashed his ladder, descended to the floor below, tugged on the line that sent it back into the roof, then crossed the corridor, opened a window and stood out on the third-floor ledge. Blending in with the wall, he moved as the clouds moved, a faint shadow at sunset.

# ❧ 27 ❧

Red was delighted to discover that Karen had accepted a job with the killer. Like her, he figured that it gave them a chance to get closer to the fat man. Like her, he was also beginning to wonder about the connection between a rich professional from Boston and a whore in Panama City. He continued to speculate about the fat man.

"For God's sake, Red, could you stop calling him the fat man."

"What do you want me to call him? The thin man?"

"Harry. 'Cause if you don't, I'm going to forget myself, and wind up calling him 'Fat Man,' right to his face. I don't know how strong his ego is, but I suspect I'd be in trouble if that happened."

Agreeing that this could put a crimp in employer-employee relations, Red began to rethink the whole picture that he had built up of the fat man—sorry, Harry, and of his brother. Most of his criminal experience was in a circle of petty thieves and con men. He had never encountered any murderers until he met Wayne and Harry. He wondered if real killers enjoyed their work, and thought that there would, instead, be a center of coldness, of detachment.

He was about to follow this line of thought with Karen, but she had moved on to discussing the station that she had seen in the afternoon, going over her reasons, despite the fat man's beliefs, that it should not be purchased.

"Call him Harry," was Red's only observation. Karen's excitement grew as she went on to explain how all the things that made the station look like a good purchase were actually points against buying it. Red was impressed with her. He watched the way she rocked back and forth as ideas came, the quick spring of her legs as she had to start pacing, unable to sit still as she went over idea after idea. She talked about getting back to broadcasting, of the reason she'd always liked working in it, of how this could be a comeback, even if it was on a killer's coattails.

He listened until Karen stopped in mid-stride and stared at him.

"I'm really sorry I cut you off about the killing...."

He reached forward and slowly kissed her.

"It's good to think about other things. But what I can't figure is how broadcasting would be tied up with any of this."

"Don't ask me. Did Azucar ever go to Boston?"

"She didn't even go outside Panama City. Maybe it's got nothing at all to do with it."

"Oh shit, I've got to meet Harry for dinner. I'll bring you back a doggie bag."

And she was gone.

Red decided not to wait for the doggie bag. Not for nothing was he a con man. Picking up the phone with great confidence he used a Viennese accent to inform the desk clerk that a vital meeting was underway in Ms Chapman's suite and much coffee was required, along with the biggest steak they had, baked potato, steamed crisp vegetables, and a good red wine, as well as Sacher torte. Being told it would take an hour, he informed the desk how quickly the Sacher Hotel would provide the same thing, if only, heaven grant it, he were at home in his beloved city, and praised the hotels of that city so much that room service, stung, told Red the food would be there ten minutes after he hung up the phone. He let the receiver settle with a discreet click and smiled.

From the open window came a ghostly voice.

"Make that two steaks."

Red jumped back, just as a pink phantom materialized through the window. Pink, red or blue there was no mistaking that the ghost was Jack.

"Don't stand there with your mouth open, kid, we got a lot of catching up to do."

# 28

The fat man ate with surprising restraint. Slow and precise moves, like a piano tuner. The other thing that distinguished him from the rest of the diners was his habit of staring at his food before he put it on the fork. It was like watching a Zen master eat. The fat man also used his cutlery the way a European would, keeping his fork in his left hand, and his knife in the right.

Karen hardly touched her food. She concentrated on giving her best report about the Bermuda station. It was vital to make sure the report was good. Everything depended on her getting to Boston, so she could find out about the murder. But that wasn't the only reason. She had enjoyed thinking about the station and analyzing what the fat man had said were good reasons for investing in it. She liked taking his arguments apart. Then she wondered if she was pressing a bit too hard. After all, he had seemed ready to recommend buying it before she was sent out to do her check. So she paused, wondering if she should hold back on her comments. "What the hell," she thought, "if he wanted a toadie, Boston was already full of them."

When she concluded telling him why the station was not a good investment, she glanced down at the bowl of soup that was still untouched in front of her. It was originally chilled, but Harry remarked it had been there long enough to have steam rising from it. He raised a finger and three waiters arrived to remove his main course plate and, without a word being spoken, replaced her bowl of soup with a fresh one. A fourth waiter had a miniature vacuum cleaner, and, with a quick swipe, he cleared the table of invisible crumbs and other sub-atomic particles. The linen cloth gleamed clean and white. From outside there was the sound of a distant thunderclap.

"Well, Karen, you know that your report directly contradicts me."

"Yes, but…"

"Don't bother answering, I hate to see good soup grow warm while you talk. Besides, this is a time when you should listen. You spent one afternoon at the studio. I, on the other hand, spent months looking at flow charts, doing a mock-up schedule. I spent weeks having my experts research the island and its needs."

Karen gulped the last of her soup, so she could defend herself. But as soon as she opened her mouth to speak, the bowl was whisked away and a succulent platter filled with different hues of native fish was placed before her. She became aware, as she waited for the fat man to continue, of the recorded music in the restaurant. Acker Bilk was playing "Unchained Melody," and all the words and murmurings in the restaurant fell in with the beat of the song. As the clarinet continued she found herself eating in 4/4 time, taking swinging

sweeps of her vegetables as Harry, now thorough-
ly enjoying himself, gave reason after reason for
buying the station. He smiled as he concluded and
nodded, apparently in time to the Acker Bilk tape.

A snifter of brandy was placed before him and
he took an expensive cigar from a maroon leather
case. Snipping the end of the cigar, using a gold
clipper, he lit and savored it. Then he looked
across at Karen. She was busy trying to debone a
red, evil-looking fish. Harry leaned over and
picked up a flat silver knife and a small fork. With
three quick moves all the bones vanished, along
with the staring head.

"Karen, I want you to know that I don't need to
always hear 'yes,' I have many clever people to do
that for me. I've now told you all the reasons they
found to back every one of my theories. They
drew up splendid essays to demonstrate my
thoughts and display them back to me. But now,
after hearing you, I think all their work is," he
paused, "bullshit." And he grinned.

Karen grinned right back.

"Harry, might I sample one of your cigars?"

He watched as she went through the ritual of
preparing it. She raised an eyebrow and the waiter
appeared, almost as quickly as he did for the fat
man. A brandy was placed in front of her. Karen
warmed it slightly and sipped.

As she tasted the cigar smoke and the brandy,
she thought of her father, who had now been dead
for almost twenty-five years. She was nine when
he died and most people had thought she was old
enough to experience the grief right along with
the grown-ups. Because they thought she could understand, she had been allowed to visit him at the

hospital where he lay like a crushed acrobat. He was so weak that he couldn't speak. Sometimes he looked towards the corner of the hospital room, smiling and nodding as if he had spied a familiar visitor. But whenever Karen was brought to him, his eyes clouded over as if he were seeing a stranger.

After her father died, she spent a lot of time looking out at the Atlantic from his study. The room held tones of smoked oak, leather and the green blotting paper. The desk lamp was brass. There was a cigar clipper next to some large kitchen matches and a box of Panamanian cigars. Karen had always watched every detail of the ritual her father went through whenever he smoked and she remembered every move. Because she had a feeling that her mother would disapprove of a little girl enjoying cigars, she'd added a few moves of her own. When lighting up, she would go over to the fireplace, open the damper and blow the smoke up the chimney.

For a while her mother thought the house was haunted by the ghost of her late husband because there always seemed to be a lingering scent of cigars in the study. It was this feeling almost as much as discovering how little her card-loving husband had left behind that led her to put the house up for sale and eventually move to a small bungalow further away from the ocean.

"Who taught you to smoke cigars?" asked the fat man.

"My father."

"Ah, you were lucky. Mine was a clergyman. Not smoking fit right into the ten commandments in his scheme of things. 'Ten B' I think it was.

Whatever its number, that was one of my favorites to break."

And he and Karen smoked and then drank endless snifters of brandy. The bill never appeared and Karen suspected that was the way things were for rich people. She wondered if all the other diners paid for the process. She also began to puzzle over Red's description of what this man was supposed to have done. He appeared to be everything a civilized man should be—cultivated, witty and good company. The thought of his cutting a woman's throat, and still being the person that he appeared to be, didn't fit into anything that Karen had ever seen in her life. The fat man had offered her a job, a real one, something that she'd have killed for. When he heard her destroy a plan that he had spent a great deal of time and energy on he didn't get angry, instead he complimented her.

Their smoke swirled in gentle spirals. The brandy tasted of lined cigar boxes and Karen liked that. Liked? She loved it, and not just because she was feeling light headed.

"What about your brother? Are you leaving before you find him?"

The room changed in tone as Karen realized what she'd just asked. Nothing altered in the fat man's posture. The ash that he'd been tipping into the ashtray still dropped in at just the right angle. He smiled as gently as before, the music continued, other diners talked and laughed, but something had shifted. Something so deep that it couldn't be seen. However, like a subterranean stream, its cold could be felt even through summer's hay. The trembling would be sensed. Karen knew that Red's story was true. The fat man looked at her and smiled.

"My brother? I wasn't aware that you knew my brother."

Karen blushed. She hadn't done it in years and years, but she managed. Somehow, she felt that her life might depend on her being able to.

"You caught me out."

"I did, indeed, Karen. Tell me how I caught you out?"

"Well, suppose a stranger came up to you, and offered you something you'd been wanting for years, just when your whole life had bottomed out. Wouldn't you check out his story?"

The fat man said nothing, he just looked at Karen, and he took a sip of ice water.

"So I waited till the desk clerk was away, checked the register, then chatted him up about you. He said you were driving him crazy about your brother—Wayne."

Things seemed to ease a little as the fat man continued to sip ice water. He nodded gravely.

"Wayne has a habit of vanishing, but usually not seconds before I turn around. Maybe you've seen him, you're a girl with an eye for detail."

And the fat man described Red for Karen, not only giving a pretty good physical description, but including a couple of mannerisms that Karen hadn't consciously noticed herself. As soon as the fat man described them, however, she remembered that Red did have a habit of stroking the edge of his chin when he was in thought and that he always slouched into himself when it seemed he was being watched.

Karen shook her head, and Harry looked sad.

"What a shame. We'll probably see him in Boston, when we get there. Speaking of which, I've booked us out on the early morning flight. Time to call it a night."

They left a bowing group of waiters and strolled through the lobby. As they took the elevator he punched the third-floor button.

"My floor too."

She didn't ask how he knew it was her floor. This didn't appear to be a time for small talk. The fat man studied his cuff links until the elevator door slid open.

She walked to her room and unlocked the door, turning to say good night, although Harry didn't appear to be ready to leave. However, she decided that this wasn't the time to ask him in. Through the half-open door she saw Red and a strange pink man in a loincloth vanishing into the bathroom. The pink old man paused long enough to blow her a kiss.

"Karen, perhaps we should have a small night-cap to celebrate your new job?"

"How about waiting until we get to Boston? Right now, sorry, but I'm exhausted. Otherwise I'd ask you in."

"I understand. Good night."

She nodded good night and then rushed inside her room and slammed the door before Harry changed his mind.

"It's okay, Red, I'm alone."

And he popped out of the bathroom, followed by the pink man.

"Karen, this is my friend Jack. Jack, this is my friend Karen."

She stared at him.

"Red told me a lot about you, but he didn't mention that you were pink."

"The kid always forgets minor details. He did tell me that you were a knockout, and had guts. He was right."

"I like this old pink man."

"Hey, not so old. This color adds twenty years."

Suddenly there was a knock on the door, and both Red and Jack vanished, once more, into the bathroom.

When Karen answered the door, Harry was there. He was dressed for outdoors and looked very excited.

"Wonderful news! I've just heard from my brother, he's here in Bermuda. And you're going to meet him!"

## ❀ 29 ❀

The wind blew across the cape and around jagged rocks lining the shore. Pretty as the island might be, it still had a sharp edge that had caught ships and lives for hundreds of years. Right now that edge pressed against Karen and the fat man. She didn't know where they were going, and was very nervous about why. As Red had claimed to have killed the brother they were now supposed to meet, she had a distinct hunch that nothing good was about to happen. Harry assured her this was going to be a pleasant surprise, but she doubted it.

As they bent their shoulders against the wind and the rain they stayed close to the rock wall that, slippery with moss, gushed water onto the narrow paved road. The fat man had outfitted himself in a dark rubber raincoat and rubber hat which seemed to be keeping him perfectly dry, thank-you. Karen had a fashionable raincoat which had ended up being soaked through. She felt relieved when, as they rounded a corner, a small dark car was waiting for them.

The fat man nodded towards it and opened the door, getting in the back seat while she climbed in the front. A young black man who didn't glance at either one of them started driving fast with no lights on as soon as the doors slammed shut. The car skidded sideways a few times and Karen put her hands in front of her face. The fat man didn't seem to notice and the black man laughed.

When the car stopped, Karen and Harry got out. She found that she was trembling, her hair was soaked through and she felt as cold as the day before she left Boston.

Red and Jack watched them from the shelter, if anyone wanted to call it that, of a swaying, buckling coconut tree. The wind spun the tree's green fruit in great land-mine spirals to explode directly behind Red. No matter how many times he told himself what it was, he'd still give a jump every time one landed. He was already pretty uncomfortable and his suit had soaked up all the water in the vicinity, while wrapping around his legs like the first damp layer of a plaster of paris cast. Jack was quite pleased at the amount of rain in the storm because the pink color was beginning to wash off.

Karen wasn't enjoying the rain. She paused long enough to shake a fist at the sky.

Red whispered that he didn't think they should let Karen go into whatever trap the fat man was setting, but Jack shook his head and shouted full volume.

"They ain't gonna hear us, kid, matter of fact, we ain't gonna hear each other."

"What?"

"Save your breath. Way the wind's growing it'll suck your lungs right out of your mouth if you try to talk."

"We should make our move now."

"Why? I don't see no guns, I don't see no knives."

"Whose wives? She's not married."

"I said, SIT STILL! See what the hell they're up to."

A fluke of the wind brought the words true and clear to Red.

"I can't sit still, the wind's whipping my ass around."

Karen and the fat man felt the wind claw their bodies and pull them towards the mouth of a near-by cave. There was a sign that was warping back and forth while its legs made small sucking nois-es in the mud. There were pictures of smiling, happy people on the billboard all lined up like the seven dwarfs ready to descend into the "Crystal Caves." Karen didn't feel very much like those happy people. The wind buckled and rocked the sign, the bulbs strobed, reflecting against the edges of the cave's open maw. Flickers of lightning helped illuminate a sloping wet tunnel. Karen hes-itated, but the wind made up her mind for her, dragging her into the cave.

Inside, the wind howled even louder, while the tinted lights made the walls heave as if they were alive. Harry started off at a brisk walk down into the earth while Karen edged her way down what was beginning to look more and more like a whale's slippery throat. The rain poured in and roared down the slope in sheets that caught the shade of the wall.

Karen not only felt every bad moment of this de-scent, she also had the strong feeling that she was being followed. She kept looking back, but all she could see were lightning bolts dancing across the exit of the cave. It occurred to her that this wasn't the vacation she'd planned! The Bermuda that had tugged at her through the winter translite in Boston, was a place of daylight, of warm yielding sand and water as warm as sex.

She kept thinking about why she had come to Bermuda, and of where she was, and every step down the slippery rock that was the cave floor made her angry. When she rounded the last bend of the tunnel, Harry was waiting patiently beside a pool of green water. He glanced at her as if they were in the middle of Boston Common and she was two minutes late for an appointment.

"Karen, something wrong?"

"Listen, this may cost me my alleged job, but knowing you has been one of the worst things that ever happened to me."

"You don't like this part of scenic Bermuda?"

"Do I have a job? If I do, is this sort of crap part of it? If it is I want to know why!"

"It's very simple, and I owe you an apology. We're here because I thought my brother was going to be. But I was mistaken. The phone call I received must have come from someone pretending to be Wayne. I must confess that I also wanted to see if you would be surprised that he could join us. I had my own reasons for that little test, and I apologize."

"You couldn't recognize your own brother's voice?"

Harry didn't appear to have heard her question. He turned his back in sorrow and gazed at the reflection of the stalactites. He leaned against a stalagmite. The tip broke off and splashed into the pool. The fat man didn't notice.

Red looked around the bend in the tunnel and eased his own throwing knife from the sheath that was suspended between his shoulder blades. Looking at the fat man he placed his fingers on the heft of the knife, finding its balance point. Jack shook his head but it was too late for Red to stop. He could see the perfect target of the fat man's back and prepared to throw his knife. Before he could, he felt excruciating pain and despite what his brain wanted to do, his arm wouldn't follow through. His forearm flopped as if lifeless. The knife fell towards the floor. Before it hit, Jack scooped it up with one hand.

Red's arm felt a pressure which made it easier to retreat instead of thinking of attacking. Suddenly they were outside the cave mouth. He hesitated, wondering if he should go back inside anyway. While he paused, he heard a shot that, despite the wind, was clean as the bullet itself. It was followed by a scream. As quick as the shot, Red felt new pressure on his neck. He collapsed as all the darkness in the world seemed to be expanding, with him at the center.

The fat man squeezed off another round that blasted across the wall like a stone skipping on water. It echoed and nestled and rang in Karen's ears. Harry stopped and shifted his gun to cover the turn in the tunnel that led to the entrance. But nothing happened. No one came, and slowly he lowered his gun and reholstered it. Karen had stopped screaming.

"Sorry, my dear, but I thought we might have visitors—it's all over."

"Like hell it's all over. I want an explanation"

"Actually, the explanation is quite simple."

And so it was. Simple and reasonable. Harry explained that what started him worrying was the disappearance of his brother, a man who could not hurt, as the saying goes, a fly.

Karen looked doubtful, but he paid no attention to her because he was launched on something that he'd obviously said a great many times. According to him, it seemed that leaning to the right, even though most of the world was going that way, was still unpopular amongst people with power. Timothy Shepherd, his boss, received hate mail and threats every time he took over a station. For that reason there were people out to get the organization. There was another crasser reason, the millions that the system was worth, the millions that the top members were worth. When the phone call came from someone who sounded like his brother, Harry thought it might be a trap, so he had to act as if they might be murdered any moment. He brought Karen down into the cave making it look as sweet to a killer as wild horses in a box canyon.

"And you brought me here, anyway. Even if I might be killed?"

"No danger in the world, my dear, the turn in the tunnel and the reflective pools everywhere means I'd have seen anyone and squeezed off a shot before they moved. Besides, now that it's all over, don't you feel more alive than you have for a long time?"

Karen nodded.

"Better than Channel Five?"

"Actually, a cleaner kind of danger. But what if they'd, assuming there is a 'they,' decided to roll a grenade down the slope?"

"And damage public property? That isn't done in Bermuda. A good point about the grenade though. Perhaps, from now on, I should describe danger to you before we encounter it?"

Karen agreed.

"However, there is never any jeopardy when you are with me. There is only peril, and mortal at that, when you are my enemy. I don't believe yet that you are my friend, but I do consider that you are not my enemy. That will make for a pleasant trip to Boston."

Karen doubted it.

# ❦ 30 ❦

When Red came to, it was daylight. He was resting under a grove of splintered trees, and the early morning was filtered by torn fronds. Lemon color lay on the gray as day moved closer. Jack was asleep with the remains of some abandoned picnic blanket pulled over him. Black, gray and white checks covered most of his body, all except his buttocks which gave the moon to a Bermuda morning.

Red figured that if Karen had been killed there would be more action around the area, and that Jack would have done something to stop the fat man from leaving. Aside from the upside-down remains of the sign for the Crystal Caves, there was no other indication of violence. Fragments of coconuts littered the entire area where the trees were snapped and bent. Jack yawned at the day as Red looked sourly at him.

"Give me one good reason why we didn't kill the fat man."

"I can suggest a few, kid. The first is, he'd have killed us if we made a move."

"Like hell he would. I had my throwing knife."

"How many?"

"One. How many do you carry?"

"Suppose it had missed. He was there with a gun, and a woman you seem to care for. Unless you're from the planet Krypton, you didn't stand a chance."

"His back was towards us, perfect target."

"Too perfect. This guy is not an asshole. The whole thing was a setup. He was waiting to dance. Besides this is Bermuda, they go to a prime tourist attraction and find a guy with a shiv in him, they'll check."

"You may have a point. So, let's get back to the hotel. Then with any luck we can get off to Boston before they do."

"Yeah, good idea, kid. Only there's a few problems. I'm wanted for theft and for a jailbreak. You may be on the most-wanted list in Panama for making away with yourself in your identity of Wayne Murray, which is a hell of a charge. This isn't Boston, we can't just wheel up to the expressway. We're on an island, and we got no airplane of our own."

"The way I figure it, Harry hasn't said anything about me to the cops, so that leaves only you to worry about. He's killed one person and he's not going to draw the heat his way."

"So?"

"So, let's get back to the hotel. I can change in Karen's room, and you should be able to steal some clothes for yourself, unless you've grown fond of the loin cloth?"

"Only if it comes with a vine. You'll have to steal something for me, 'cause I can't get near anything wearing this outfit. Pick something nice."

Red found himself back at the Elbow Beach Hotel, rumpled, but unbowed. That's when he discovered Karen had already checked out and must be on her way to Boston. He broke into her room before the next guests arrived and found his clothes under the mattress and some money in the cistern of the toilet. He changed before anyone else could enter the room. Even though his cash supply was lower than he'd have liked, he bought Jack a natty outfit. Blazer and flannels, bright yellow tie and pocket handkerchief.

The outfit was perfect for the airport, where the barman concentrated on constructing a foaming drink that held huge chunks of pineapple, pale spirals of coconut, a neon-colored swizzle stick, and a tiny parasol that spun about in the fumes that rose in gray vapor from the frosted glass. This was the sixth such cocktail he'd been forced to make in the past fifteen minutes for a table full of dog lovers. There had been some sort of screw-up in the loading area at the terminal which meant that dog owners, cages and all, were crammed into every inch of space in the bar. Every time there was a bark or a whine the bartender would make a sour face, and other paying customers would raise hell.

Jack looked around and began to curse every dog that had ever been known to mankind. As he kept on, Red's eyes sparkled. Jack stopped his tirade and stared, puzzled, at him.

"I've got a great idea. We're going by dog team, and you're going to be my father."

"Where's the dog team? And don't you think it would cause me acute embarrassment to claim such a relationship?"

"No bloody more than me, but this way we can travel together as a team."

"That's the dog team you referred to?"

"Look at all these little doggies going home. I think some of them might need helpers."

"Good plan. Barkeep, some more drinks, *real* drinks."

The bartender looked up from his collection of tiny umbrellas and swirls and foam and decided he liked these guys. They kept quiet, knocked back their booze with no sign of ill effects, and also looked with disgust at the parasol-laden libations that kept being ordered over the din of the caged dogs.

Red went on to tell Jack that the authorities were looking for single fugitives, not a pair, and that a father-son combo was an easy way to avoid attention. He also pointed out, even though he was sure that Jack must have been the ugliest thing on two legs when he was a young man, there was a kind of freak resemblance between the two of them.

Red couldn't help feeling that in some weird way the old guy was enjoying himself. He'd even gone so far as to ask Jack if he'd ever had kids. But the icy look that the old man had used to chill him off the topic prevented any more questions.

Over the bar there was an angled full-length mirror, and running along the walls were patterned squares of mirrored tile that allowed someone at the bar to check out the entire length of the room. Most tables were full of excited people and of foaming drinks. But off to one side, at the edge of a minuscule table which had been jammed into a forgotten corner as an afterthought, sat a leathery old woman who was knocking back boilermakers.

Both Red and Jack joined the admiring glance of the bartender who kept sending more alcohol over to her whenever she neared the bottom of another sudsy glass. The other dog owners seemed to specialize in small yapping breeds that bounced around their plastic cages as if they were six feet tall. Some of the more aristocratic of the tiny dogs had huge ribbons.

The old woman was different. Her vast mastiff didn't think he was six feet tall, he just was. He also didn't bark, or growl or hop around, and his cage was not of tinted plastic, but of no-nonsense steel. There was no ribbon on his cage. On it a sign told the world he was "Bruno, Pride of Boston." Once in a while he opened a lidded eye, looked pissed off at the scene, and snored again. Red liked the look of the dog and the owner. So did Jack.

The PA system made the same unintelligible murmurs that such speakers make in every language all over the world. The only people who paid it any attention were the old woman, Jack and Red. She kept turning the pages of a Dick Francis paperback while smoke from her Gauloise curled up her cheek and into her eyes. Without stopping her reading, she tossed a twenty on the table and stood up. She continued smoking and reading, as with one hand she began to drag the huge crate and dog along behind her. It scraped and groaned its way towards the stairs that led to customs and caused thin muscles to tighten along her freckled arms.

The other dog owners frowned at her, and tut-tutted as the cage crashed into the little palaces of the minor breeds. The tiny dogs set up a frenzied barking, which didn't get even a raised lid from

Bruno until his way was blocked by an assemblage of spotless cages. The old woman, realizing that something was amiss, looked up from her book and let her smoke drift across the No Smoking sign.

"Excuse me, chaps, but could you move your fucking dogs?"

Red and Jack moved over to stand by her side and listen to what was going on.

"By God, if you weren't a woman, I'd make you apologize to the ladies in this company," said a fierce looking middle-aged owner of a prize-winning Pomeranian.

Jack stood very close to him and cleared his throat before he spoke.

"Aside from all that, can you move your fucking dogs for the lady?"

She smiled, while the owner of the Pomeranian retreated after catching the look from Jack's eyes. The little dogs were shifted and Red and Jack each gripped a side of Bruno's cage. The scraping and bumping stopped and Bruno licked Jack's hand.

"He's just getting a taste, you know, to see if you're good enough to eat. My name's Dot."

"Dot, you tell Bruno that if he bites me I'll bite him back, right where the sun don't shine."

"I've tried it. Don't do no good."

They grinned at each other. Even Bruno curled his lip.

They arrived at customs where long lines of non-drinking passengers had been waiting for hours, standing behind a large tack box. Its vivid red seemed to reflect in the eyes of the irate people lined up behind it.

Despite the long queue and the vicious looks they received, Dot and her two helpers crashed straight into the front of it. Before anyone could say anything she turned to the line and shouted at it.

"My tack box, my helpers, my dog, my bloody place in line!"

Every eye in the airport looked at them.

"Good choice, 'Dad,'" Red smiled gently at Jack, who was endeavoring to look inconspicuous. They busied themselves polishing a faint lustre into the dull metal, and trying to appear as if they were busy doing something or other with the tack box.

At this point they became aware that the owner of Bruno was talking to them.

"I don't care if it's only because you're skipping out of town that you're helping me, I appreciate it."

As this was delivered in a stentorian gale fueled by the boilermakers, both Red and Jack flinched. They wondered if her voice had carried as far as the nearest policeman. Their looks must have shown their concern, for Dot promptly lowered her voice to a force-six whisper.

"Can I help you lads escape?"

"Actually, my hard-drinking darling, you can."

"Then you don't pretend that what you're doing is not escaping, if you know what I mean?" she asked Jack. Red had paled as the conversation developed.

"Why lie to you? I'm taking a chance that you're enough of a sport to help us out."

"What's the crime?"

"I stole some money from a rich man, and my son is supposed to have made himself disappear."

"Will you carry the dog whenever I want you to?"

"Yes."

"And the tack box?"

Red nodded yes, just as the ticket agent opened up for business.

"Do you have money?"

This time Jack nodded.

"Lots?"

It was Red's turn to nod.

By this time the ticket agent was anxious to get down to business and the murmur from the lineup behind the trio, or quartet if one included Bruno, had risen to cries of protest. Dot turned her attention to the moment.

"Don't try to rush me, young man. My brother and his son need first-class tickets to Boston, and I'll be upgrading to first class as well."

Finally everything was worked out and Red and Jack struggled with Bruno towards a door near the ticket counter. As Bruno was whisked away by the luggage handlers he began to whine piteously.

"Scared of flying," said Bruno's owner, adding only, "hey, fifteen minutes left, we can all grab another drink." But she noticed her new friends glance at the policemen who were now moving towards the bar area.

"On the other hand, let's get aboard the goddamn plane while we still can."

When the security check for the flight to Boston was announced, the trio moved towards the metal detector, the last obstacle before they could escape Bermuda. Jack maneuvered towards a wastebasket where there were a number of clangs and clinks as he removed knives and other homemade weapons from his body, slipping them into the trashbin. Red reached inside his jacket and waistband, and there were two clinks from him. His father looked at him with disapproval.

"After what you said this morning, 'Dad,' I figured I should have at least a couple of throwing knives, in case I missed with numero uno."

The old woman listened to this conversation, looked at them both and smiled. This was going to be an interesting flight.

## ❧ 31 ❧

Boston looked gray to Karen. The snow had mixed with slush and scraps of paper. Cabs skidded, bounced off each other's fenders and honked as they bumped away from each other, while rows of civilians raced through Don't Walk signs. The streetlights could feel darkness tickle their photoelectric cells, making them sputter on. Clouds broke and sunset bounced through spilled milk over Boston Common.

From the moment that the airplane had shadowed along the slate ocean and aimed itself at the icy asphalt Karen felt like a stranger arriving in what should have been home. The warm beaches gave way to chill underwater sand, and echoes of the gunshot in the crystal cave clanged along the edge of her memory. She couldn't stop thinking about Red, wondering how the hell he was ever going to make his way to Boston. She smiled as she thought of Jack in his pink loincloth trying to clear customs.

As she looked at the carousel revolving she tried to come up with a plan to avoid going into Boston with Harry. She didn't want him seeing where

she lived, she didn't want to be near him anymore. His luggage had been first off the plane and
a redcap whizzed it away.

Karen's suitcase appeared along with a few extra
bangs and scuffmarks. While Harry was glancing
towards the redcap, she whipped off her suitcase,
putting it behind a stack of cartons. It was easy
then to stall and pretend to look for her missing
bag. Harry tried to talk her into forgetting about it
until the next day, but she wouldn't be persuaded.
Reluctantly, he left her at the carousel. She waited
there for another half-hour just to be sure, then
plucked her suitcase from behind the cartons and
strode towards Boston.

She ended up, as always, having to open the luggage and display her worldly goods to the lineup
that grew like fungus in her footsteps.

When she got outside things began to improve.
The limo driver sensed that she didn't want to talk
so he remained silent. As Boston began to invade
the night hours she watched it anew, starting to
feel a little better.

All the way in from Logan the driver had been
surveying Karen in his rear-view mirror. Finally,
after stopping in front of her apartment building,
he grinned as she laid on a ten-dollar tip.

"I thought it was you, Karen."

"You know me?"

"Hell, everyone knows you. You're the dame on
Channel Five."

"Not anymore, bub. They fired me, I'm with another station."

"Yeah? Still in Boston?"

"Where else is there?"

"Way to go."

And he spun his wheels very slowly, with that precise grace of the Boston cab driver, spraying an old man behind her from head to toe with an armor of snow and ice, but avoiding putting even one flake on her. He tooted his horn in farewell as she slipped inside the building. The old man shook himself so the shell of slush shivered and slid to the sidewalk.

Karen set her suitcase down in the hallway, took out her keys and tried to unlock her apartment door. That's when she discovered the lock had been changed. At first she thought that she was inserting the wrong key. Then she realized what Scott must have done. She kicked the door, but all that did was hurt her foot. Still lugging her suitcase she went out in the Boston night to the only place that resembled home.

The bar was warm and smelled of good booze, of clean sawdust and of Brasso. Vilmos, or "Dooley" if you wanted to dream along with him, was leaning towards the television as if being sucked into the picture tube by an enormous vacuum. Usually it stood mute and demanding with a blank screen, but Vilmos now proved beyond a doubt that the set could actually work. The faces of three hairy men peered out of the screen with enough volume to shift glasses. PBS was running a tribute to Ireland, and when this group called "Ryan's Fancy" sang about The Dark Island, Vilmos's eyes filled with tears. He appeared not to see Karen, but as she moved closer, he reached out his hand, without looking, and curled a glass of Laphroaig down the counter. Only a few drops spilled out to amber along the dark walnut. Karen picked up the glass as Vilmos, still watching the screen and harmon-

izing with the lead singer, swept his own tumbler
under the bottle, filled it, and then clinked it
against Karen's without losing a beat. She set down
her suitcase and they drank while Denis Ryan
from the television and Vilmos from the bar did
fine service to the song's dying notes. The show
went to credits and Vilmos vaulted the counter to
pull out the plug of the TV, after carefully hanging
an Out of Order sign over the screen. Only then
did he hug Karen.

"How can you go to Bermuda and come back so
pale?"

"I don't look all that pale. Besides, one insulting
comment like that and I know you're not Irish,
Vilmos. The Irish know how to flatter others, Hungarians are only good at flattering themselves."

"Nobody is perfect. So tell me of Bermuda and
how you found love. Also tell me why you carry
such a large purse now."

"Who said I found love?"

"Why else would you be pale? I am sorry you
found love, because I had hopes that together we
could stroll hand in hand along the Shannon."

"Danube more likely. You want to hear my story or you want to give me more of your blarney?"

"What's my name?"

"Dooley."

"The right answer. As sure as my name is Dooley,
I'll settle in and listen. But first, more of the drap."

And over a few more "draps" she spun the tale
of her new job. There was enough story to last
them until darkness battered its way against the
stained-glass windows, to be halted by the warm
and cosy light that made the inside of Dooley's
feel like a warm mitt. She told of romance and

then she told of danger and then she told of getting back to the apartment and finding the lock had been changed.

The last item was dealt with very quickly by Vilmos. He picked up the phone, dialed a well-worn number, and spoke rapidly in Hungarian. He smiled as he replaced the phone.

"An old friend from the wrong part of Budapest is a locksmith. He is now on his way to your apartment and will replace the lock. Your new key will be left in your mailbox."

Then she told Vilmos more about Red, about his quest, and how she was helping. He began to look very worried.

"My advice about this, Karen, is to call your mother, go and stay with her in Gloucester."

"Call her yourself, and say hello."

"Is she single?"

"Don't be obscene."

Just then a group of customers came laughing into the bar. She frowned at them and so did Vilmos, but they didn't pay any attention.

"Should I throw them out, Karen? They're a rowdy bunch."

"Time for me to go."

"If you have trouble, come right here, as fast as you can, and as straight as you can. It is safe in Dooley's."

She bundled her way out of the bar. Snow was spun by streetlight, and that hurt her eyes. She drifted into a dented cab and slammed the door with a half-closing clink as it skidded away.

She didn't notice the long blue car that slid smoothly into traffic behind them as she moved along Mass Avenue towards her apartment.

## 32

Red and Jack would have liked a better welcome to Boston. There was some sort of air-traffic controllers' dispute at Logan and the plane was forced into following the downward funnel of a holding pattern for an hour or so.

Red spent tedious moments while the plane lurched around wondering how Dot could continue to slurp down champagne while keeping up a chatter about dog shows, ticks and the best sort of flea shampoo. The plane moved out of the holding pattern for a while giving the steward a chance to catch up with her for a few moments. He kept running back and forth. Dot looked at Red and knocked back another split.

"It's not for the booze. I like to watch his buns."

The plane began to circle once more, but, despite this, the steward didn't buckle himself back in. Instead he kept up the marathon of supplying Dot. Red looked out the window in the beginnings of despair. Despite himself, he started thinking again. He stared at this strange city that kept going round and round beneath him. Everything looked cold and gray, and he was missing Karen.

He looked back from the window to see Jack and Dot grinning away at him. Each passed him a split of champagne. Jack, smiling even more, reached across Red and lowered the little excuse for a blind. It did shut out the reeling world in front of the wing lights, and he felt grateful. He knocked back the two splits of champagne and looked at Jack and Dot who had their arms entwined.

He felt better when he saw the two old farts hugging. Despite the sign that warned everyone to keep their seatbelts fastened, Jack and Dot, hand in hand, made their way towards the front lavatory. The steward moved forward to escort them back to their seats, but before he could reach them they'd both gone into the same washroom. The light over the washroom door came on and the steward stared at it with disbelief. Then he too smiled and buckled himself in.

Red discovered a small cache of bottles tucked into the seat pocket in front of Dot's place, and by the time he had finished the last one he felt content enough to raise the small blind. Night had arrived in Boston and their plane wasn't far behind it. The wing dipped just as the washroom door opened and a very disheveled and happy looking Dot and Jack strolled up the aisle.

He lifted his glass to toast them. Dot reached inside her seat pocket and, seeing all her booze had gone missing, looked up with a quick anger. Jack saved the moment by pulling another hoard of small bottles out of his pockets. He poured for Dot first and then all three raised their drinks as the plane bounced its way to a landing in the middle of a snowstorm.

In the terminal Red and Jack tried their best to look inconspicuous. They were helped by the huge crowd waiting for planes, as if everyone in the world had decided to come out to the airport to meet aircraft. Babies cried, children whined, a drunken convention sang and kept dropping their funny hats. The air conditioner came on full blast, making everyone huddle in their winter outfits. Into the middle of this clanked Dot and Bruno.

"Well, are you two sons-a-bitches going to stay there with your fingers up your rear ends, or are you gonna help a little old lady?"

Despite the crowd, Dot's voice was sharp enough, clear enough and loud enough to cut through every other sound. Heads swung round to look at her and to identify the two "sons-a-bitches."

Red and Jack sprang to Dot's help and together with Bruno they managed to punch a hole through crowds where porters feared to tread. The dog woke up long enough to growl at a pony-tailed boy who was wearing a private school uniform. The boy screamed, and, satisfied, the mastiff went back to sleep again.

They exited through a door that had a picture of a dog with a line drawn through it, and approached a group of limousine drivers who shuddered and looked away hoping instead for a party of drunken Texans. Dot stepped out into traffic, directly in front of an old van that bore the legend "The Grateful Dead Still Live." As if a time machine had come to a stop, the van jerked to a halt and disgorged some aging hippies. Dot told them about her plight, while they smiled and threw flowers at her.

Dot ignored the carnations. "Screw the flowers, got a joint?"

Now the hippies also smiled at Bruno. Two of the younger men, one balding, the other with gray hair, opened the van doors, revealing a day-glo interior. Dot, Jack and Red gave the cage a mighty heave and with a muted clatter Bruno and cage landed on the lime-green carpet. Dot gave Jack a passionate kiss, telling him it was the best short-term marriage she'd had in a long while, and advised Red to help dishonor the family name. Then she climbed into the van next to Bruno and leaned over to close the door.

Her parting words wafted through rusty tin, as the van squeaked its way into traffic.

"I have always relied on the insanity of strangers."

Jack watched until the van disappeared around the concrete island of the terminal. Red looked around at a place that didn't feel like home anymore.

"Now that we're here, what the hell are we supposed to do?"

## 33

The locksmith had done a good job. The new key was in the mailbox and it worked perfectly in the new brass lock. But as the door swung open, Karen saw that there were some changes a locksmith couldn't fix. Against the windows, along the walls, on top of tables, everywhere she looked she saw dead plants. Dried, yellowed, bleached and curled, all withered away. She sat on her suitcase and looked at them. Some of the plants were recent purchases, others came from cuttings that went back to college days, and some African violets that she'd been especially proud of had come from her mother's house.

Karen knew what had happened. Because the locks had been changed by Scott no one could get in to water the plants.

There were other changes too. All the stereo equipment had vanished; the furniture, including a huge master bed, had been taken away, and the remaining records in the collection had been smashed. On the mirror that hung over the fireplace had been written in lipstick (that of Scott's sweetie, Karen presumed) "Fairly divided. We're on holiday, so don't try to reach us. Scott & Brooke." A happy face had been drawn above the message.

Now, with the plants gone, and with her records shattered Karen began to feel a strange sort of joy. This was the last remaining trace of who she had been, of where she used to travel. It was all gone, destroyed. While she was falling in love with Red, Boston—at least the part of it that she had always known—had melted away. She was left in an empty room with a battered suitcase, and she felt good about it. What had happened to the plants still angered her, but she had other things to think about, and all of her new thoughts were about Red.

She began clearing up the apartment when she saw a figure approaching her still-open door. As the man walked into the light, she could see it was Harry. She had no fear, no worry, just a feeling that she was about to enter someplace new.

He stepped over her suitcase.

"Karen, I'm sorry to bother you like this."

"How did you know where I lived?"

"These things are easy to find out. As I said, I'm sorry to bother you, but Timothy wants to see you. Tonight."

"The last time you used a line like that was about your brother."

"I don't want to discuss my brother. I've only tonight discovered that he's dead."

"And you came here to see me?"

"Everything seems to go together, doesn't it? I've never been a person for grief, so I find it best to put it aside when there is work to be done."

"What happened to him?"

"He was murdered, brutally. But I will not talk about that."

"The police?"

"Are useless. I am not. Now, Timothy really is demanding to see you. It's about the job I offered, and I'm very afraid that it's dependent on your seeing Timothy, in ten minutes. Otherwise the offer is over."

"Well, Harry, perhaps I can tear myself away from this homecoming. I'll meet you there..."

"Timothy insists that I drive you. He calls it 'The Personal Touch.' Shall we go?"

Karen clicked off the light. They walked out of the apartment towards the waiting elevator where identical twins in black alpaca coats were holding the doors open. Harry didn't bother introducing the two men but Karen smiled at them both.

They didn't smile back.

## ❧ 34 ❧

She was expecting Timothy's office to be electronic, high-tech, metal and glass, something that spelled twentieth-century power. What she got instead, after an entrance way of mirrored steel and curved glass, was an out-of-the-way time-machined corner of a modern building.

Even though the elevator was all mirrors and metal, when Harry pressed a coded number pad the door swung open into a world of wood and warmth.

She was left alone while he vanished to track down Timothy.

"Welcome to Rockwell-land," his voice echoed back.

The elevator doors shut, and the small security panel on the closed door was the only sign of the current decade. The rest reminded her of nothing so much as the attic of her childhood home. This *was* Rockwell-land. To begin with, the room had been done in the same sort of wood that had been used to finish the attic of every American house. Karen didn't know the name of the wood, but she knew its texture, smell and look in soft light.

The walls had some very good paintings, placed cheek by jowl with framed Norman Rockwell originals. It all worked.

When she crossed over to the waiting area, she found, next to a working penny gumball machine, issues of *The Saturday Evening Post* that went back further than she did. She picked up a copy that showed on the cover a red-headed kid of a soldier coming back home to a neighborhood that was more familiar than anywhere she'd ever lived.

"That's my favorite, too."

Karen looked up and saw Timothy Shepherd in the flesh. He was tall, craggy and wore a seersucker suit that was supposed to make him look relaxed and casual. Instead, he reminded Karen of a knife folded into a pocket.

"What makes you think you're good enough to work for us?"

"I know that I'm just fine for you, the question is whether or not you're good enough for me."

Timothy sighed and turned away, walking towards a big easy chair. He slouched into it and gazed out a bay window over the city.

Karen followed because she suspected this wasn't the end of the meeting. However, Timothy simply continued looking over Boston, while Harry crunched gumballs. She decided to wait to be spoken to. A large dog of mixed breed came over as she sat down, putting a cold nose into her hand. It snuggled up to her and thumped its tail on the floor.

"All we need is little Opie," she ventured.

But there was no response. She spent the next while looking quite openly at Timothy. An impression of raw sex that she'd felt in the first few seconds continued, and grew stronger. She couldn't understand why. His looks were more like the effect of a patchwork quilt than an obvious force. Somehow, she figured, it was connected with the combination of being homespun and also giving off a sense of danger. She crossed over to a series of photos that showed Timothy posed with various television preachers. A grandfather clock bonged away in the distance. She felt like she'd been in the room a few hours too long.

"I'm surprised to see these photos."

Now that got his attention. The gaze returned from the middle distance and focused on Karen. When he looked at her she felt the sense of danger increase. She didn't know how he was connected with what had happened in Panama, but she felt he was. There was the sense of a greater threat from him than from Harry.

But as she looked at Timothy, there was also a return of the same spirit that had led her to squirt Scott with the plant sprayer, moved her to Red's arms and now to this room, high above Boston. She thought of Red and remembered the look of fear and pain on his face when he woke from nightmares. She knew it was time to stir things up.

"Do you have any interests in Panama, Mr Shepherd?"

"Now that's a very peculiar question, Karen. Isn't that a peculiar question, Harry?"

"Odd."

"I was wondering, because it's a place I'd like to visit. All these plants made me think of it."

"Did they now? Perhaps you'd like to do some reports from there?"

"Love to. Who knows what I could find out?"

He stared at her. Karen's heart was beating so loudly that she had trouble hearing Timothy's next words.

"I was wondering why you were surprised about the photos of my friends. You don't approve of Christians?"

"It's not that. It's the autographs. I didn't know these guys could write."

From Harry she felt a shudder, from Timothy she got a series of gut wrenching laughs. He laughed so much that he was on the edge of tears. He stood up and slapped her on the back.

"You're all right, woman. Now go and do the news."

"That's it?"

"What did you expect, a secret oath?"

"It's just, well, aren't there any words about your concerns?"

"My concern is good news. That's it. Period. Anything else you hear is crap."

The phone on his desk rang. Still smiling at her, he answered and then gave a shrug as if to say, "What can I do?" and turned away.

"Mr President. Good to hear from you."

Harry touched her arm, and without a word he walked her to the elevator. He pressed the buttons quickly and when the doors opened let Karen get on alone.

"He likes you. I have to stay to see what that's all about. Congratulations."

And the doors closed before Karen could think of anything to say. Harry went back to the inner office, making one quick stop at the gumball machine. When he returned, Timothy was off the phone. He wasn't smiling when he looked at Harry.

"You're right, we should watch her. Continue surveillance, because I'm sure that someone from Panama will try to contact her. Whoever that is will prove to be the person who killed Wayne. You can have him as soon as he's near. I want Karen alive for a little while until I find what I'm looking for. Then you'll have to deal with her, unless it pleasures me to do it myself."

He swiveled around to look out over Boston. Harry knew enough to leave without saying anything. As he walked towards the parking lot he thought that Karen might have a very short time left to live.

## 35

The bus terminal was pretty near empty as Jack dozed. The newspaper that he had been reading was crumpled and refolded making the creases spider-web as it fanned to the floor. There it tented and dipped against the bare marble when the cold winds blew in from north of Eliot.

He awakened to the steady whirr from the cleaning machine that an old black man was sliding back and forth in tight, controlled arcs across the floor. The man didn't waste any looks from side to side, no taking in of the Pillsbury Doughboy teen who was sleeping next to an ashtray full of the smokes he'd gone through at a tense three A.M. waking, no sidelong look for the two aged winos who were sleeping as if glued to the coffee machine. Every time it made a noise they cuddled closer like a puppy to an alarm clock.

Red was up and fiddling with the coffee machine. He had his back to the ticket agent and the cleaner didn't pay any attention to him, so he had a pretty clear field. He wedged the blade of his pen-knife into place.

The two winos, who appeared to be wired to the inner workings of the coffee machine, felt the strange stirring in its cash-sensing mechanism and stood in line to get their free coffee. Red moved over to the automat. It took a few minutes there, but he was able to get a fairly good breakfast without paying. He returned to the bench with assorted doughnuts and, for health purposes, two speckled apples.

"You still think this is better than the Ritz?"

Jack smiled.

"Well, no one's come looking for us here. At the Ritz anyone looking for us would find us. Besides the price is right."

"Room service isn't bad either. And the other guests are an interesting bunch."

The winos vanished through the front door. Each one carried a couple of coffees and a mountain of doughnuts. They didn't seem to worry about their health. Jack thanked Red for the bounty and then dug in. For a while neither said anything. They were content to munch and watch the day begin as sounds of arriving buses began to razz their way into the building.

"So, Jack, what next?"

"Wait till eight. Then we go to Standard Telecasting and ask for Karen. Simplest way."

"I thought you were the one who didn't want to check into the Ritz in case anyone noticed us. What do you think is going to happen when we show up in the lion's den?"

"That was yesterday. This is today."

"You ever consider writing for a fortune-cookie company?"

The PA system sprang into life calling out the destinations of departing buses. "...New Bedford, West Haven..." and the list went on and bounced off the gray floors. Jack listened.

"Brings back a lot of memories, kid."

"You never said you had anything to do with Boston."

"Why should I? Lots of stuff I never told you."

"But you knew I was from here, only natural that you'd say...'Hey, kid, I'm from Boston too.'"

"I just did. More or less."

"Gives us a lot in common."

"Depends on what part of the city you come from. Beacon Hill's different than right here."

"I'm from right here."

Jack grinned. "Me too."

"Three streets over."

"I know the place. I used to live near an establishment named Andy's Bar. You know it, Red?"

"Know it? My old man used to take me there. We'd pitch pennies with the piano player."

"Who won?"

"My old man. Then we'd take over the piano. He'd hit a couple of chords. 'Play that when I give you the wink!' he'd say. Then he'd put his beer on top of the upright, and sing. 'A Splinter from My Father's Wooden Leg' used to be a favorite. You know that one?"

"No, kid. But it sounds like my kind of song."

There was a pause, before Jack spoke again. "Even though you keep calling him an old fart, seems you had a good time."

"Until my mother gave us hell, but, yeah, that was fun."

"So he wasn't as much an old fart as you let on?"

"Sure he was. Just that he had his good moments. Even Attila the Hun had his good moments. I only remember my father was always leaving."

"You got itchy feet, so do I. What's wrong about that?"

"We don't have kids, that's the difference. Look, I'm sick of talking about my old man, what about yours? You had one didn't you?"

Jack began to look a little uncomfortable.

"What was he, a whorehouse piano player?"

He laughed, loud enough to make the ticket agent look up.

"No. Pretty close though. He was a clerk."

"Clerk?"

"Yeah. In an old store—department store. Worked in the same place, same store all his life. Till he dropped dead where he worked, in the boys' clothing section. Croaked right in the middle of listening and nodding to some great-great-grandson of some fucking Welsh ironmaster who was giving him shit."

"He got angry?"

Jack shook his head.

"I used to watch my father at that store. There were hardwood floors with lots of shine to them because the clerks had to take an hour each weekend and polish them. When it came to money, he wasn't allowed to make any change himself. Minor employees weren't trusted. Put the money in a little brass trolley on wires. It chugged off to an inner office and brought back the pennies for him to give to some snotty eleven-year-old and say, 'Your change, sir.'"

"Jack, I think that's the most I ever heard you talk."

"Yeah, well mark it in your diary, kid. 'Cause the topic is now closed."

"At least your father didn't run off."

"Too bad. The old fart might have had himself a good time. Now, time to go and find your sweetie."

They spent a few minutes in the public washroom making themselves look as presentable as they were likely to get. Then a subway ride to the center of town, a brisk walk and they were outside Standard Telecasting. The building, designed to awe, didn't. Jack glanced at the main door to see what kind of locks it had. Red, his thoughts were only on Karen. Now that he was this close he began to worry again. They hadn't been able to find her name in the phone book because it was unlisted, Channel Five claimed they didn't know where she was, and so this direct approach was all that was left. If things were going all right for her they should have no trouble.

However, according to the woman at the reception desk, the station had never heard of Karen Chapman.

The overhead camera monitored them while Harry watched from his office. He pressed a button and recorded a close-up of each man, printing them out in crisp black and white. Harry studied the portraits, remembering the time he'd seen the younger man in the lobby of the Elbow Beach Hotel. That meant, of course, that this could be the man who had killed Wayne. It also meant he was connected with Karen.

For some reason the younger man had brought an old guy along with him for company. Harry looked back and forth from one print-out to the other. There was a slight physical resemblance.

Most people wouldn't notice it, but Harry did. The age span meant it couldn't be his brother, so it must be his father. Why would this guy bring his father along with him? Especially when the father was so disreputable looking? Another thing was now obvious: they didn't know where Karen was, but he'd have them followed anyway.

After he'd set that up, he buzzed Timothy's private line, only to discover that the computer was on holdcalls mode and wouldn't let him through.

Deciding it was time to do things the correct way, Harry filed his info in the computer, attached a flashing beeper code to it, and then walked over to his room's built-in bar. He lifted the door and pressed a small knot in the wood panelling. The back came down and he reached inside to take out a doctor's satchel. It was time for Karen to answer some questions.

## ⚜ 36 ⚜

Karen had been shopping. She'd spent the night tossing around on a makeshift bed with her suitcase for a pillow, and decided that a sleeping bag would be a better arrangement. That had taken the entire day to track down. She also picked up a frying pan and some bacon and eggs and was looking forward to a huge breakfast for supper. Staggering down the hallway, about to put her new key in her new lock, she hesitated when she noticed how quiet everything was. That was a bit of a surprise because before she'd left the apartment that morning she'd turned the intercom's radio on, good and loud. Now there wasn't any noise leaking out from under her door.

Beginning to feel that she was going to spend the rest of her life sneaking around, she crept towards the two elevators down the hallway and pressed the button to descend. Nothing happened.

She tried to calm herself by looking at each elevator door and then making up her mind, picking the one she thought would arrive first. When she was little, she and her mother would come into Boston to shop at Filene's. Always, while they waited for their elevator they would lay a small bet on which one would show up first. Now she checked the one on the left and laid her mother's bet on the elevator to the right. That was the one closest to her apartment. She kept looking at her door as she became more nervous, moving back, blending in with the plants and brass pots.

Suddenly the elevator door opened and Harry came striding out. He went directly to her apartment and, new lock or no new lock, took a key from his pocket, unlocked the door and vanished inside. Karen's nerve was gone, so she decided to walk the fifteen flights down the stairwell.

All the way downstairs, she was left with the urgent question of what to do. Even more urgent—where to go. She suspected that all this attention was a result of her comment about Panama. She also began to doubt the wisdom of stirring things up just to see what would happen.

She came to the bottom of the stairwell and made her way towards the front door. No sign of anyone following her. They were all probably in her apartment trying to glue her Elvis records together. There was a new janitor mopping the lobby and she tracked through an area he'd just cleaned. He glared at her as her boots made little sucking sounds and left a trail of dirt right through the cleanest part of the floor. She gave him her most dazzling smile before she went outdoors. He continued to glare.

Karen flagged a cab and leapt aboard, but when the driver asked her where to go she didn't have an easy answer. The apartment wasn't safe, neither was Standard Telecasting. The only place she could think of was Dooley's.

The driver was South American and played a cassette that was all guitar and flute. It made Karen think of jungle, and of warm beach and of Red and of how much she missed him. Remembering the little time they'd had together, she thought how such a tiny space now felt longer than the rest of her life, and better. Looking out the window at a Boston going gray and dull in damp snow, she could see only green, yellow and the face of Red.

"Shit!" she said aloud, getting a disapproving glance from the driver.

Karen Chapman, who always liked to leave her options open, had moved into a world where choices had been made permanently. She was now on the side of the angels, and so far the angels had not shown. The driver turned his tape up louder and didn't look back at her until they arrived at Dooley's.

To her dismay there was anything but peace and quiet inside the bar. A berserk group of hockey fans were celebrating a Bruins victory. Someone had ignored the Out of Order sign on the TV set and it was blaring out a repeat of "20 Minute Workout." Clouds of smoke drifted blue and fat over the screen. Everyone except Vilmos was singing. He picked up the Out of Order sign from the floor and hung it over the bar, as he pointed towards the ladies' room.

The only thing that distinguished this washroom from the men's room was a series of plaster crumblings where the urinals had been ripped from the walls. Karen glanced at the broken mirror and brushed the snow flakes off her hair. Through her reflection she could see Vilmos enter.

"I phoned your mother. She didn't answer."

"You called my mother? Why?"

"Because I know the ways of the world and I knew that sooner or later you would need a place to duck. You've got that look now and I figure she's your best bet. I have to tell you why she didn't answer the phone."

"There's something wrong with her? She's not..." But she couldn't finish the question.

"No, she's not. I thought you didn't care about her?"

A woman opened the door, Vilmos was irate.

"Do you mind?"

"Not a bit," was the answer, as the newcomer shouldered her way past him towards one of the cubicles. Karen turned her attention to Vilmos.

"I didn't say I didn't care. My exact statement on the subject was that we fight all the time."

"Ah, I understand. Just like in Hungary."

"So how is she?"

"She has only a broken bone."

"Thank God. Only?"

"It could have been worse under the circumstance. The neighbor who was in her house to clean the dust that had gathered in the less than a day she had been in hospital answered the phone, and told me..."

"Em is obsessive about dust."

"...told me that your mother was cleaning the ice off the path that goes by the cliff..."

"Why didn't she hire someone?"

"...when she slipped and fell, but grabbed a small tree before she kept sliding..."

"...down to the ocean. My God. How is she?"

"In hospital, couldn't reach you. Didn't know where you were..."

"I have to go and see her, don't I?"

"Look at it this way. If all the things you have told me are true, you have a difficulty. Do you still need to avoid certain people?"

"More than ever. They're letting themselves into my apartment. But no one followed me."

"How do you know that?"

"Why would they follow me if they could get into my apartment?"

"Were you in your apartment?"

"I didn't go inside, but I went in the building. Oh, I see what you mean. They may have followed me from the building, they might even know I'm here."

"That we can deal with. Leave it to me, and wait."

Vilmos departed, his arm crooked as if he might be carrying a Molotov cocktail. Karen walked over to sit down on the metal chair that wobbled near the broken mirror. As she moved, her boots stuck to the floor, giving off a slight sucking sound, and she remembered crossing the lobby of her building, while walking across the newly washed floor. The question was, "If the floor had just been washed why was it still sticky?"

She didn't realize she'd asked the question aloud until the woman who'd earlier gone into the cubicle stood over her shoulder and looked into the mirror at her.

"Do you find the floor sticky, luv?"

"I'm sorry, I didn't mean this floor, I meant the floor where they started following me. So it means there's something on my soles, something they can see."

"Don't go on about being sorry, dear. Yours is the best conversation I've overheard in a long time. Someone's following you, right?"

Karen sized up the woman. Who knows, perhaps this stranger was crazy enough to help out.

"How'd you like to trade boots?"

"Super. But I'm not into anything kinky, mind."

Deciding to take a chance, Karen explained what was happening to her, why she figured the people trailing her could follow her anywhere, what danger there might be and how the woman could help. She also told her how much she could pay.

A beer truck pulled up outside Dooley's, and Vilmos himself came out to guide it back down the alley. While it was unloading, the young woman came out the front door. She was bundled against the night and looked very much like Karen. Arm in arm with two Bruins fans she made her way towards a 4x4 where they all piled in together. The 4x4 wavered towards the center of town.

Before the pursuit car followed, its driver first looked at the sidewalk where the woman had walked. To do this he put on a pair of specially tinted glasses. The footprints glowed with the tracking chemical and he rushed back to the follow car. As it pulled away a beer truck left in the opposite direction. The two guys in front were smiling and counting over some bonus cash for Christmas. Karen sat behind, in with the beer. Vilmos had thoughtfully supplied her with an opener. She used it on a Narragansett as the truck turned towards Gloucester.

# ❧ 37 ❧

Harry was getting tired of Karen's apartment. He disliked the dead plants, was annoyed by the crunch of the smashed records when he paced around, and was disappointed to discover that there was no food in the place. He wanted to phone out for a pizza but didn't want to tie up the phone.

The first report from Zeb and Abel, the twins doing the tracking, had already come in, and Harry was now waiting for an update. According to them, Karen had visited every club in lower Boston, and then had gone to an after-hours place, ending up, still with the guys she'd picked up at her first stop, at a jazz club on Kenmore Square. After that the threesome had checked into a nearby hotel. Harry's men were gaining access to the building.

While Harry was waiting he decided to go over everything that he and Karen had discussed from the time he met her until the time he had last heard her. This didn't present any problem in terms of memory, for he was blessed with total recall. Or to be more precise, he was sometimes cursed with total recall. For most of his life he had regarded this as a problem. He couldn't go to sleep after a party, without replaying every word of any conversation that he'd been involved in or had overheard. Each moment would be played in his mind. But now he was glad of his gift as he went over all his conversations with Karen.

It wasn't a question of not remembering. The problem was making the right associations, spotting connections that might give him clues. She hadn't mentioned anything other than cigars when it came to family, so that didn't tell him where she might have a home to run to.

Then Harry smiled as he played back a fortuitous section of her dinner conversation. A bar had been mentioned, "Dooley's" was its name. The same bar where Zeb and Abel had seen her last night. When she had mentioned "Dooley's" the tone of the word was so warm that it must represent a place of security, perhaps even a place of confession and atonement.

The phone rang again.

He listened while one of his men, half of the twins Zeb and Abel, he couldn't tell them apart, told him of the latest about following Karen. The twins had entered the lobby, gone up the staircase and stopped outside the room. Before entering it they put on their specially tinted glasses, looking quite foolish, and checked for footprints. Sure enough the footprints had led to the door. They crashed it down, and entered to find a young woman in bed with the two guys. That was all okay. However, the woman was not, on closer examination, Karen. The two guys with her were very tough and the woman herself had hit Abel with a chair. Zeb had managed to steal her boots, which did have the chemical on them, but the woman was another person. They sure couldn't figure that one out, could Harry? Right now he should take his brother to get the wound closed if that was all right?

There wasn't a whole lot that Harry could say, so he remained silent. Zeb hung up.

The phone rang again and Harry discovered that his other men had lost the trail of Red and Jack. Not only had they lost them, but when they returned from looking down a laneway where they'd seen them enter, their own car, a new Lincoln, had been stolen. They wondered if they should report this to the cops. Harry told them no, and hung up. He buzzed Timothy's private line, but the computer was still on holdcalls mode and he couldn't get through. There was only one place left for Harry to go.

Inside Dooley's bar, time was slow and easy. Vilmos had tracked down an audio tape of "Ryan's Fancy" and their music floated on the winter's day. He looked fragile and sipped on warm soda water. Once in a while he would massage his temples and shake his ponderous head slowly from side to side, stopping quickly as if something inside had broken loose and was clattering around. There was the sound of drumming fingers on the bar keeping time with the music but Vilmos didn't look up. The fingers tapped louder and louder, slightly out of time with the music. Vilmos covered his ears and looked up.

"Pity for the sake of the blessed virgin!"

The outside light burned his eyes as he tried to see the strange man who was at his bar.

"Eyes hurt? I can fix that."

And the fat man moved towards the windows pulling down the green roller blinds until they were in near darkness. Vilmos moved down the bar, as the man returned.

"This bar is closed."

"That suits me fine, but why is it closed?"

"Because I have a hangover. Now go away."

"I thought the Hungarians could hold their liquor."

"Us and the Irish. That's the problem. If we did not hold it so well, if we didn't keep it inside so to speak, then it couldn't do the terrible damage that it does. Who are you?"

"I'm a friend of Karen's. She wants me to ask you some questions."

And Vilmos reached under the bar in one quick move grabbing and swinging a baseball bat towards Harry.

He missed by a fraction and the momentum of the swing carried him across the counter. Before he could recover his balance a small, nickel-plated, .32 pistol was held against his neck. It was tiny and the circle of cold metal felt no larger than a ballpoint pen, but Vilmos stayed very still.

And Harry stepped back, the pistol still pointed at Vilmos's head.

"Like a toy isn't it? I like toys, more subtle toys."

With his left hand he opened the doctor's bag that he placed on the bar.

"You left Hungary when?"

"After the revolution when bastards like you came into our country."

"Please, don't mix us up. They were communists, I'm a capitalist."

"Same thing."

"Really?"

And Harry took out a disposable syringe and a paper pack of needles. Then an assortment of vials were placed along the bar. They made a clicking sound as they touched against each other.

"I think, dear friend of Karen, that you will discover the toys are much better now. They always find what I want to discover. Could you please roll up your sleeve?"

And Harry reached for the tape machine. He turned up the volume before crossing the room, smiling at Vilmos as he slid the bolts across the door.

## ✿  38  ✿

Em Chapman was sleeping, tucked into a turned-down, severe, white hospital bed.

Karen rearranged, for the fourteenth time, the bouquet of flowers that she'd picked up in the gift shop. Someone there had the good sense to keep daisies in stock and they made a cheerful spring-like face against the winter cool of the room. Her mother stirred a little and turned towards the wall.

Karen was not used to seeing Em helpless. Whenever she did think of her mother she remembered hands that could never stay still. If they weren't peeling vegetables, then they were cooking, if they weren't cooking then they were writing letters, otherwise they might be gardening, or making a fresh compost heap, or nailing up crooked shutters or, if it was a quiet day and all the chores were done, the clever hands of her mother would be picking up brush and oils and beginning to paint until the light failed. Those paintings would all go through certain phases. You didn't need to know color, tone, nor evolving brush strokes, nor changing use of perspective to determine what period of her painting life Em was in.

Nineteen fifty-eight, for example, was the year of Sloane's Mill. That was all she did for the year, and each canvas (all twelve of them) was exactly the same. It was always summer in Em's paintings. The snow might come and go in real life, but it never drifted into her art.

Somehow, between the last time Karen had seen her mother and now, Em's hands had gotten old. They were wrinkled and pale. Karen didn't want to follow that thought any further so she looked for something to read. However, there were no books in the room, no newspaper, no fruit to eat. Only the flowers, and she was sick of rearranging them. She walked towards the drapes and stood there wondering whether or not she should open them.

"You never could sit still!"

Karen swung around and looked at Em, who was now decidedly awake. As a matter of fact, she looked as if she'd had time to brush her hair, clean her face, lose five years, and appear as though she hadn't been asleep at all.

"You were sleeping so peacefully that I was trying not to wake you."

"Nonsense! I wasn't sleeping, just grabbing forty winks. What are you doing here?"

And Em opened her night-table drawer, pulling out two knitting needles along with some yarn of a peculiar golden color.

"You're my mother. Why shouldn't I be here?"

"Because you never visit!"

"I've been busy."

"Me too. Very busy."

There was a pause and her mother began to cry. Another startling moment for Karen. First her mother's hands had grown old, now she was crying in front of her. She moved towards her and took one of the tiny capable hands. Em squeezed back using a longshoreman's grip.

"Oh, Karen. That's when you really get old, when you get broken bones. That's when it happens."

It was her turn to say "nonsense," but Em continued before she got the chance.

"I remember my own mother..."

"Grannie wasn't a bit like you."

"She got a broken hip, which I admit is much worse, and she just gave up on life, let it take her quicker than a chariot right to the grave."

"That's what I mean. No goddamn way Em Chapman would do that, is there?"

"Karen, you've been in the room for ten minutes, can't you contain your swearing for that amount of time?"

"No."

"But you do have a point."

"Goddamn right I do. Sorry, Em, I just mean you're not that sort. You die, it's better if you kick the bucket while skidding off the cliff, or falling off the roof, something worthwhile like that."

"I was waiting for a lecture on my hiring someone to do the path for me."

"I was going to give it. But so much has happened to me, I can't say things like that anymore. I'm in love."

A look of horror crossed Em's face.

"You and Scott aren't back together?"

"Don't make me throw up."

"That's what I want to hear. So, who is it?"

"He's called Red, he's from Panama, people are trying to kill him, and I'm in it up to my ears."

"You're actually telling me something! All my life I've longed for you to tell me something and when you do it's this kind of stuff. These people, are they likely to try and kill you too?"

"They'll try."

"Then we should go to the police!"

"We can't, because there's no evidence. Besides, Red doesn't get along with policemen."

"That's a good sign, neither did Henry Thoreau. This Red, you're sure that he's better for you than that jerk, Scott? Name like a tissue, I never trusted him."

"They don't know I'm here. The bad guys."

"How about the good guys?"

"They don't know either."

"Then you should stay for a while. It would do me good, and it sounds like it would, sure as ... heck, do you good."

"I've got to find Red."

"Why not let him find you?"

"You don't mind I'm in danger?"

"Of course I do. But I tell you, there's nothing like a skidding fall on ice towards the edge of a cliff to give you a new look at things. I clawed the ice, I tried to grab a stump, and then I figured it was all over so what the hell."

"You said 'hell'! Mother, I heard you!"

"Don't go all prissy on me, I'm only saying what I thought at the time."

"If you figured 'what the hell', how come you grabbed a tree?"

"My point exactly! Now I've got to rest, so why don't you go home, and think about the tree."

And Em was sound asleep once more, but this time she didn't look as tiny, or as old.

## 39

When Karen entered her mother's house she felt like she was seeing it for the first time. Whatever change had come over Em seemed to extend to the house itself. The white clapboard that was rimed with the edge of salt was sharper and brighter. The green storm door with its square deepset window cupped a dusting of spring snow, as if it had never held any before. She saw the house like she was seeing it with Red, and she longed for him to be there. It was all very well for Em to go on about his finding her, but now that she was alone again, she began to have her doubts.

Inside the house the drapes were all pulled back and the sun was full. It reflected off the waves and was caught by the whitewashed walls. Her mother's summer paintings were prominently displayed, joining the celebration of light.

Karen sat in her father's favorite armchair and looked out to sea from his old study window. There was a brass telescope left in position near the port side of the panes, but she didn't bother with it, choosing instead to look at the wide view. She was glad that her mother's most recent move, some ten years ago, had taken her once more to the very house where Karen had grown up. It had suddenly come on the market and Em had bought it right away, for more money than the house was worth. After Karen's father died, she'd sold it, then had kept moving all around Gloucester, gradually working her way, through five other houses, closer and closer back to the one she'd shared with her husband and daughter. She'd said only one thing to Karen when she bought it, and that was "Don't laugh at me!" She'd never talked about her reasons, but Karen had figured out that it had taken that long for Em to go into the house without its memories killing her.

Feeling restless, Karen got up from the armchair and made her way into the kitchen.

This was a wonderful room with good strong tile on the floors and a huge working area of rich board over the countertop. The board was glowing from its usual treatment of lemon and cooking oil. There was a round pine table, made from a solid block of wood. Thick armchairs, also of pine, surrounded it and vivid dried flowers were in the center of the table.

Em had made one change in the house. She'd had a huge ceiling-to-floor window installed on the cliff side of the kitchen. Karen looked out and down to the ocean swirling in a mixture of green, gray and white ice as it jellied around the rocks. It made her feel dizzy and she moved away from the sheer drop back to the safety of the cooking area.

In the cupboard under the counter top she found an ample supply of dried salt fish. It was sealed in a plastic container and as she opened it there was the aroma of summer and the small flake in the backyard where Em still dried her own cod to perfection. Now Karen knew what to do to help take her mind off her worries. She put the fish in to soak in a big white enamel pot, letting the water run over it. Then, looking on another shelf, she smiled, glad that Em always kept everything in the same place because there was, imported from Newfoundland, the bright red bag with the caribou on the front that meant there was still a good supply of hardtack, or fisherman's biscuit as the cook books called it. In the fridge she knew there would be a block of fatback pork, as white as the whitest snow. She put the hardtack in to soak. If all went well she'd be able to fix Em's favorite meal and smuggle it into the hospital. As a matter of fact, thought Karen, this is *my* favorite meal.

The rest of the afternoon was spent in roaming the house and dusting it as obsessively as ever Em would have done. She came across a half-finished painting. The easel was set up near the small bedroom dormer facing out towards the harbour. The painting was correct in every detail to the view through the window, except on canvas it was summer and tiny sails dotted the July ocean.

When night arrived she busied herself turning on lights. She was about to close the drapes but decided against it, despite the sensation of being vulnerable and exposed.

From outside the house the windows shone their light in squares onto the snow in clean white and black silhouettes of line and form. Karen stood out as clear as a moth against a summer's lantern.

## ✿ 40 ✿

Red and Jack parked the stolen Lincoln on a back street. It had been a pleasure to have liberated the car from Harry's men. It was big, fast and throaty, with wonderful upholstery, but it was also very, very hot. With a slight regret they left it. As they were walking away, Jack had a better idea. He went back, unlocked the car, turned on the ignition and left the doors ajar. From a nearby window shifty eyes looked at them.

"Seems a shame for Standard Telecasting to deprive the needy of transportation, doesn't it, Red?"

But even this inspired moment wasn't enough to lift his son's spirits. He was still trying to decide how to find Karen. The same receptionist who claimed never to have heard of her had told them that Harry Murray was still in Bermuda. Jack didn't believe this, but Red was beginning to suspect that anything was possible.

The day was damp, and the mild front had come and gone, sucking in some colder air behind it, making him feel even worse. A brightly colored bar shone out at the afternoon, and Red spun on his heel to lead the way inside.

They picked a booth that was near the back, far away from the TV set. The bartender who came over to the booth had hands that were big and pink from polishing shot glasses and wore a clean apron. Good signs. Jack ordered bourbon neat and Red heard himself asking for Laphroaig. The bartender didn't know what it was, Jack didn't know what it was and, to make matters worse, neither did Red. He asked instead for some Narragansett. As he'd never ordered Laphroaig in his life before, he tried to puzzle it out.

"You don't know what that stuff was you ordered?"

"I never heard of it, Jack, swear to you. Maybe I used it in a con once and it stuck with me."

"It's a drink?"

"Yeah."

"So how do you know that?"

"A good question. But what difference?"

Jack ordered two more shots, this time bourbon for both of them.

"Because, kid, we've been racking our brains for something that might lead us to Karen, and you sit down and order a drink you never heard of before. The two things go together. You ever hear of Sigmund Freud?"

"Of course I have. I was a psychiatrist in a scam in Montreal once."

"So nothing's an accident. Have a bourbon, and it'll come to you."

"I got a fancy we should move around, go to some other bars, ask for the drink there. Maybe that'll trigger something."

They spent a couple of hours touring bars, which Jack allowed was a very good way of being a detective. Most of the bars hadn't heard of Laph-roaig, those that had heard of it didn't have any. They finally found a Japanese restaurant-bar that did carry it. This joint had every kind of Scotch in the world. The bartender left as they pronounced the name and came back, his face beaming in a very scrutable manner.

"The best, isn't it?" he said, and left them to look over towards the corner where the new music machine was in full blast. This gadget allowed a customer to sing along to any song, while a computer with perfect pitch fixed up the voice and made the client sound like, in this case, Tom Jones. The older Japanese businessman who had the microphone was busy belting out the chorus of "Green, Green Grass of Home" when Red took his first sip. The bartender was right. This drink was the best.

"I don't think it tastes like peat moss." He stated emphatically to Jack.

"I never said it did," Jack replied.

> Yes they'll all come to meet me
> Arms reaching, smiling sweetly
> It's good to touch the
> Green, green grass of home,

sang the businessman.

Red knocked back the glass of single malt, and pointed to the empty tumbler. In mid-point the bartender had the glass refilled. Red now sipped.

"I've got it. Karen was the one who said it tasted like peat moss. She told me that's what Dooley said, or did she call him Vilmos? But said he liked to be called Dooley?"

Jack beckoned towards the bartender.

"You ever hear of a bar called Dooley's?"

"Sure, but he doesn't have a machine like this."

"Does he have Scotch?"

"Only ten kinds."

"Where is he?"

"Couple of blocks away."

Jack paced while Red paid the bill with a rapidly expiring stolen credit card. Then they left on the run.

The wind cut at their open jackets as they jaywalked to Dooley's, only to find it firmly closed. The door was bolted from the inside and a sign hung at the window saying "Out of Order."

"No bar I ever heard of closes early on a Friday night."

Jack punched in the glass, reached through the broken panes and opened the door. It was done so quickly that no one passing by paid any attention. They stepped into the bar.

The blinds flapped in the night air. Someone had been there before them, and there'd been a fight. The mirrors were shattered in crazy cracks that left fragments hanging from brown backing and torn silver.

They didn't find Vilmos until they entered the far room at the end of the wine cellar. There were no cases of wine in this room, but there were bolts set in the wall to hold extra shelving. He had been strung by rope from various bolts in the wall, his massive head bent to one side, blood congealed on his left leg. Red felt sick but Jack moved closer under the overhead light bulb that starked shadows along the stones.

"He's alive."

Red moved quickly towards him and reached under Vilmos's arms. While he struggled to hold him up, Jack broke a bottle of Tokay, and cut the strands. The sudden release of the strain from the ropes tipped Vilmos forward and he and Red crashed to the stone floor.

After picking himself up, he and Jack managed to lug Vilmos up the stairs into the bar. They put a jacket under his head, and poured a little brandy into his mouth. Vilmos coughed, sputtered, and began speaking Hungarian.

This didn't bother Jack, who listened closely, while Red watched him.

"Can you speak Hungarian?"

He shook his head.

"Just a little. I once had a sweetheart in Budapest and Magda at the Blue Goose taught me a few more words."

"So what's he saying?"

"I can't hear him. You're talking too much."

As soon as Red stopped talking, Vilmos began to sing.

> *János Bácsi,*
> *János Bácsi*
> *Keljen fel...*

Vilmos went back to sleep.

"What was it? Is it a clue?"

"Not really, kid. He was singing 'Frère Jacques' in Hungarian."

Using a little more brandy, he was able to revive Vilmos once more. This time his eyes were a little clearer and he looked startled as he saw Jack and Red.

"We're friends of Karen."

"How do I know that?"

Red thought for a moment.

"I know your real name is Vilmos, but you like it best when Karen calls you Dooley. My name is Red and I'm guessing that she told you about me, and I'm making another guess that someone came here and tried to get information from you. Did they?"

"*Igen.*"

"That means yes," offered Jack.

"In Gloucester because her mother is in hospital there. That is all I know, and that is all I told."

Jack was already on his way to the door.

"What about you?"

"I'm alive, I can reach a phone. I'll tell the cops someone robbed me. How are you getting there?"

Jack stopped at the doorway.

"We'll steal a car."

"Inside the coat hanging over there, you'll find my keys. My car is yours. Tell Karen that I'm sorry."

Jack went over to an immaculate green topcoat hung neatly on the brass coatrack that stood in the shadow of the door. It had a lucky four-leaf clover pinned to its lapel. He reached inside the pocket and found a set of keys for a Morris Mini.

Before they left Red kicked the shards of glass from the window into the gutter. Across the street there was a small bright-green car.

The engine caught on the second turn of the key. Jack waited patiently until the heater came on, waited until the windows were all defrosted and then began to drive away, picking up speed while making his way towards the expressway.

"So now we know how to find her. And we've only got one big problem—whoever got here first knows where to go."

"The fat man."

"Yeah, and I figure he's got a few hours' head start on us."

## ❧ 41 ❧

Em had finished all of her salt fish and brewis, so smuggling the food into the hospital had been worth it. The fish had been cooked to that glorious moment where the flakes separated and yet stayed firm, while the brewis still held the flavor of the soaked sea biscuit, white and golden brown. The pork fat was cut up into tiny cubes of scrunchions, fried till the perfect moment and then poured over the tender flakes of fish and brewis. About an hour before preparing this Karen had remembered how much her mother loved gingered beets, so she'd taken the forty minutes needed to make the dish. In the root cellar there'd been fresh ginger that she could mince to give the whole meal its proper taste. Now, Em was eating chocolate poppyseed cake with great swirls of mocha frosting. Her daughter was beginning to feel hungry.

"Karen, you always could cook!"

"Take after you."

"That's for sure. Your father couldn't cook worth a hoot."

"Men weren't expected to cook in those days."

"Who in the world told you that? My father

baked all the bread in our house. I wish I could make brown bread that had half the taste. Your father was a different story. He used to work summers as a cook in a lumber camp."

"In a lumber camp? You're kidding, he was always so fastidious."

"You don't know a thing about your father, Karen. Anyway, it was in the woods that he found out all he'd ever know about cooking. But only for fifty men, he never could get used to working with anything under a ten-pound sack of sugar. He learned to smoke in the woods too ... cigars."

And Em yawned.

"Not the company, it's the hour."

Karen collected the empty dishes and kissed her mother.

"You saved the trouble of washing the plates."

" 'Give them to the dog to clean,' that's what your father used to say."

Em laughed to herself, and yawned again.

"Good night, Em."

" 'Night, Karen, that was a perfect meal."

And as she left the room Em's sleepy voice drifted after her, "Good to have you home."

Karen felt warm all the way across the parking lot, and it wasn't only because she was wearing her mother's thick down coat.

As she unlocked the door of Em's Pontiac, the moon came out from behind some dark clouds. It was full, with a mixture of milk and crystal in its color. The lot lit up the key sharply against the lock. The night felt colder than before and Karen shivered. During the drive towards the house she couldn't shake the feeling that she was being followed, but no matter how often she checked her rear-view mirror there were no headlights reflected in it. Once she thought there was a glint of moonlight on metal, but when she pulled over nothing passed her. After waiting ten minutes, she began to feel foolish so she drove on.

She tuned to a country-and-western station, finding some cheating songs and crying ballads that took away most of her fears. When she arrived at the house she remained in the car a couple of minutes longer to hear Bill Monroe and The Blue Grass Boys finish their number.

Getting out of the car, without locking it, she moved towards the house. It was after crossing the driveway that she first noticed the light on the telephone pole had gone out. But that didn't bother her as the moon was still full and there weren't any clouds sloping towards it. About this time she also realized that she had gone away from the house in such a hurry that she'd locked the house key inside, and swore at herself until she remembered Em's old trick of hiding keys all around the property. Much as Karen had lectured her mother about the danger of this practice, she was now quite glad of it. The first place to check was under the front door mat. No luck. Karen's heart sank, because this was the one place where there always was a key. She turned towards the back door, without much hope. As she rounded the corner she could see lights from the kitchen streaming towards the abyss of the cliff edge. She knew it was wasting electricity to leave them on, but she hated coming home to a dark house. When she lifted the back-door mat she was relieved to see the moonlight caught on the edge of the house key.

Inside the house the hall light was off, so Karen had to grope her way along the wall towards the kitchen, crashing into a passel of brooms and mops. She fought her way past them and opened the door into the kitchen. She moved towards the stove to light the gas burners, feeling ravenous.

She jumped as Harry's voice echoed through the kitchen.

"Better make enough for two."

When she spun around Karen could see Harry smiling, with a bigger smile than she'd ever seen on his face before. He was dressed in black and carried a doctor's bag.

## ❧ 42 ❧

At first Red had wanted them to steal a larger more powerful car, but Jack talked him out of it. It was windy and it was icy, and slush that held other cars' tracks began to freeze into ruts that their smaller car could straddle. The front-wheel drive whipped them around curves that would have spun a larger car out of control, while the manual gearshift allowed Jack to wind the car through rpm's that wouldn't have been possible in another auto. Jack's decision to drop down to Highway 127 proved to be a smart one, as the radio later let them know that the Interstate had been closed because of whiteouts caused by blowing snow. The little car had fog lights and the road shot yellow stripes beneath them.

When they neared Gloucester the wind began to die down and the clouds shifted away, torn in streamers from the moon. Jack shut off the fog lights and shifted into high gear. The ocean caught moonlight and bounced it on to 127. There was enough light for Red to lean back and sift through the mound of papers and books that spilled around the back seat of Vilmos's car. He grabbed volumes at random from the shifting mass. The first book was in Hungarian, by a poet called Faludy. Red glanced at the dense pages of a different language and put it back. The book was well thumbed with frequent corners turned down. The next volume was of Yeats, which Red tried to read until Jack told him they were entering Gloucester.

"No time now, kid. Look for a hospital sign."

In her room, Em was wide awake, regretting having yielded to her earlier desire for sleep. She was a creature of habit. Bedtime was at ten, reading time until midnight, and then sleep. To doze off at eight or so was a mistake, and a sign of weakness that could, she mused, keep her leg from mending as it should.

She had been sleeping well, she did admit, until she was awakened to take a sleeping pill. She'd put it in her mouth and dutifully swallowed. The nurse had smiled and as soon as she'd gone from the room, Em had taken the still intact pill out from under her tongue. She had learned a lot by watching *One Flew Over the Cuckoo's Nest.*

The overhead light was off and she didn't feel like turning it on because she knew it would bring some watchful nurse to inquire about the sleeplessness and perhaps deduce that the sleeping pill had not been taken. So Em lay there and watched the ceiling and thought about Karen, marvelling that a broken limb had got the two of them talking again. If she'd known that's what it took she'd have broken all her bones years ago.

Somewhere in the middle of this thought she was aware that two men had entered her room. As soon as she saw the look on the younger one's face she thought of her daughter. There was something

in the eyes of this man that reminded her of
Karen, and she realized who he must be.

"Red?"

"She talked about me?"

"Never stopped. Is she in worse trouble than she
thinks?"

Jack stepped out of the shadows. "A whole lot.
They know she's here."

"Can we call the police?"

Jack and Red looked dubious.

"Then you've got to go and help her!"

Red nodded, "Only one flaw in our rescue
plans, we don't know where she is."

Em reached into the night table and took out her
writing pad. She began to sketch a small map to
her house rapidly on the front. As she drew she
kept glancing up at Red. Her daughter had chosen
well.

"If you stop whoever's there now..."

"His name is Harry Murray, a fat man, with
Standard Telecasting. Just in case we have
trouble."

"Once you get him, is that the end of it?"

"Once we get him all hell could break loose and
we might have to leave. Your daughter would have
to scram as well."

"Here's the map. I wrote a note for Karen at the
bottom. Here's my credit card and my code number. Bank's at the cross on the map, on your way
out of town take what you can. I've got a five-
hundred dollar limit. Tell Karen I love her."

And the two men slipped out of the room. Em
lay there. The cool white sheet that covered her
made her feel like a prisoner. For the first time in
over thirty years, Em Chapman started praying.

## 43

Mealtime was over and Karen hadn't enjoyed the food that she'd been looking forward to all day. The only reason that she'd forced herself to eat was because she knew that she was going to need every bit of strength she could get.

Harry, on the contrary, had relished the meal. Once more he paused and examined every morsel before he took a bite. He savored each dish and commented wisely on what she must have done to achieve its flavor. He'd even looked in the pantry and found a bottle of dogberry wine which he proclaimed to be one of the miracles of Massachusetts. He'd taken some time out to tell her that if he hadn't made it for this special meeting then Timothy would have come himself. He went on to chat about how, compared to Timothy, he was a kind man. However, Karen wasn't listening closely. Instead, she tried to think of weapons.

On the counter there was a wooden block and in the block stood an array of gleaming sharp kitchen knives. She'd casually glanced at them and was convinced she could get there with only two steps. She also tried to remember a class she'd once taken in self-defense, one that she'd dropped after three weeks. She had decided, at the time, that it wasn't worth the energy to rearrange her workload. She regretted that decision.

Harry stopped talking and there was silence as they finished their cake. His fork scraped against the plate when he captured the last crumbs. The sound was like chalk on a blackboard. From the corner of the kitchen the ticking of the world's ugliest clock continued. On the hour a small wooden cuckoo creaked out and gave twelve clacking sounds. The ticking continued as the tiny oak doors ground shut.

Harry reached under the table and took out his doctor's bag. He opened it and, to Karen's horror, began spreading a white gauze sheet across his side of the table. On one corner of the material there was a dried bloodstain. He began laying out scalpel blades that came in a neat package which he unrolled upon the cloth. While he was doing this, he began to talk.

"Vilmos made the mistake of thinking that he wasn't going to tell me where you lived."

"How do you know about Vilmos?" A more important thought struck her. "What did you do to him?"

"I made him tell me about you, and about everything that you had told him. Which was not much, so the beginning of this session may be painful. Perhaps, pretty Karen, you'll suffer well?"

"Fuck you, Fatso."

"A good start. Perhaps you'll do better. I need to know about the man in Bermuda. I also need to know what else you know about the trip Timothy and I took to Panama."

"I don't know anything."

"You are going to be very, very surprised about the number of things you know."

Harry took out a length of rope and then a small gun.

"Karen, we really should begin."

As he raised his gun, she remembered something from the third week of her self-defense lessons, just before she had quit the course. It seemed silly and unlikely, but she had the harrowing thought that it was going to be her only chance.

As Harry walked from around the table towards her she began to cry and he smiled.

Karen pressed one of her feet against the other and slipped off her right shoe. She felt with her toes for the bottom rung of the unused armchair, moving closer to Harry as if she were going to ask his mercy. He smiled even more and lowered the .32 slightly. When he did, she pushed the chair with all her strength.

It slammed into Harry's shins and the top caught him right in the crotch. He gasped and buckled over. Karen took the two steps to the counter and pulled out a long carving knife. Harry was now groping for the gun that he'd dropped. He found it, grabbed it and began to aim as she jabbed. Her carving knife hit a rib and Karen's hand slid down the handle. The blade cut deep into her fingers. She could feel the blood run down and over her nails. It didn't feel sticky or smooth, it just felt warm.

And now Karen was sure she was going to die. It was the brief pause between action that did it. Until then, everything had been so fast, running on instinct, that there was no time for thought. In this second she could see the texture and tone of the room as detailed and intense as a slide projected on snow. It wasn't slow motion, it was more like being aware of living inside a snapshot.

Harry pulled the trigger and Karen felt a distant thud on her side. Shifting the knife to her other hand, she plunged the blade into him. The gun dropped and Karen slammed him with the chair again. He staggered towards the window, where he tripped while trying to get his balance and fell backwards. His huge weight took him against the glass where, with a crashing, tearing splinter, the lower section ripped out and spilled, along with Harry, into the ocean. There was the start of a scream which was cut off by a splash and then quiet, except for the tinkle of small fragments of glass falling on the kitchen tiles.

Karen felt weak but calm. She noticed, as if it was happening to another person, blood leaking from her hand. She ran the water but it wouldn't go away, lying in lazy brown red ribboned circles against the metal basin. Then she noticed the wind whipping through the kitchen. Just as the lights brightened she heard a strange ringing noise in the running water and turned off the tap. But the ringing noise continued. As it did the sound filled the kitchen and then the light was gone and she fell to the floor.

# 44

The morning's wind was from the nor'east, bringing the ice onshore in thick blue and gray and green that rolled and dipped with the waves. It covered Harry's body. His white cuffs were shot beneath the crystal as the ice chafed along his wrists.

Inside Em's house the wind whistled towards the thermostat and the furnace lost a growing battle with the cold. Upstairs in the bedroom there was a small fireplace where a coal fire glowed round and deep. The heat kept Karen cozy and asleep until the middle of the morning. When she did wake it was to see Red dozing at the corner of the bed. He had put his feet up on the coverlet and one of his socks had a hole in it. Karen moved her hand to touch him and a sharp pain went through her hip. She sucked in her breath and that was enough to wake him.

"Karen. You're in pain?"

"I'm in bed and you're here and I'm alive, who cares about the pain. What happened?"

"We were hoping you'd tell us that."

And she did. As her memory returned, so did every ache and pain and cut. So did fear as she described the last moments of Harry being pushed and staggering backwards towards the window. Then she stopped talking and leaned back deeper into the feather bed. It closed and held her. Red stroked her hair and slowly ran the back of his hand along the bone of her cheek. They kissed gently, and then he checked out her many bandages and plasters.

"It was real easy fixing you up, with all the medical equipment that Harry had along with him. His bullet worked its way through your flesh, didn't hit the bone."

"Where's Jack?"

"In town talking with Em, so she won't worry about you."

"You know Em?"

"We met her last night. That's how we knew where to find you."

"He's not going to tell her about how I'm busted up? It'll kill her."

"Nothing's going to kill that woman. Her and Jack just phoned to see how you are. She's happy you're alive and glad I'm with you. The wounds are mild compared to what might have been so she rambled on about taking each thing on its own. Also she and Jack have hit it off. He threw the head nurse out of her room when she tried to tell him about visiting hours. Em understands. She also knows everything about what's going on and has fronted us cash so we can make a getaway."

Karen's eyes started to close and she had trouble opening them again.

"Red, darling, it's not you, it's just, I feel so sleepy...."

And in the middle of whatever else she was going to say, her head slid back into the drifted pillow.

He heard the sound of hammering and made his way downstairs. Jack had returned and now was busy ripping out whatever was left of the window. He'd rented a propane space heater which roared towards the space where the window used to be. All around him, in orderly heaps, were panes of glass, nails, wood, putty and whatever else it would take to get the house sealed up again. He pointed towards one bag from a toy store. Red opened it and found a Fisher Price nursery monitor. He smiled and made his way back to Karen's room. She murmured a little as he came in and set up the listening half of the monitor. Then he made his way downstairs where he turned on the other half of the device. It worked perfectly. He could hear the crackling of the bedroom fireplace mix with the sound of Karen's breathing. With that worry off his mind he pitched in to help Jack.

By the time that first afternoon had vanished the window had been fixed, with every seam double caulked, and every corner plumbed straight. They stood back and admired their work. The timer on the stove pinged gently and Jack went over to add vegetables to the soup. One of his in-town purchases, a range-fed hen, had been simmering for most of the afternoon.

When all the tools had been put away and the kitchen cleaned up, the furnace had begun to triumph over the elements. The soup smelled wonderful.

By the time Karen had finished her fourth bowl, everyone felt better. The house was back in working order. Jack had earlier driven Harry's car towards a cliff a half-mile east of the house. He'd put the Caddy in drive and let it bounce its way down the winding road towards the cliff drop. It had gone over with the door staying open and crashed through the ice. It hesitated and then sank. He figured that this way there was a chance someone might read accident for the whole event.

Harry's gun had clattered its way across the kitchen floor to end up jammed under the fridge. But other than that no damage had been done. So, Jack took the time to clean the weapon and oil it. The gun had not been looked after and as he got it into perfect working shape he shook his head and tsked a lot. He reloaded the .32 and then tucked it, safety on, into his belt. Earlier he had found the entry hole through the drywall of the kitchen and had then traced the path of the bullet until he was able to dig it out of a beam.

Now he went into the study, turned out the lights and sat next to the spyglass. From here he could see the ocean and by leaning to the side the land approaches to the house. He knew that upstairs Karen and Red would be sleeping, so he decided to spend the night awake. Everyone else might think that most of the danger had gone. He had been through too much in his eventful life to ever allow himself the luxury of relaxing. He knew that Harry was only the beginning of new trouble.

## ❧ 45 ❧

The road back to Panama City began at the Gloucester hospital.

Jack was on his way to join Karen and Red who were visiting Em. The front seat of the Mini was jammed with a huge floral display that he'd liberated from a church on his way. As he approached the hospital he noticed a group of expensive-looking automobiles at the gate, so he slowed and peered through the fuchsia and roses, the carnations and baby's breath, at the people sitting in the cars.

There were Zeb and Abel along with some other very clean-cut men who looked like Mormons except for the eyes. Jack wanted to make plans to leave town, but before that he had to make plans to get into the hospital.

Outside the side entrance there was an ambulance unloading, and just down from that, with its motor running stood another long blue car of the variety favored by the heavies at Standard Telecasting. Jack kept driving until he rounded the building, where a rural hearse had pulled up to the service door and an elderly undertaker with two black-suited, zit-stricken apprentices walked into the gloom of the loading room and approached the full casket. It had no frills, no brass, no polish, designed only to transport a corpse to the funeral parlor where the replacement would be more "appropriate." The undertaker waited for his apprentices to seize the moment and the casket, but they appeared to be unable to figure out how to move it.

He lost his temper.

"Rotate the deceased a hundred and eighty degrees, lads!" he said sternly.

The lads looked puzzled. The undertaker kept repeating the instructions, but nothing happened.

Jack stepped forward and addressed them.

"Slew the bugger round, boys."

And they did. He then helped carry the casket, and watched the hearse vanish before walking back towards the staff entrance as the watchman gave him a nod. Jack always liked to blend in with the locals.

A white coat got him past two more spotters and then once inside Em's room he held his fingers to his lips and motioned for them to use pen and paper. All this might look silly, thought Jack, but with a lot of money chances were there would be some kind of listening device pointed their way.

Em took the pen and swore she'd be careful until she heard from them.

This was a moment they had discussed and planned for, so they were ready. But when Karen hugged Em there were tears in her eyes. Her mother stayed dry-eyed, she'd made up her mind to save the crying for later. Red kissed her cheek and Jack kissed her full on the lips, which surprised everyone in the room except Em.

Red and Karen followed Jack to the back entrance, where for fifty bucks they had the pleasure of leaving the hospital in a laundry truck.

The truck stopped near the transit station long enough for some anonymous and wealthy dentist to donate his or her car. It had tinted windows, smelled of cloves, and looked less obvious than a bright-green Mini. And it blended in perfectly with traffic that headed towards Boston.

They took a roundabout course that brought them over a little-used border station into Canada. From Montreal they flew to Miami Beach, where they all stayed at a cheap motel called "The Happy Adventure!"

Then they waited until Jack could make a couple of contacts and buy the makings of false papers. Red felt very nervous all the time they were in Miami Beach. The last time he'd been there he'd also been in danger of being arrested. It could seem to a perceptive person that no progress had been made.

When they checked into the motel they were given a glossy brochure. It showed a fun-time nineteen fifties party in faded greens and yellows, where a brush-cut beach bum was saying "Every room has a view of the ocean!" It was the truth that if someone in the opposite room left their front door and rear drapes open at the same time, then, by squinting into the other person's motel unit, it was possible to see the beach.

In the room there was also a defective TV and a series of cards arranged on top of it advertising the charms of various local beauties. Red invented a game, a variation on blackjack, that involved adding up the real ages of the ladies, but after two days they all tired of that.

While Jack was looking up old friends who might have the proper makings of false papers, Red and Karen spent time at the local library. Not to catch up on the classics but to do some reading on Timothy Shepherd. Every mile of the drive and well into each night, they'd talked about what it all meant. The fact that they'd been tracked down by more heavies to Gloucester meant Timothy was after them. The numbers who had turned out were impressive. It was also significant that no police at any level were involved.

Red and Jack thought Karen was crazy to have mentioned Panama to Timothy, but had to admit they had learned one important thing. Timothy had been there, Harry had told her so himself. That meant that Mr Clean himself might have been in on the killing. Proving it was something else.

Red knew he should feel that he had now avenged Azucar—the two men who had taken her away from the casino were dead. In the warm lapping night of Miami Beach he looked through two motel rooms towards the ocean and thought of her. Sometimes in his dreams the three of them, Red, Karen and Azucar, glided into the jungle towards a purring ocelot and a cursing cockatoo. But just as they all arrived and the sun was dappled and folded, Azucar would start running away, and neither Red nor Karen could make her stop.

When Red told Karen about the dream she sighed and told him it meant the quest wasn't over yet. That there was more to learn. They were sure Timothy had been involved in the murder, but still didn't know why. She also told Red that the only place she could think of to find out more was at the library. The one they visited certainly was not high tech—it specialized in the collected works of Pearl Buck—but did have a wonderful periodicals section, and in a humungous storage room, back copies of most major magazines back to the time of the building of "The Happy Adventure!"

In the middle of dusty old papers, of yellowed pages, of frail newsprint, Karen was at home. Red also felt better. He read the racing pages and gained a greater understanding of the lineage of horses that he was fond of today. He gained so much extra knowledge that he wanted to go to the track and put his new perceptions of horseflesh to work, but Karen kept him at work looking for stories about Timothy Shepherd.

By the third day they'd put together a better picture of the man. There was a lot of junk about what a good guy he was, and what wonderful friends he had and so on. There was, however, a slew of editorials against him and the simplistic views he held about the way to run the U.S. The real goldmine occurred in an early *Miami Herald*. It was reported that Timothy gave a youth address to the JayCees, right in Miami Beach. The story only took up a few paragraphs, but that was enough for Karen, because the speech was full of praise for the late Huey Long and the idea of forming a third major political party. Now, Red did not consider this to be a goldmine, but Karen told him that it was the key to everything. She became so excited that she spoke loudly enough to wake up three sleeping derelicts. She was in the middle of telling Red, at top volume, that the killings had to be connected to Timothy's political desires, when a librarian threw them out.

Once they were outside, Karen kept on in the same vein while Red dreamed about the track. When she had finished telling him that Timothy planned to form a third political party, as far to the right as you could go after shoving Republicans out of the way, he pointed out that Azucar knew nothing about politicians, other than going to bed with them, and that was no crime, at least in Panama. Karen maintained she was correct, Red that she was wrong, and in the early hours of the evening the discussion sputtered out over cold coffee and the "Happy Adventure!" club sandwich which seemed to be made entirely of lettuce.

Jack returned with all the papers and forms needed to make them fresh passports. He was missing only one seal, but Red showed him how he could duplicate one using ink and a peeled hard-boiled egg. He was so anxious to get out of Miami Beach that he felt very nervous as he began his various forgeries.

However, his nerves didn't affect his skill and the makeshift papers that he constructed with the help of the hard-boiled egg worked long enough to get them all visas.

It was just in time, because the *Miami Herald* had as its lead story the death of Harry Murray. The body had finally rolled ashore in Gloucester, coated with light skim ice. Police said that foul play was suspected.

There was only one place to go. Panama City itself would be too dangerous, but if their papers worked well enough to get them out of the States and into Panama outside the city, there was somewhere they could hide. Jack told them about it each night, like a bedtime story, and in the morning the thought of it rose with the sun.

They didn't start to relax until their flight taxied to the end of the runway and lifted off towards their hiding place—Jack's jungle hut.

## 〰 46 〰

Timothy Shepherd usually enjoyed nothing more than the murmur of a Sunday morning prayer breakfast. The chiming of the crystal, the faint clink of silver on china, the sailcloth sound of linen napkins being unfolded with vigor. It always made Timothy think of King Arthur's court and allowed him the chance to study every face, while keeping his back away from any possible danger.

But today he felt that it had all been rolled in ashes. Harry was dead, and Harry had always been his link to the world, his arranger of events. With those cat eyes there was never any dark, no hidden traps, the shadows could hook but never hold. Now even this bright room, this place of light where conversations and loud comfortable laughter rolled across the round table, held shadows.

Wayne had been killed while on the special assignment. That same job had spun Harry out of Panama City, through Bermuda and back to America and his death. And all that Timothy had were two computer printouts of an old man and a younger one, and the knowledge that these people were connected to Karen Chapman. When they were brought to him he would find out what they knew about the secret, and then would kill them himself. Nothing could be allowed to get in the way of his dream. The world, he knew, would be a better place because of it. And he would do anything to help the dream.

The morning papers lay discarded on the crisp linen of tables, prayers had been heard and food consumed, servants in blue and gold removed the plates and scraped the remains of the eggs, bacon and sausage into large plastic bins that were in turn whisked away to an inner kitchen. Coffee was poured as huge video screens were placed around the room, lit up in garish color, displaying a huge cathedral of redwood and glass. The television image showed an artificial island in the middle of an artificial lake. Water shot up one side of the cathedral and cascaded down until it shimmered back into the lake in such a fine mist that it turned sunlight into rainbows.

On the tape, the camera moved closer and closer as the world's largest pipe organ rolled sound towards the screens and in a dissolve the whole beauty of the structure held for a moment while the video-enhanced face of Timothy Shepherd emerged. He was singing with the massed choir and as he sang his eyes remained half-closed while he squinted at a superimposed image of Jesus. The hymn ended and Timothy turned towards the camera.

"Ever wonder where all the real people are?" he asked, and went on to answer his own question.

"They're in hiding. In hiding because there aren't many real churches left, no real political party left for us to call our own. Only airwaves that are polluting the minds of our children. This Sunday, sit real close to me, because I have for you, and for the country—An Answer."

The politicians and the businessmen who were watching the monitors started to applaud until the real Timothy held up his hands. He glanced towards his image on the screen and suddenly looked very shy, too modest to stay and watch his own speech continue on television. He bowed and retreated to his office.

"I know what I said, the rest of you call me when it's done, if you're still awake!"

Through the laughter he went to his inner office.

Once he got inside the smile left his face. He'd known something was wrong when a small blue light at the top of one monitor had begun pulsing. That meant something urgent was going on. As he entered the office he could see Zeb and Abel both standing near the blue switch. Timothy clicked it to the Off position.

"You two assholes haven't lost them again, have you?"

"I wish you wouldn't talk that way, Mr Timothy," requested Abel while Zeb shuffled from one foot to the other.

Zeb finally spoke. "He didn't mean nothing by it, Abel. If he thought we was assholes he wouldn't keep sending us on jobs, 'cause that would make him even more of an asshole than we're supposed to be."

Timothy had nothing to reply. It was, for the twins, a long train of thought, and it was quite correct.

"Well, did you get them?"

"No sir, they slipped out of Gloucester before we could get to them, but we found the girl's mother. We thought she'd have lots to tell you so we brought her here."

"She's in this building?"

"We put her in your private office."

"I am an asshole. Let the world know it."

Zeb and Abel backed much closer to the exit. Abel thought it was his turn to speak.

"We bundled her into the car just as she was leaving the hospital. We gagged her and we went round so many corners she's gonna think she's in Disneyland."

"Take her back."

"Back where?"

"To wherever you found her, and spin her around a few times on the way. I will not meet her, I will not allow her to hear my voice. But I will allow you to ask her three questions. If she answers them she can live. Did her daughter mention any specific name? Where has her daughter gone? Who are the men with her? Pretend you are with the CIA, get a shave before you talk with her, put on some Brut or something like that, things she'll remember. If you're satisfied bring her back to the hospital."

"That's pretty difficult, they might spot us."

"Does the old woman have a house?"

"Yes. She sure does, a real nice one."

"Good, put her there, and even after you've finished getting answers to the questions, leave an all-purpose bug in the house, along with a wire crawler for the phone-activated calls. Crawler with tracer. Okay?"

"Right on, boss. Only one other thing. She's kind of feisty. You got something to help calm her down?"

Timothy went to a wall safe and took out a vial of pink liquid along with a couple of disposable syringes. He gave them to the twin incompetents. Then he returned to the prayer breakfast. The applause began as soon as the door opened.

Zeb and Abel went into the inner office, where Em had just finished chewing through the kerchief that was gagging her. As soon as she heard footsteps she began to yell, "This is Boston, I know it's Boston, I can tell by the smell. Now, you must let me go!"

But by this time Abel had the gag replaced, and Zeb injected her with the pink liquid. Em relaxed, slumped and began to snore. Zeb and Abel put her back on the makeshift stretcher and made their way to the freight elevator.

Em felt one jolt and almost woke. She tried to think but all she could come up with was Boston and the fact that her daughter wasn't there.

"No matter what they do to me," she thought, "I'm not going to tell them anything."

Back at the conclusion of the prayer breakfast the coffee was gone. In previous years the air would have been thick with cigar smoke, but now everyone was quite aware of health dangers, so instead they drank down tea and munched their way through mounds of cheese Danishes. There were lawyers, politicians, some show business personalities—all of whom had, through drink or drugs, bottomed out and found their way back again. They would tell stories about themselves that would have allowed at least twenty blackmailers to retire in a more innocent age. Whatever the profession, former sinner or present clergyman, or a combination of the two, they were all praising the guest sermon that Timothy had given. That sermon had also coincided with the takeover of ten more stations, putting him closer to the position of becoming head of the most powerful network in the country. His influence was enormous.

No one in the room doubted his next step. The Presidency. Only a few knew the way that he interpreted that particular job.

The last of the well-wishers had left, except for one clergyman who had stayed long enough to request a video copy of the address. He was handed one on the way out the door, and then Timothy was alone. He walked slowly back to the office. His face was on most of the newscasts displayed on the monitors, but he didn't bother looking at any of the screens. He went past the scanners into his inner office, where he opened his desk and took out a grimy letter. It smelled of lilac scent and was addressed with violet ink. It contained something he thought he would never see again. The same request as was made before, as if no steps had been taken to deal with the problem. All this power and still the constant danger. His headache began to go and he felt himself coming alive. He looked at the envelope and its postmark—Panama City.

It was time to go visiting.

## ❧ 47 ❧

Time had not been kind to Jack's hut. The bright white clapboard had warped and buckled. The chimney had nests of mud leaking from it like pendulous tears. Mushrooms sprouted on the overgrown path where small green frogs with bright red backs made peculiar sounds. The tin roof had fried layers of mosses and strange glowing growths that looked like psychedelic lichen. Tiny eyes peeped from all this. They stared at Karen.

Jack was trying to open the door, but it too had warped. As it shook, the edge of the roof began to quiver, the tin shaking like thunder. The same tiny eyes blinked again and there was the distinct sound of claws scrabbling on the roof. Karen stepped back, just in case something fell off the roof and onto her, but when she moved she felt something resting on the arch of her foot. She looked down where grasses and vines covered her feet and stopped walking.

The men had finished opening the door of the hut and Jack reappeared holding a small net. With two quick "whoops" he lifted out a couple of very ugly spiders, depositing them into a small wooden cage.

Karen was just about to go towards the hut when another slithering motion went over the arch of one foot and then across the other. She felt very glad that she hadn't moved. As she looked down she could see the undergrowth skid and shag in a long shimmering line across her feet. Then the feeling was gone and the green stood still. Karen didn't. She shot from the undergrowth and in three long kangaroo-like bounces was at the door of this horrid little hut. She arrived just as a beaming Jack looked out.

"No place like home, is there, Karen?"

To which she could only make a feeble nod in agreement.

"Better come inside while I clean up out here, all kinds of poisonous snakes and creepy-crawlies around till I get things shipshape. One thing to remember, you don't bother them, they aren't going to bother you."

"Like dogs?"

"Everything's like dogs."

And he emerged from the hut, machete in hand, a polka-dot bandanna strapped around his forehead, and began to attack the jungle where it had invaded territory that was clearly his. Karen heard a few extra scrabbles on the roof and jumped quickly inside the hut. Whatever was on the roof might not be poisonous; however, she still didn't cherish the thought of those little claws scampering around her neckline.

Inside, the hut was bright and cheerful and some of her shivers began to leave. There were vile-looking leaves scattered before the doorway and on the window ledges. They smelled sharp but not unpleasant.

"They keep the bugs away," said Red, as if he'd heard her ask the question. He was over near an old rocking chair where he ran his fingers along the headpiece. From the crest down it was carved with strange feathered and scaled creatures rising from a froth of small wooden waves. Karen joined him to look at the chair.

"In an odd way it's beautiful. Fits in with all this doesn't it?"

"Yeah. Except the creatures don't move."

"So all that stuff," she pointed outdoors and looked up at the scratching roof, "bothers you too?"

"We used to have mice in the house when I was a kid. I'd lie there at night and hear them scratching away, sometimes right over my head. I got used to that, but this sounds a lot worse."

Red walked over to the rocker.

"What I find really peculiar is that this chair looks familiar."

"Maybe you saw one somewhere else."

"Are you kidding? No one in their right mind would make another piece of furniture like this. Believe me, this rocking chair's one of a kind, made by a madman or drunk."

"Want to know something, Red? I like this place. Not the outside, but the inside. Even the rocker is okay."

And Red moved away from the chair to look around the hut.

It was tidy and everything that was inside was needed. For that reason the place looked much larger than it actually was. The mats on the floor were of an Aztec design that had probably started out as sparkling as a toucan's eye. Now they faded in comfort across the rough floor. Red smoothed the surface of one of the rugs. He felt a hard circle under it, a circle that felt like iron. When he lifted the mat he saw an iron ring set in the middle of a pale wooden hatch cover that was set flush with the floor. When he lifted the cover there was an unpleasant odor of earth and fungus. He hastily closed it, and slid the mat back to cover it. Karen looked disapproving.

The machete hung oiled and sharpened from its nail on the wall. Red looked out the window at Jack, who was working steadily outside. He swayed in his too-big shirt of linen white and moved as regularly as a scythe while he cut the underbrush. A tiny path was emerging from his struggle with the green and brown. Red picked up the machete and went outside to help him.

Karen watched him join in slashing at the greenery. Ever so slowly, like a shadow growing out of noon, the jungle began to shade back while they worked. She was impressed. Not so much by the details of what they were doing or by the technique—that she couldn't judge. What made her smile was the essence of it, of these tiny pale men scratching away at this giant and making it move slowly away. There they were, dwarfed by the trees, out-veined by the vines, surrounded by things that waited to eat them or sting them or grow over, under, and through them, but they didn't pay any heed. She felt like joining them and came close to going out the front door until she heard some extra scrabbling from the edge of the roof. So she turned her attention back inside the dwelling. Neat the place might be, but the weeks of neglect had left it grungy and mildewed.

Karen found the closet where cleaning materials
were kept, a surprisingly well-stocked cupboard.

She spent the afternoon scrubbing and cleaning,
dusting and shuddering as various things fell flail-
ing through the air whenever she moved the
feather duster towards the ridge of the house. But
that didn't make her stop until everything was
shipshape by the time dark fell. And here in the
jungle it did fall, with a crash. One second it was
afternoon, and, the next, it was a night where she
found herself groping her way towards the kitch-
en. She discovered what felt like matches and
what seemed to be a candle. Jack clicked on a
flashlight just in time to avoid having Karen strike
a match to a twelve-gauge shotgun shell.

They brought in fresh water and Jack went to
the open hearth where he struck up a fire faster
than anyone outside of Lord Baden-Powell could
have managed. He heated the water and filled a
huge galvanized washtub, and they took turns
washing off the day's sweat. Then, all scrubbed
and glowing, they sat around the wooden table.

Jack had been the first to bathe, and, while the
others cleaned themselves, he'd been busy making a hearty supper. Karen didn't have the faintest
idea what she was eating, and she was too tired to
ask about the ingredients. All she knew was it was
delicious. Everyone was too tired for conversation.
They were content to give thanks for the meal by
taking second helpings. Red watched the way that
lamplight lay in smoke and shadow along the
neck of Karen as she ate. She watched the way that
the golden light leaned over the ridges of the two
men's hands. Their meal was finished and the
dishes washed without a word being exchanged.

Jack pointed to their cots, each separate. First to tumble into the amazement of flannel sheets was Karen, and he ran a canopy of cheesecloth over the bed as she snuggled down like Guinevere. Red collapsed into his cot and Jack adjusted the mosquito netting. There was some scrabbling on the roof, but by now Karen was too tired to care and she began gently snoring. Red joined in seconds later.

Jack removed his boots and walked around in the most comfortable pair of slippers in the world. Tomorrow he would be the one to go into Panama City and see what he could discover, but tonight he could sit in the rocking chair and light a pipeful of Erinmore Flake. It pulled true and strong and the glow circled up to join the lamplight. He rocked slowly as he smoked and watched Red and Karen. He rocked until the pipe went out, then he knocked the dottle into the dying fire of the hearth and lay down, after blowing out the lamp and allowing the netting to settle. The room still smelled of good tobacco.

That night Jack went to sleep with a machete folded like a baby in his arms. His old legs were drawn up, and there was a smile on his face that lingered till the morning.

# 48

If Em weren't being held captive in her own house things might have seemed almost normal. The replacement window was working better than the old one ever did, the furniture was all back in its proper place, and all the dusting had been done. Not only was everything spotless, but there was also the smell of good home cooking. Em's only problem was that it wasn't the shoemaker's elves who were responsible: Zeb and Abel had done the duties and they weren't about to go away when morning came.

It was a very odd existence. After the corkscrew drive back to Gloucester Em had ended up inside her own house. Despite the blindfold she could tell by the sound of the ocean and the particular way the wind aeolian-harped through the old spruce tree that she was near her cottage. There had been little hesitation by the front door so they knew where she had hidden the key. Or perhaps, Karen was correct and any fool (or set of them) would have little trouble discovering her hiding places. Then she'd been carried up to her bedroom and the next thing she knew large, though gentle, hands had undressed her and placed her in bed. She felt padding being placed around her and there was a new sensation through the flannel sheets as she could feel the warmth and softness of sheepskin under the covers. She relaxed into it all with the firm thought that there wasn't a lot that she could do about this particular situation. She was also sure if this lot were taking the trouble to cart her to Boston and back, it meant one thing—Karen had gotten away.

When she heard the curtains being drawn, Zeb told her that he was going to remove the blindfold. He did, however, warn her not to open her eyes right away. He also told her that he had drawn the curtains because stray sunshine should not enter the room, and warned her that for a while her eyes would feel the light like a cut. Zeb was correct.

But oh, then it was such a relief to gaze at the sun and the sea, even if the slob ice was still onshore. The clouds, slate and solid, held up the sky and pressed down the ice with a crunching grinding sound. In front of the window, on opposite sides, staring out at the gray of the day stood Zeb to the right, and Abel to the left. In that moment, even though they remained identical twins, she could see the difference between them, her eyes sharpened by the enforced darkness that had lain two days upon them. Zeb and Abel looked as different to her as day and night, chalk and cheese, poem and cliché. "Whatever the hell you can think of for opposite," thought Em.

Despite the danger, despite the absence of a summer sun, despite the lack of a firm future—all based on the fact that she didn't have the faintest idea of what the twins might be planning—Em

wasn't worried. For one thing she knew her
daughter must be far away, and safe. For another
thing she was sensing the beginnings of a new
painting. She could see Zeb, the dour one, and
Abel, he of the cheerful vision, each on his own
side of the window while, in the background,
summer would churn the ocean with its light, the
waves would hold small gulls of boats and larger
schooners would catch the clouds in their topsails.

Zeb cleared his throat.

"We're with the CIA...," he began.

"Of course you are," said Em, absent-mindedly.
"Tell me, what's your name?"

"We don't have names in the CIA."

"Well, I need names so I can talk to you. Even if
they don't give you real names, they must issue
you with aliases. If they don't, at least make up
something!"

"Zeb."

Em snorted. "Can't you do better than that?"

"What's wrong with Zeb?"

"Nothing at all, it's a wonderful name. The
more I think of it, the more Zeb-like you become.
Your brother is called...?"

"Abel."

"Zeb, have you and Abel ever posed for a por-
trait?"

"We used to get snaps taken a lot."

"Snaps don't count. Couldn't tell you two apart in
a snap."

"Couldn't tell us apart in a painting neither." But
Zeb was curious. He was watching Em quite closely.

"In my painting people would have no trouble
telling you apart. Cause I'd do the work and I can
tell you apart."

"No way, lady. Not even Mom, God rest her soul, could tell us apart."

"I can. You're Zeb, he's Abel."

"Oh, sure, that's easy enough. We already told you who we were and we haven't moved since. Close your eyes."

Em did and she heard shuffling and shifting. Then Zeb spoke again.

"Okay. You can open your eyes now, lady."

She did and looked at him.

"Zeb, you can call me Em."

It took ten more trials before the twins were convinced that Em could tell them apart—always! And that made her the first person in the world ever to do so. They'd spent their lives waiting for her, the woman who could tell that Zeb was Zeb and Abel was Abel and always would be. Until that moment they were the only people who knew that fundamental secret, and that was from the inside out. They had dreamed of meeting someone who would see what they saw, the total absolute difference between them. And suddenly here was this old woman with a cast on her leg—and she was the one.

"Even shadows are different," ventured Zeb.

"How could anyone ever confuse you with Abel?"

Abel smiled.

"Even a snowflake is the same."

"Abel, how could a mother not know you?"

"We'll pose for you, won't we, Zeb?"

Zeb nodded. There were tears in his eyes.

"What do we have to do?"

"Undress," said Em, "and then stand by the window."

They didn't hesitate. Neat as a pin they folded their black jackets and laid their gunbelts on top of them. Next their trousers, along with the white shirts and black string ties. Stepping out of their underwear they leaned towards the window. Zeb looked out at shadows and Abel watched snowflakes. Em took her sketchbook and charcoal from the night table and began her study.

That night, as Zeb was about to go to sleep, a thought crossed his mind and he turned towards Abel.

"Abe. Are you asleep?"

"No, Zeb. I was just lying here thinking."

"She's the real goods, ain't she?"

"Yep, I can't kill that lady."

"She told us to call her Em. I can't kill her either."

"It's agreed then. She's special."

And they fell asleep within seconds.

So, over the next couple of days they didn't bother getting dressed at all. To save time they wandered around the house nude. Every morning they would pose, and then break to make lunch. Early evening, after a hearty supper, Zeb and Abel would play cribbage until Em called them.

They would pose again for an hour or so in the nighttime while lamplight played over them. Then Em would sleep and dream. Sometimes in the early hours Zeb and Abel and Em would dream about each other.

A full week passed while Em worked on her paintings. For, to save time, she had been doing both paintings simultaneously. In front of her as she painted, side by side, were the two canvases, her brush stroking each so they would be finished on the same hour.

Em presented them to Zeb and Abel on the evening of the year's final snowfall. The paintings were exactly alike except for the subjects. Each one showed a totally different brother looking out to sea. There was, as Em had promised, no mistaking which twin was Zeb and which twin was Abel. They had sunlight in their eyes while their bodies were covered in lamplight. Each looked out a window that held eternal summer.

They kissed Em and cried, then dressed and went down to the kitchen where they wrapped their paintings in brown kraft paper which they sealed with masking tape.

Before they left they made a new pot of beef and barley soup for her.

She heard the door shut, and felt the quiet. Now all she could do was wait until she heard from Karen. Her leg was feeling better, she believed that her daughter was safe, and she sniffed the smell of fresh soup rising from the kitchen. Before the twins had left they'd removed the all-purpose bug and re-spliced the phone wires, so she could call anyone she felt like. Instead of reaching for the phone, however, she picked up her sketchbook. Before the memory left she wanted to do her own painting of Zeb and of Abel.

## ❧ 49 ❧

Timothy Shepherd didn't like being back in Panama City and he didn't like being the secret guest of General Santos. The general was not only the meanest man in Panama, but also the ugliest. He was about the same height as Napoleon and resembled Richard III. Timothy tried to think of this as bestowing leadership qualities.

He was feeling restless. For one thing he wasn't in his own house and for another he had to stay hidden so he could not be connected with a man who was known as an opponent of the current regime. The general had been shifted to the right of power, but he still might become ruler of Panama someday. It was this potential that made Timothy seek him out and stay in his villa. Despite the usual tensions, he and Santos got along fairly well as each sensed that the other shared desires and flaws that were very much alike.

Last week had been futile. The general assured him that when he needed the manpower to eradicate these three little nuisances there would be no trouble. The only problem was finding them.

Thanks to a fingerprint left in Gloucester, Timothy had finally identified Red. That seemed promising. However, by now most thought that he was dead and still more didn't care one way or another. Timothy had to content himself with waiting back at the villa while numerous sleazy types came and went with very little news. At first they had even less information about Jack, but some of the soldiers knew of him and his reputation. Word then went out to those mercenaries who had allied themselves with the general. They all knew Jack, but it would take a while to find him. There was a rumor that he had some sort of hideaway near the coast, but no one was able to come up with an exact location. Some off-duty soldiers were sent to track it down. As for Karen, she was described and photos distributed. A customs guard remembered her because she had entered Panama in the company of two particularly disgusting drunks. He had been so interested in her that he didn't pay much attention to her father or brother so he let them all through without any questions except to ask for the phone number of the beautiful young woman. That number turned out to be phony, but so was the way of the world. Anyway, he did let them through, and now wished he'd detained the pretty woman.

Timothy was prepared to put out a contract on the customs guard, but the general only laughed. The guard's information let them know that all three were in Panama and that meant, Santos said, that things would be very easy.

"Panama is like a little backyard. Everyone knows where everything is. There are no secrets, only delays!"

Then the general tried to press Timothy about reasons for having the trio killed but got no believable answer. He tried to explain things by saying that his security system had been breached, with vital data being taken, even secret information about the general. At night Santos would wonder about the real motive, but he knew enough not to ask those specific questions again. He also knew enough not to poke around. Timothy would be a very useful friend when the right moment arose. With him as President of the United States, all sorts of things would be possible. Central America, to the general's way of thinking, should really be "CentralAmerica," one country, one leader.

As days went by and no real information came in, the general noticed that Timothy was becoming restless. He had a black harsh-looking computer with him and would hook up to a phone line and listen as it made small whirring noises. That would use up two or three hours a day. Then a courier would arrive with video tapes. Timothy would slap them on the VCR and scan the day's news. When evening fell and insect noises mingled with the guards' gossip, Timothy would pace and look through the heat of the garden. He didn't like the climate so he stayed in and looked out while the general worried about how to cheer him up. It was on a Wednesday that the solution occurred to him.

That night, as a surprise, General Santos arranged a small party of three women to entertain his guest, but as soon as the women began taking off their clothes Timothy stalked from the room. When the general followed he screamed.

"You goddamn idiot. First of all, my morality does not permit this, but even more, what if it got out?"

So that was it.

"If, Tim, the news got out, people would only envy you three women at once. Even I, who have only gone as high as two, feel slight envy."

"Things don't work like that back home. There, I would be dead meat. Besides, it is simply wrong. If you wish to keep my friendship, never do anything like this again. Otherwise, I cannot support you, otherwise I can't ever again ask your help."

And he walked away. The general decided not to waste an arranged evening, nor what he hoped would be well-spent money. He began undressing as he walked back along the hall towards the bedroom. But he was puzzled. The only reason he'd ordered the women was because he noticed the way his guest had glanced at whatever magazine showed any woman of any age, even in an innocent ad. He'd also noticed that whenever the news cassettes were being scanned, at any hint of flesh or of sex the tape had slowed.

"The Americans," thought the general, "all white men are silly when it comes to that." He shook his head and, now totally naked, opened the door. As the three women were also naked everyone smiled at everyone else.

In his room, Timothy wasn't smiling. He undressed but only to step inside the shower with the water turned as cold as it would go, which was just tepid. He leaned against the tiles and pressed his face as hard as he could hoping for some pain, hoping—although he knew better—that it would take away his desire. The danger had brought back all the old feelings. He tried to think of other things, of God, of the takeover of the Network, but that didn't work. All he could see was blood, all he could think of was being naked.

He opened his eyes and looked right into the shower head, but that only made him feel more aroused. Kneeling down he tried to keep his hands clasped together, praying for a release, praying for power. Even as he began touching himself he kept praying, until, through the sound of the water and the surf of the blood, he heard the phone. He used it as an escape, throwing open the shower door. The water spilled over the floor. Timothy walked, still erect, and grabbed the phone. He didn't say hello, just listened. As he did he began to smile. It was a simple message from the general, who for some reason sounded irritated.

He'd been interrupted, "...during a vital activity," he told Timothy, "with some news." And despite the urgency of the activity he thought he should phone Timothy with this information.

His men had located Jack.

## 🪷 50 🪷

The week stroked Karen and Red with a wet warm sponge. For the first while, Karen had been restless because she'd never before spent more than a day without keeping busy. So she got up each morning wanting to rearrange the jungle. At night she tried to sweep away the shadows.

It was only after three or four days of green time and filtered skies that she began to relax. The feeling of relaxation was so new to her that she worried it might be a sign she was going crazy. Her arms wanted to float while her mind watched every thought vanish at the same instant, to be replaced with clean sky and the shadows of leaves.

It took a few days longer before Red noticed some strange changes taking place. He stopped talking all the time, no longer having the need to describe or comment on everything that he looked at. Soon even the little voice inside his head that planned, dreamed and prepared sentences in case he had to fast talk his way out of danger, stopped talking. Red and Karen now spent a lot of time in silence, and an entire morning could go by without their bothering to speak at all. When they did talk it would, more likely than not, have something to do with when they were little. Then they'd go back to watching the jungle quiver, and when they did speak their talk began to sound like the words of contented old people.

When night came they would light the kerosene lamps and watch the shadows flicker across the walls full of dark and gold. The scurrying noises that had kept them awake on the first evenings now seemed a familiar part of the little hut, warm and woolly.

They read from an old copy of *Swiss Family Robinson*, sometimes Karen would read aloud, but more often Red would read to her. She liked resting on the sound of his voice. There was also a battered copy of *Treasure Island*, and she held her breath as Red put Jim halfway up the mast holding his two pistols pointed at the sea and his opponent. Then just before the next page both would feel snug and cosy. Sometimes they would make love and then snooze in a tangle of sheets. Other nights they would hardly have enough time to blow out the lamp before sleep overtook them.

Another week went by and they grew into the shifting jungle. They rooted. Once in a while they would wonder where Jack was, if anything had happened to him—but, like a bad dream vanishes when one turns over, the thought would mist and fade. Their days were quiet and full of soft shadows, so how could anyone's be different? Their nights began with lamplight and ended in gentle covers.

They thought they were secure and safe.

# 51

Jack was in a beaten-up Panamanian bar that was too cheap to afford a sign. He was also ready to doze for an hour or two, after he'd looked around the place and squinted with a fairly open curiosity at everyone.

A hooker almost as old as him gave a forty-watt smile and then, seeing no action in his look, turned her attention to a cockroach that was making its tortuous progress up a sticky section of the far wall. It was the kind of place where a few other patrons began taking bets on how long it would take the bug to reach the ceiling. When the cockroach eventually arrived, everyone forgot what their bet had been except for two feeble old men who got into a fight that collapsed when they were unable to regain their breath.

All this activity bored Jack who started thinking he was safe in getting some shut-eye. Just before he drifted off he was aware of a face looking down from street level into the bar, but he was too tired and had too many drinks inside him to pay any attention.

The nap was progressing very successfully when something strange made him wake up. It was the silence. He continued to breathe in the same rhythm as before, while keeping his eyelids from showing the slightest flutter. The sounds in the bar had pretty much stopped. He could hear the creak of the door as it closed, but no more old men arguing over the cockroach bet, no more greetings or small talk from the hooker. Instead there seemed to be only three other people in the bar besides Jack. He kept his eyes shut, trying to remain calm so his heart sounds wouldn't get in the way of the noises from the room.

He cursed the drink as he tried to remember the layout of the place. He knew there were steps down into the basement and then one large room, but there was no sign of any back exit. So he was trapped. There was the bar itself, flimsy and made of planks and wooden crates covered with thin cloth curtains, and that was it. The way in and the way out were exactly the same. What the hell they were waiting for, Jack couldn't figure. He did notice that they weren't too good at waiting. One guy lit a cigarette.

There was the hiss of a match from a corner, while near the door someone cleared his throat. Now he had the positions of three people mapped out. His big worry was that there might be someone else in the room who was very good at waiting, so good that there was no indication of his presence. If that was the case then there wasn't a chance. He decided to risk opening his eyes a little.

No one moved near and he lowered his gunhand closer to his boot. All he'd been able to get in the way of weapons was a .22-caliber pistol that dated from World War One. It was small enough to fit in his boot. It took .22 short, and Jack had criss-crossed the tips so they had about the same impact as a .32 when they got inside. He'd spent most of one night fixing the pistol as best he could. The firing pin was filed sharp and straight, the heaviest part of the decades of rust had been scraped from inside the barrel and he'd oiled every part. He'd even managed to load it. The one thing he had not done was to fire the gun, but he was going to get his chance.

After opening his eyes the width of an eyelash, it took a few seconds for his pupils to react to the light. This was the hardest time to keep his eyelids from fluttering, his eyes from watering. But he did and then he saw a fourth person in the room: the bartender, who seemed to be pissed off at the intruders and waiting for his chance. Jack knew for sure whose side he was on when a fly landed on his own eyelid. He couldn't help blinking as he felt his eye begin to water. The only person in the room who noticed was the bartender. He gave Jack a wink and moved up along the bar away from him. One of the soldiers, who looked like an anemic water rat, took out a gun and raised it towards the bartender. As he did, Jack slipped the .22 from the hiding place in his boot and squeezed off a shot at water rat. He aimed for the neck and the bullet went high catching the rat in his temple.

Another soldier got his gun out and Jack swung towards him pulling the trigger and aiming lower to compensate for the gun's high sight. The trigger pulled and the firing pin hit, but the cartridge must have been a dud, because nothing happened. The bartender swung a galvanized pail of papaya juice from under the bar and over at the gunman who was shooting at Jack. The bucket clanged, metal on flesh, and sprayed a pale orange liquid over the soldier and his friend behind him. His shot went wild, lodging in the earth walls. Jack succeeded in getting his little gun to fire again and dropped the second soldier. It was the third man who was too fast.

That shot caught Jack in his left shoulder, smashing through bone and splashing the wall behind with blood and splinter. The bartender tried to vault over the bar, but slipped on spilled beer. The lean soldier swiveled and bellyshot him. Jack still held on to his gun even though it weighed a thousand pounds and the heat of the barrel scorched his hand. He lifted it through what seemed an hour of pain and pulled the trigger three times at the thin mean soldier.

He felt blood pour over his own head, washing down his neck and chest, covering and folding in his eyes until he realized that the last shot of the soldier must have hit the shelf of bottles over him and that it was alcohol not blood pouring down over him. As the liquor spilled into his eyes it made them burn and the room was lost to sight. He grabbed a bar towel and mopped his eyes. The room's lights started to dip and raise, and the pain made him curse. He staggered up the steps into the humid night, which wrapped around him while people moved out of his way. They stared at him.

Jack knew what he must look like as he moved along the side of the road. He thought he heard something in the ringing that sang around him and when he squinted back he saw dark faces and eyes looking at him. He glanced down at the road and saw the damp of his blood as it spat on the dirt. Finding himself by a vendor who was selling brightly colored cloths, headbands and kerchiefs, Jack couldn't find any money so he just reached towards him.

The man was young and his face showed no expression. He backed away and then vanished into the shadow that reached out from an alleyway. Jack staggered off the street into a narrow lane that smelled of shit and piss and meals and cats and dogs and perfume, and that tipped with balconies towards him and that dropped more shadows of shutters and that had a bright red door, like the door to hell. He knocked on it. It opened and he fell through. Someone was moving towards him from behind. He tried to turn and the pain hurt and he cried and he was afloat on the night.

## ❧ 52 ❧

Before the car stopped, Timothy threw open the door and jumped out, skidding when he tried to keep his footing on the sidewalk. Santos tried to stop him. From the way the crowd was pushing towards the bar he knew it was time to be cautious. These people wouldn't push close unless the shooting had stopped and the killing was over. Now they were using their eyes and might remember things they shouldn't. It wasn't a good time for Timothy to plow his way to the center.

Santos watched the tall American tower his way over the blood to the man sprawled over the cement.

The general swore and went after Timothy to get him back inside the car and then to the villa. He hoped that the next step would be to get him back stateside where he belonged. When he was President that would be the time for a visit. Not now.

Timothy was leaning over a dying man, Roberto Aguirre, one of Santos's men, who lay very still, holding his gut with his hands, trying to keep himself alive by stroking and pressing his flesh.

Timothy was asking question after question in English, but getting no answers. Blood blossomed through the soldier's fingers and he shut out the sound of Timothy Shepherd like it was distant traffic rumble. Then, Santos arrived and Roberto's eyes looked at him. He stopped stroking and kneading his own belly and gathered his strength for the talk with his general.

Santos and Roberto talked in fast Spanish, the general speedy in his questions so there would be enough time for answers. He had seen a lot of men die and he knew that there were only a few answers left.

Roberto knew that too. He sucked in his breath and listened to General Santos. He was also aware of the tall American leaning over him and distracting his thoughts. He lifted one hand from his belly so he could see the general better and shield his vision of the crazy one. As Roberto held his hand up the blood made it stick to the side of his face. It was easier to leave it there and not pull it away.

"The man, you knew him?"

"For a long time. Sometimes we fought on the same side, sometimes against each other. He is a good soldier, one of the best, now he was, I thought, he was, he was, I thought he was..."

Roberto coughed and the hand that was shielding his face unstuck from his cheek and he moved it down to his belly again. He couldn't feel pain there anymore but he wanted to hold the blood in. Lights flashed at them and he thought he was in the jungle. It was warm and wet and through the leaves he heard the voice of his general. The crazy American was trying to tell General

Santos something and the general was not listening but kept asking a question.

Roberto finally heard the question. It was an easy one and he could answer it now.

Before this time he'd forced his mind to think of the vague memory of a face. But it wasn't until he'd actually seen Jack that any memory had come back. Now with his life steady in his hands he could remember everything, even when he was a little kid, he could recall.

So the question of where Jack lived was now an easy one to answer.

People were yelling and a flashbulb was popping and the American was running after it, and Roberto remembered a whore telling him about where Jack lived. This whore and Magda, who always smelled of lilac, had visited there. Now Roberto remembered every word she had said, and he told the general. The questions stopped and Roberto decided to sleep. His body was suddenly heavier on the sidewalk, and he did not move even the tinest bit.

General Santos stood up. He called two of his guards and told them to follow anywhere the faint drops of blood might lead in a small trickle. He motioned to Timothy who was returning from the futile chase of the photographer. Neither man spoke to the other as they got in the car. Santos wound down the window and called over three more guards. He told them where Jack's hut was. He told them to go there and bring back anyone they found. If there was trouble those people should be killed.

Then as the auto drove away General Santos put on the earphones from the car's CD system. Faint-

ly the sound of the Concerto for Guitar leaked from
the headphones to reach Timothy.

Timothy stared at the darkness as they sped
back to the villa. He looked tense, tired and folded.

The general watched him.

Santos decided he'd tell him the news back at
the villa, but right now he liked seeing him worry.

Perhaps he wouldn't bother telling him until his
guards brought back the bodies from the hut.

# ❧ 53 ❧

A thunderstorm was building clouds, turning the light into cream and spinach while Karen slept. Red felt the storm growing when the hairs along his arms began to rise. He got up from the cot without waking her and then walked over to the window where he could see the reflection of his face against the leaves that pushed close to the hut. The roof scurried while the jungle parted and shook as the wind gathered.

Near the log by the smoking stream, parrots jawed at signs of movement by the water. One man who was approaching the water raised his rifle at the closest parrot, until the leader reached over and stopped him. The parrots kept calling and the men crossed over the log.

Red and Karen had made love after lunch and she had dropped into sleep. Every now and then she would start to smile, but then it would fade and her face would repose against the pillows, flushed and gathering the shifts of the changing light. Red felt restless, and all through last night's late hours had been unable to sleep although it was still and, for the jungle, quiet. The moon had been filtered through the overhead cover and lay upon the trees with the color of spilled skim milk.

In the morning all the shadows of the moon were chased away and Red looked out the same window. The only thing he could compare this mood to was childhood, with its rib-aching boredom of a Sunday afternoon waiting for cold chicken sandwiches. He would look at the pale white meat that lay on a bed of wilted lettuce where it was coated with congealing mayonnaise, and wish that he was with his father somewhere in the exciting jungle.

Well, here he was, in the same jungle, and he still had the familiar feeling that had always rolled around every Sunday afternoon as sure and certain as a dressed-up button-down town.

Thunder rumbled on a distant hill and the echo of it rolled into the clearing. There was a hint, at the corner of his eye, of lightning. He looked back at Karen who used the thunderclap as an extra blanket and snuggled further into sleep. Red walked over to what he'd been trying to avoid and stared into the brass-bound face of the trunk he'd noticed the first day he arrived at the hut. He knew it belonged to Jack and he knew there were probably ten thousand devices to keep him out of it, but the thought of that danger lifted his spirits. Enough of calm and tranquillity, here was a challenge.

He went to the cutlery drawer and then over to a small tool chest where he made his selections. The thunder echoed and swirled from a distant, different direction, as though the storm were circling them. The daylight was still good, but even so, Red brought a small lamp close to him as he began his work, inspecting a lock that seemed suspiciously easy to open. On closer examination, he noticed that two ornamental swirls of metal surrounding the keyhole were in fact the ends of wires. He was patient and soldered another wire to the tips of each.

When the trunk gave a small click, he paused long enough to change positions.

The lock snapped open, the top was raised, and no explosion! There was, however, a blob of plastique glued inside the top cover, which made Red glad that he'd taken so much care. He used an extra few minutes to rearrange all the wires and detach the bomb.

Opening the door, he took the explosive outside, trailing wires and all into the clearing. He left it there, propped against a nearby tree, facing away from the hut, and told himself that he'd look after it later. On his way back to the hut, the wires tangled around his ankles and he plunged headlong through the doorway. At last, Karen woke up.

"Nureyev? You've come at last."

Red picked himself up, trying to look as dignified as he possibly could. Considering he had landed flat on his belly and skidded to a stop under the kitchen table this was pretty difficult to achieve. Finally, he gave up and joined in Karen's laughter. It took a few minutes for that to die out, just about the time the thunderstorm stopped circling and zoned in on them. Water poured over the hut making it shake in the heart of the thunder. Red and Karen lit some lamps and it was as they finished putting the chimney back on the last one that she noticed the open trunk.

"You found where Jack hid the key?"

"Not exactly."

"You broke into his trunk?"

"I helped the lock along."

"That's disgraceful. What was inside?"

"I haven't looked through it all yet."

"I won't have anything to do with this, Red, and I don't think you should either."

"You're right. So I should close it up, and not check out the wedding dress?"

"Wedding dress? Jack has a wedding dress in his trunk?"

But Red had already eased the top of the trunk down again and was in the process of closing the lock. Thunder pealed while Karen hesitated.

"I don't think we should look in the trunk, unless we get some sort of omen."

The thunder gave another tremendous clap, vibrating the top of the trunk and making the lock hum.

Red smiled.

"What sort of omen, Karen?"

"That sort of omen, Red."

And as the thunder banged at the hut and spilled rain all over it, they moved the lamps closer and began to unpack the trunk.

"Besides," added Red, "the old bugger's been gone a long time and maybe we're going to have to go looking for him. Might get a few clues here."

Karen stood up and held the wedding dress against her. She walked over to the window to see her reflection. The rain formed a solid back that caught and shimmered the lamplight. In the reflection Karen appeared to flashback her way into the forties. The dress had yellowed to the color of old ivory and the lace had browned. It flipped dust and lint into the air. She was already naked so it was only a minute's work to try on the dress. Holding the train in one hand, she moved and the fabric ripped slightly. The sound made Red look up from the trunk. By this time the thunder had crashed its last peal as quickly as a movie ends, and silence came dripping down the panes.

Red looked at Karen like she had a frame around her.

"How come it fits?"

"Kismet. If you follow my drift."

"Karen, are you asking me to marry you?"

"No. It wouldn't last. Even the dress wouldn't make it to the ceremony."

"Neither would I. Come see what I found."

"Pieces of eight?"

But as she walked around to look in the trunk, her wedding dress trailing across the floor, all she saw were some old photos. Red had taken them out and spread them around the trunk. There was a photo showing a woman with dark cascading hair. She was wearing the same wedding dress that Karen had on. But in this shot it was as white and new as a cloud. The woman held a bouquet loosely, letting it dangle and scatter petals on the floor. Karen touched the dress that she was wearing.

"Who is she?"

"My mother, and that's obviously her bridal gown. So tell me what the hell it's doing in the middle of nowhere, along with this?"

He took out a photo of a small boy. Despite the fact that the child was wearing a cowboy outfit and stood, brandishing a huge bandage around his thumb, in a defiant pose for the camera, there was no mistaking that the snapshot was of Red. He tossed the photo next to the holster of a toy gun.

"That snap was taken by my father one day at a picnic. I'd cut my thumb on a tin can, and instead of crying or screaming or anything like that, I came over to him, held up my hand and told him to fix it. He did, and took that picture to show the world I was a real little soldier. Two weeks after that he was gone again. This holster is the one I wore in the snap. Know what it all means?"

"Jack's your father?"

"That old fart is my old man."

"Are you sure?"

"Tell me another way to explain it."

"Perhaps he killed your father and lives here now?"

"No way anyone could have killed him, he's like a cat. Nine lives. Besides if you need any more proof that Jack's my old man, he's gone away again and hasn't come back."

"Then there's something wrong, really wrong."

"Why?"

"Red, if you know that he's your father, then he sure as hell knows you're his son. No way he wouldn't come back. Not now, with him knowing that. That explains how he found you in the first place, he must have been looking for you even then. I tell you something's wrong!"

As if on cue there was a sound from outside the hut, not the usual animal, insect or bird sound but the noise of clumsy human twig-bending approach.

For a moment they were sure it was Jack, and turned towards the door, neither knowing how to react to him this time round, when Karen suddenly tackled Red. Just as they sprawled behind the trunk a spray of bullets smashed through the windows sending splinters of glass into the walls and some into Red's hand which bled in small points, leaking blood in tiny streams. The gunmen lowered the aim of the automatic weapon to cut beneath the windows but none of the shots came through. There was the sound of sharp ringing and ricocheting as the bullets deflected.

"Jack's had the wall reinforced," said Red. "How the hell did you know someone was going to shoot?"

There was some cursing outside as a particularly long burst got a rolling echo of the gunfire, and for a moment the shooting stopped.

"Jack would never make as much noise." Now the cursing outside turned into commands given in Spanish.

"What are they saying?"

Red listened.

"One guy thinks they should rush us. The other thinks we've got weapons. Most people, thank God, are going along with the one who thinks we got weapons."

"What happens when they find out we aren't shooting back?"

"We've got trouble."

Red rummaged through the rest of the trunk but all he could find was his toy gun. It was better than nothing and he took it out. He hung his little holster and gunbelt from his shoulder. Then he bellied over to the kitchen where he reached in and extracted a flashlight. Rolling a battery into his hand he moved towards the door. He opened it a crack and held the barrel of his toy gun outside the edge of the doorpost. There was a spray of bullets all around him but nothing hit. He slammed the door shut and winked at Karen. "They'll think I didn't get to fire off a shot. Think it was all their doing. Here's what I was after."

He held triumphant the wires that he'd earlier kicked away from his ankle. If his luck held, they would still be embedded in the plastique.

"Get over to the hatch, and when this goes let's beat it."

"Red, I'd...I'd rather die running."

"See these wires? They're connected to some explosive..."

He was about to continue with more details when a tear-gas canister sailed in through the now empty window. It took one last fragment of shattered glass with it.

"The man I loved would set off any and all explosives just about now!"

And Red touched the wires to the battery, but nothing happened, no explosion, no outside screams. Instead the gas swirled making them cough and cry. Red reached for the flashlight and shook out the other battery. This time when he applied the wires there was an enormous explosion from outside the hut. And there were screams and more curses from the clearing. There was no time for any self-congratulations from Karen and Red, they were too busy coughing.

He held tightly to Karen's wedding train as she led the way to the hatch and then down the stairs into the vegetable cellar and along the earthen tunnel that seemed to drop forever. It was at first lit by the hut as it burned behind them, but then turned into total darkness, where other creatures scurried beside them.

Then there was a sudden increased smell of more damp and fungus as they found themselves blinking, coughing and crying, near the muddy edge of the river. From the distance they could still hear shooting, and as darkness moved in they could see the glow of the burning hut in the night sky.

## 54

Blackmail had never bothered Juan Chinchilla, and the idea of becoming rich had always excited him. But on the morning the two things came together, he didn't get up and dance around. Instead he stayed sitting behind his little desk. He seemed not to have moved since Red asked his questions about Azucar. He looked as dirty, he looked as lazy, the only thing that was different was the presence of a paper. Juan Chinchilla seldom read a newspaper.

Sometimes, however, he would take it with him to the bathroom, other days he would use it to shield his eyes from the harshness of the midday sun. More often he would hold it in front of his face, during the restful late afternoon hours while he caught forty winks. The drooping of the paper and the lowering of his arms would make him wake up and he would shift his weight from massive buttock to massive buttock trying to look alert for a few minutes until he felt exhaustion come closer. Then the paper would tremble aloft again.

Today was a very different day for Juan, he actually read the paper, at least one section of it. He'd

261

just settled in with his coffee when he slopped the cup over his small desk making a wave of coffee surge over the edge of the saucer and onto the newsprint. He moved the cup and that's when he saw the photo. There was General Santos, which was no big deal, that guy always had his photo in the papers for one thing or another. He was on the sidewalk in front of a lowlife bar, one that Juan knew well. Even that wouldn't have prompted him to read the story. It was the other hombre in the photo who caught his eye. The man was trying to hide his face from the camera, but he was a second too late. Juan nodded his head in appreciation of the photographer's skill, knowing this was the work of another gifted amateur.

Juan had one hobby, besides picking his teeth, and that hobby was taking and processing black-and-white photographs. He didn't believe in color, feeling that at its best the very most you could expect was a cheap tint, even in nature. That's how he knew the snapshot had been taken by an amateur. Too grainy and too much contrast, all printed on the wrong film stock. But that wasn't why he looked at the photo, there was a better reason. He recognized the man who was trying to hide. He didn't know him from the news, or any fancy magazine; instead, he'd seen this guy in another photo, a special photo that he had taken.

Now he read the article, but what was frustrating was there was no mention anywhere of who this other person was. The story dealt with a killing that had taken place at "Balboa's Bar." The bartender had been shot dead, and so had three of the general's aides. Santos was trying to maintain that the killings were politically motivated. Then there was a long extension of the story where all the general's political foes had told the world they'd had nothing to do with the killings. Big story but no mention of the mysterious man.

The desk clerk looked up with surprise. For years he'd followed the progress of Juan Chinchilla, fascinated. Juan was like the lazy man's Kant, you could set your watch by how long he sat down. In the morning he never budged for three hours and twenty-five seconds. Today, however, he was getting up from his seat after reading the paper for only ten minutes. Then he crossed over to the phone booth and dropped a slug into the phone. The clerk shook his head in consternation, there was nothing you could depend on anymore.

Juan waited on the phone, with great patience, for George MacPherson, a dour, hard-drinking, married Scots journalist who had willed his way into Panama City. He couldn't seem to will his way out of the country again after marrying a very jealous and heavy-set local woman. Juan took pity on him, having been married once to a similar lady himself, and often set up a night or two of whoring for George. Last night was such a time so Juan knew that the reporter would have returned to the paper, showered there and gone to sleep in the office so he would have an excuse prepared for his wife, telling her that he'd had to stay behind at work. There was a long bony indentation in the thin carpet near George's desk that was a direct result of years of sleeping on the floor. When he came to the phone it was with a sleepy gloomy voice.

"Hello, Juan? The wife is coming over looking for me. She phoned and she didn't believe me..."

Juan interrupted.

"George, I have a question."

"There are no questions when a man faces death..."

"I read a story on the front page of your illustrious paper..."

"What are you doing reading the paper? I thought you reserved it for more personal functions."

"In this photo there is a man with General Santos, but the story says nothing about him."

George groaned.

"Are you asking me, at a time of peril, to actually look at the rag I write for?"

"You are an intelligent man, George."

The phone clunked down on the table and there was the sound of cursing mingled with the rustling of paper. He returned to the phone.

"There's a hundred people in the photo."

"Look in the back, past the old whore, to her left."

"I can hardly see him for Christ's sake."

"Get a loupe."

Another clunk, the sound of a desk drawer being opened and then a distinct whoop.

"My ticket, my ticket, Juan, you just bought me my ticket."

"You know this man?"

"Give me a break. Everyone knows this man."

"He is rich?"

"And powerful and supposed to be in the good old U.S. of A. right now, and having nothing to do with fallen generals. That's..." And he paused for dramatic effect, "Timothy Shepherd!"

"This Timothy Shepherd, you know him, how to reach him?"

But George, with another whoop and some re-mark about the story of a lifetime had hung up the phone.

Juan smiled. This man was in Panama City, again. He was rich and he was powerful, and Juan knew his darling name. Timothy Shepherd. There was a good chance he'd be staying with Santos.

There was a relative who cooked for the general, a cousin who—like all of Juan's cousins—owed him. Perhaps he could get a message to this rich and famous American. For he had a very impor-tant matter to discuss with him.

## 🪷 55 🪷

When Jack woke up it was night and he had time only to think he was asleep somewhere in Boston, where the summer heat made his skin burn and where molasses ran down his arm. Someone was speaking Spanish in a distant room and he wanted to call Mary so he could get his trunk packed and ready for travel.

"Don't forget my underwear!" He called out until he heard children laughing. Despite the heat and laughter he fell sound asleep.

He woke up again when someone shoved a knife into his shoulder. He was soaked in sweat and someone had bound his shoulder in bloody bandages, and he wondered how they got the bandage on so quickly when he had been stabbed only seconds earlier. The pain went away after a woman placed her cool hand on his forehead. He couldn't remember seeing any woman at the front when he first arrived and so he tried to recall her name. She was speaking Spanish and he understood every word even though he was quite sure he had never spoken the language in his young life. Perhaps this was his mother?

Jack thought that he'd been standing on the night table next to his bed and trying to light the lamp. He'd been sick and his nightgown was soaked through so he didn't know if he'd wet the bed or if he'd been sweating so he had to find out, but before he could reach the lamp it felt like he had set his shoulder on fire and it was moving down his chest. He heard his mother's voice and cursed again, in Spanish, but she didn't mind, she laughed. Then she threw more water over him and it put out the fire. Ice was on his shoulder and how could they find ice in the Boston summer? Jack touched it and it was as smooth as a thigh, it had sawdust all over it and he worried that the sawdust would get into the wound and he held the bandage tight when his shoulder caught on fire again and this time it set fire to his hand. He buried his hand in his hair until his hair caught on fire, like the old man when he got drunk and fell into the candle flame. There was more water and more ice and the fire moved down into his leg, and a doctor was looking at him.

The doctor was drunk and white and fat and old and he smelled of tequila and vanilla. Jack saw a large beautiful brown woman who reached into his own trouser pockets taking out money and giving it to the doctor. The doctor took out a black satchel and pulled out old packets of powder just before he began cutting away the bandages. After they were removed he took out a bottle and sucked down a few mouthfuls before pouring it over the shoulder. This time Jack was ready for the pain and sat to one side of the ball of it, watching it grow.

He suddenly remembered Red, and he wanted to warn him that the soldiers might know about the hut and to tell him to run, run fast and deep into the jungle. Then the doctor did more things with the shoulder and he sat like a cat in a shadow watching the pain. The doctor sprinkled powder into his wound and the woman appeared with what looked like a bread poultice.

Jack fell asleep, dreaming he saw the large woman in bed next to him. She was with a Yankee sailor who was naked except for some anchors tattooed on his arm and over his chest. There was a knock on the door and there were strange voices in the room, the voice of guards, but the sailor and the woman didn't stop, they pulled the covers closer over him. The bed bounced and he rocked like he was at sea with the sailor in a hurricane and the guard's voice faded as the door closed.

"Hang on, matey, hang on before we're washed overboard," shouted Jack, and for some reason the sailor laughed out of the center of the storm and he knew they would drown, so he kicked and kicked and was above the water and sucking in the air and coughing and almost too tired to reach the riverbank but did and lay there panting until it was morning and he was naked and there was water on him and once more he opened his eyes and saw...

Saw a big brown woman smiling and rolling a soaking sponge over him. She dipped up more water and looked on his nakedness like he was a baby.

"You going to fool us all and live?"

Jack decided that sounded like a very good idea.

# 56

Juan Chinchilla was a patient man. He sometimes watched the moon for hours. His balcony, like hundreds rusted onto the side of the pink apartment building, faced the lights of the town's center. So all he ever could see was the moon, because stars paled and faded against the man-made glitter of taillights, leftover Christmas decorations, and streetlights.

Tonight there was no moon and Juan was glad because he had work to do inside his darkroom. As he hung pictures up to dry and slid others back and forth in the fixing solution, he felt a calmness descend. He was not a jolly fat man, and the photos always soothed him. Whistling, he watched the images appear clean and as crisp as a copy of a copy could ever manage. However, what the photo lacked in style it made up for in content. The shot was from the series that Juan had shot from inside the hidden room.

He stopped smiling and listened. He thought there was a sound outside the door, but he had three more photos to take from the bath before he could look outside the darkroom to see if anyone was there. Every time he did this sort of work his imagination took off and made the floorboards creak, the hinges squeal, the nighttime cats shriek over his mother's grave.

When he dragged on the last of his reefer it glowed, making the paper run ragged in waves until the tip of his finger started to hurt. As the smoke hooked its way into his lungs he dropped the butt into a small dish of water, where it hissed and continued to glow for what seemed to Juan to be a minute or so. When he smoked up and worked he was always sure to put plenty of preset timers around the room. They were bright red and yellow and white and now began to ring and chime in different colors. One by one Juan reached out to turn them off. His motions were slow and regular and floated on the warm amber air. He was ready to pick up the last photo when he realized that he'd smoked too much dope, because the man in that photograph had walked out of it.

Timothy Shepherd was naked, just like in the snapshots. But in real life he carried a knife curved like a kris. As Juan blinked, he began to spin it around his finger like a windmill. The blade strobed into a propeller circle and Timothy began speaking, his words all mixed up inside the blade as it spun.

"Are you Juan Chinchilla, the man who sells dirty pictures?"

In that divided moment Juan decided he'd made a mistake telling his cousin what he'd told him. He had only time enough to begin saying "no," before the spinning knife touched and tickled and cut his throat wide open, gouting blood over the naked man.

Later, a trail of bloody footprints led from Juan Chinchilla's corpse, across the carpet, towards the bathroom where the shower mingled with the sounds of Timothy singing. On the balcony, smoke curled from burning photographs and negatives. The moon had come out full and sweet, stronger than taillights, brighter than forgotten Christmas decorations.

## ☙ 57 ☙

A few blocks away, Jack looked out at the moon and wondered what he should do next. His shoulder was still wonky and his fever had only subsided fully this morning. The woman who was looking after him was busy feeding her children, about a dozen of them as close as Jack could reckon.

In exchange for money she had nursed him back to the beginning of health, and he was grateful for that start, and for her aversion to stealing. He was also old enough to know that it was going to be a while before he could do anything to help anyone. If even the youngest of the dozen kids in the room decided to attack him there'd be shag all he could do to defend himself. He was under no illusion about what would happen when it came to Timothy Shepherd and the general. He felt very old, his joints ached, his head was splitting and his shoulder burned. Even standing here watching the moon tired him out. He heard a siren making its way along the road towards a block of pink apartment buildings and felt exhausted. Turning back towards the bed he lay down as the children and woman smiled at him.  He tried to explain about how to help Red, but he was so tired that he couldn't remember the Spanish words for "my son" until a second before his head touched the pillow, and then when he tried to say them he was sound asleep.

## ☙ 58 ☙

In the morning, Red and Karen woke up at the edge of the jungle. They'd been wandering for two days and nights, clothes torn, their flesh covered in insect bites of varying sizes and colors. The day was already hot enough to bring steam off their clothing and to make them blink when they arrived at the edge of a clean wonderful-looking asphalt highway.

They whooped, they danced and they pounded each other on the back. In the middle of their last whirlaround they saw a car approaching, on its way towards Panama City. Both stuck out their thumbs and waited to be driven to civilization. The driver of the car took a good look at them. It seemed he didn't like what he saw because instead of stopping he sped up and skidded away down the road.

After shaking their muddy and bloodied fists after the car, Red and Karen looked at each other. He was still wearing the cowboy belt and holster hooked over his shoulder at such an angle that the toy gun sparkled in the sunlight. The rest of his clothes were in tatters and resembled rejects of

Emmett Kelly's wardrobe. Karen's hair was matted and twined with various leaves and dead insects, her face was swollen and smeared with mud and the juice of many vivid berries. She was still in the wedding dress. Its train had been totally ripped off and tied around her waist, the veil had been used to unsuccessfully patch a rent that exposed her belly, and there was altogether too much of her bosom on display to the world. They began to laugh with great wheezing whooping breaths until they fell to the dirt beside the highway.

That's how they missed the next potential ride. Red helped Karen to her feet as the wind from the transport swirled the heat in loops around them. She wiped her eyes and stared at the departing truck and then looked back at the jungle and up to the clean blue sky. She took a deep breath. Leaning over, she kissed the stubble along Red's cheek, putting her arm over his shoulder.

"This is a beautiful day, Red. You're beautiful, too."

"It's the toy gunbelt that turned your head."

He kissed her, then turned and began walking towards a faint smudge of gray on the horizon.

"You know where we're going, Red?"

"Panama City. We got nowhere else to go. If we walk real fast we can be there by this afternoon, if we take our time we'll get in at nightfall. The way we look, maybe that's the best time to arrive."

"No kidding? Anyway, I like walking slowly. We got a place to stay?"

"The best, nothing but the best for you, kid."

## 🌿 59 🌿

Not many people knew that the Blue Goose had a front door. The main entrance for the whores and their customers was in the back, off a dimly lit alley usually full of dope dealers and condom salesmen. Another group of vendors offered sure-fire cures for the dose. They did a brisk trade with departing clients and kept up a steady chatter with each other, a banter with arriving whores, and sometimes entered into knife fights with rival salesmen.

The building had deep blue board the shade of a popular ointment that was supposed to be the avenging killer of crabs. Two once-white pillars tilted to either side of the robin's-egg blue of the front door. This was lit by spotlights covered by azure gel that managed to give a murky surreal wash of light concealing more of the building than it revealed. Red held Karen's hand tightly as he knocked twice, paused and then twice again.

"Is this a hotel or have you got rich relatives?"

The door flew open and an immensely fat Hungarian woman, smelling of lilac and wearing an embroidered shawl and not much else, tidal-waved over Red. She spoke in Spanish with a strong accent on the first syllable, giving the language a peculiar sound like an organ-grinder gone insane. Taking a sidelong look at Karen she switched into the English language, more or less.

"But Red, my little boy, you have gotten so scrawny, are you sick? Have you not been eating? You are dirtier than usual. Where is your white suit? Who is this bride? Is she your wife or someone else's? She is not a whore? Would you like to be, my sweet little bride? She is dirtier than you are! Why are you outside, why are you at this door? Would you both like to share a woman?"

Red struggled free of the embrace and looked at Karen who seemed dazed by the questions.

"They call her Socrates."

"Do you want to know why? What is your name anyway? Why are you so thin?"

"I'm Karen. Do I smell food?"

"Ah, you are the right kind of woman. You smell food, good cooking..."

"Great cooking," said Red.

"Who am I to argue? Great cooking you said? From my apartment. When was your last meal?"

"About a year ago."

"Come inside, we'll eat and if you want to talk we'll talk."

They followed her down the hall, past the second shift of whores who were descending the staircase. Some wore clothes. A sailor was making his way up the stairs like a boat against the tide. From a nearby room they could hear the sound of a piano and a flute. The flute stopped and the piano continued playing "As Time Goes By." Then they were next to flocked wallpaper that showed silver flowers upon a red plush field.

"This ignorant man has not told you my name. I am Magda, known only to lowlife as Socrates."

She pushed on the nearest faded rose. The wall slid back revealing an apartment decorated red, white and green and smelling of paprika and simmering chicken.

Karen felt her mouth water and food was put on the table almost as fast as they could sit. The table was covered in a hand-embroidered red and white tablecloth filled to groaning with a molded chicken pâté that was covered in black olives. There were three different kinds of bread, some dark rye rolls filled with caraway seeds, and crackers of every description and taste. Before they had time to grab for the rolls there were steaming bowls of rich brown soup.

"*Bableves,*" said Magda.

"Bob's your uncle," said Red.

"*Finom,*" said Karen as she slurped the first boiling spoonful.

This launched a stream of Hungarian from Magda. Her Hungarian seemed to be also filled with questions. They lasted until Karen had finished the bowl of soup, which took about a minute and a half. Then she had to confess that she didn't speak much Hungarian, just a few words that Vilmos had taught her.

"Vilmos, who is this Vilmos?"

And Karen found that she was talking about her friend as she hadn't to anyone before, not even Red. The more she talked, the more she began to feel the hatred she felt towards anyone who had hurt Vilmos. She talked all the way through another three courses, until she settled back, soothed by some *palacsinta*. Magda, who had eaten and talked right along with her, now added two extra dollops of whipped cream with vanilla sugar to her espresso.

Then Red told his story, but he told it backwards. He began with himself and Karen coming out of the jungle on their way to the Blue Goose, and he took Magda back over the last weeks. When Red described the death of Azucar tears rolled down Magda's face. She got to her feet and walked towards the stove. There was an old painting that hung over it. It showed a soldier sitting outside a tavern in a small town where the roads were of dirt and shaded with the blondness of summer heat. A chicken had stopped in the middle of the road and seemed curious about the soldier. Its head was cocked to one side but the soldier didn't notice. He stared at a cloud. Magda watched the painting until she finished crying. Then she returned to the table.

"When she worked here Azucar was like a daughter to me, but she was always sad. She worried, she schemed, and sometimes she tried to cheat me. Like a daughter, right? But I knew why, she had a large family and she needed much money. She was pretty and she was popular. A lot of men thought they could cheer her up, but none ever did, they came back again and again and still they could not make her happy. Then one night you came in and after that she smiled, she laughed, she ate, she put on weight, which is a good thing, is it not, Karen? Then she went on her own, and made more money than she had friends. The last time I saw her she talked of retiring, of buying a house for you and of buying a house for her mother, she talked of future. She stayed here and asked if she could sleep in my spare room. I put her up for that night, the next morning she left and then she was dead, and then they said you might be dead, and I stared at my picture every night. She left me a legacy—some 'special' photos that she had hidden while she was here. I was to sell them and raise money, she did have a lot of brothers and even more sisters."

Karen listened to the sound of a cuckoo clock as it ticked its way towards the hour. She got up and looked at the painting.

"It reminds you of home?"

"Shit, no. I like the chicken."

Karen moved closer to her.

"Tell us about the photos."

Magda crossed to the painting and took it down.

"Azucar picked the most obvious hiding place."

Then she opened the back by lifting up a tear in the old brown paper. She extracted a sheaf of black-and-white photos, the sort that poor seamen might sell to the lecherous of cold climates. Magda shuffled them and then dealt them onto the table in front of Red and Karen. When the photos were laid out the light was harsh as it angled off their shiny surfaces. At the center of each shot was Azucar. She was naked, always with a man. With Timothy Shepherd the shots were more perverse and involved other men, and much younger girls.

Red stood up and walked away. Until this moment what Azucar did was always something that he'd hidden away. They talked about it, they treated it like she was going away to work in a restaurant, but now, caught in a photo, harsh in black-and-white, it was like the real Azucar had gone forever. The image of the photographs was like the shell of a cocoon left after a rainstorm.

Karen looked back and forth from the photos to Red. She knew what he was feeling and at the same time could not take her eyes off them. The image of Azucar was strangely innocent. She looked at the face and could see an expression of someone who had left the photos long before she died. Karen also knew why Timothy would kill to keep these photos from being shown to anyone else in the world.

She crossed over to Red and stroked his shoulders.

"There's nothing of your Azucar in these pictures. Look at her eyes, she was somewhere else. Look!"

And she made Red come back and see the photographs. This time she pointed to the snapshots, to Azucar's face, and he saw.

Magda nodded.

"Azucar told me, if something happened to her, to use the shots to raise money for her family, so the first photos I sent out went to a Mr Timothy Shepherd. I gave him only a box number. There is no money yet."

Karen looked at Red before she spoke again.

"This time I have a plan."

And she leaned back in her wedding gown and began to talk about Timothy Shepherd. As she talked she realized just how much she had guessed. Anything that she hadn't, Red or Magda was able to fill in, and the more she talked, the more Red began to nod in agreement with her plan. The key to catching Timothy Shepherd lay with what was in the photos. Red began adding details. They were so right that Magda didn't ask a single question.

She waited until Karen stopped talking, then looked at Red.

"We're going to get the son of a bitch, aren't we?"

He nodded.

## ❧ 60 ❧

The Panamanian newspaper was stacked under all the important American magazines, journals and dailies. That meant a half-hour's delay before Timothy saw the item which he knew, unless he acted quickly, was going to make its way into other newspapers all around the world. It had been put on page three by an editor who didn't appreciate the full value of the story, but for Timothy it was important enough to get the general on the blower and see what could be done about seizing as many papers as possible. He began to learn a little more about Santos's diminishing influence as this day went on. There was no way of stopping the story, short of buying every newspaper in town, so that's what Timothy resorted to.

He peeled off hundred-dollar bills and sent out every available stooge to buy copies of the *Panamanian Standard*. There was a sudden upsurge in the newspaper vendors' business everywhere in the city.

The item in the paper was enough to show that Timothy Shepherd was in Panama City and not his home base in Boston, Massachusetts. It was also

enough of a story to put him at the scene of a murder and link him with the general. That was
enough to make Timothy sweat and feel his tension rise as he paced back and forth. Just when he
was able to relax about the blackmail pictures. He
smiled as he remembered the way Juan stared at
him in the darkroom. He sniffed and remembered the smoke of the burning photos and the
price Juan had to pay for taking them. His death
had given Timothy much pleasure.

The wind began to blow softly and as the sun
gained strength, so did the breeze. It blew stronger
and stronger until dust and scraps of paper began to
blow across the courtyard.

Then the newspapers started showing up. The
general's men had managed to buy up what
seemed to be every paper within twenty miles of
Panama City, and instead of dumping them somewhere else they returned to the villa with them.
Timothy had just finished taking his third shower
of the afternoon when he became aware of the
sounds of vans in the courtyard. The last shower
had taken almost an hour and now he felt clean.
As he dried his hair he heard trucks rumble to the
front of the villa, but he didn't think all that much
of it until he walked by his bedroom window. At
first he thought it had snowed and the general's
men were in a panic because of the blizzard.

He began to sweat again, despite the open windows, and decided there couldn't be snow on the
ground. Then he saw sections fold up and blow
around the yard. The general's men chased the
sections. That's when Timothy realized that he
was looking at newspapers in flight. He ran down
into the yard where the papers flew at him,

spinning, clinging and wrapping his body while his bathrobe blew open, sailing behind him like a cape.

Outside the gate a jeep skidded to a stop. A young woman, a whore from the Blue Goose, was thrown from it and landed on the edge of the road. A couple of sailors dressed in their whites laughed and drove away slugging back some whisky. The young woman looked as if she had been beaten. She stood up and the same wind that had sailed Timothy across the yard blew open the gate. The newspapers that had wound around the wrought-iron pickets now peeled their way from them and blew across the road to float by the woman. She turned and her skirt blew up as she walked slowly away from the house. She paused and stood there licking her lips. There seemed to be blood on her cheek. Timothy was tempted to follow her, but instead he forced his way back to the house.

Once inside he tried not to look towards the woman. The phone began to ring. He didn't answer it, waiting for someone else to do so, but they were all running around the yard grabbing at the newspapers. Timothy stood with his back to the window. The phone rang and rang as the room began to go dark.

# ⚜ 61 ⚜

In the slums of Panama there was much talk about newspapers. Jack was in bed when the third youngest of the sons came home very excited and shaking a fistful of balboas. They rattled and clinked while he turned away from the sound. Since his brief visit with death he'd found that his hearing had become as sharp as a chisel and no matter how he folded the thin blanket around his head, he could not shut out the small boy's voice. He tried to force his way into sleep even though it was giving him a headache. Still, through the blanket, he heard about the soldiers buying up twenty papers.

The small boy then went to get another twenty and some of the secret police bought them. After that he sold another fifty papers to a gloomy looking man wearing a trench coat. Jack now began to stop seeking sleep. He listened and began to think. Then he asked Paulo if he had a copy of the paper. The small boy held up his souvenir and Jack tottered from the bed to read it. Sitting at the rickety table he turned to the reprint of the photograph of the general standing outside the scene of the killings. In the background he saw Timothy Shepherd. Then he read the story. When he finished he knew that this item was not going to stay in a local Panama newspaper. It also meant that Timothy was likely to try and leave Panama City.

Jack felt he had only one choice, and very little time in which to make that choice happen. On a shelf near the table his trousers had been neatly folded. His wallet was next to it, and beside it his money, also neatly folded. He reached up and retrieved the trousers, dressing quickly and with modesty in front of the family. Then he took most of the money and passed it over to the mother. From the counter near the window he took a carving knife and then picked up the worn whetstone beside it. While he reshaped the blade and added razor sharpness to it, all the children gathered near. The oldest daughter reached out to touch the blade and started back when it cut a red line along her finger. Jack sang to help distract her. Soon all the children were around him as he whistled and sang in a rhythm the same as the whetstone on the blade. The song was oddly attractive, part in Spanish, part in English. "If he brings you happiness..."

The children laughed and tried to join in.

> Then I wish you both the best,
> It's your happiness that matters most of all.
> But if he ever breaks your heart,
> If the teardrops ever start,
> I'll be there before the next teardrop falls.

Then he sang in Spanish and all the children joined in. Jack paused once or twice to heft the knife while he continued singing. He threw it towards the door and it slipped through the wood right up to the shaft. The children smiled and rushed to see who could pull the knife out. It was now so sharp that it came out of the door like it had been greased. The children danced around with the blade glinting in the fading light. Jack took it back and kissed them all like a matador saying goodbye.

They all stood by the window until they saw him cross the street.

He was moving slowly, looking like a dry leaf in a hot wind.

They blew him kisses but he didn't return them.

# 62

Timothy began to notice the housemaid while she was helping to serve supper. The general had not come home to eat, which simply meant they had a better meal at the whorehouse. Most of the flunkies were out looking for any newspapers that they might have missed during their earlier search. The night was cool, especially for Panama City, and some of the more industrious of the general's men were busy taking newspapers away from the homeless who were using them as blankets.

The huge, blue dining room was empty except for Timothy and those serving the meal. There was also a bodyguard but he didn't pay attention to anything. His gun hung limp along his side.

Timothy was feeling better. He felt like singing and shouting, he was so happy to think that he'd finished Juan and the blackmail photographs. As well, most of the newspapers had been retrieved and none of the wire services had picked up the story yet. Perhaps they never would and if they did, so what. The more he thought of it the more he became convinced that, because he had killed

Juan, there was nothing else hidden away to trap him. All the other indiscretions in his life were covered up. Now, so was this one. That didn't mean he should live up to all the vows he'd taken while under pressure. It meant he could begin to take chances again.

The cook hovered because Timothy's request for a local meal had met with her disapproval. She preferred cooking *nouvelle cuisine*, could bring the delights of Thailand to the table, manage any recipe from any cookbook or sniff a dish and come within a Madame Curie of guessing the exact ingredients. However, she felt insecure cooking the way she had been brought up.

Despite her misgivings Timothy was tucking into the meal with tremendous gusto. The "old hen" soup went in great slurps that threatened to spill over his three-piece tropical suit. He took more time with the pork on coconut rice, twirling the shredded meat on his fork and dipping up rice on top of it. Instead of wine he was drinking Coca-Cola. Not the "new" brand, not the "classic" stuff, but the real flavor that had been been captured from the fifties and held in Panama since then. A taste that made Timothy remember back to when he was a little boy, sharing a bottle of Coke with his father. It would usually be too warm and the tractor would shake the bottle until the foam ran out over the top and down the sides to make his hands feel sticky for the rest of the day. Now, of course, it was chilled and served in an iced glass with a twist of lemon hooked, Italian-style, over the lip of the tumbler. He pushed away the glass and asked to have his Coca-Cola in the bottle.

That's when he noticed the maid for the first time. She'd been standing to the right of the sideboard, out of Timothy's line of sight. Once in a while he'd heard the sounds of subdued clinking of dishes when she placed them in a cloth-lined container. It was only when he asked for the bottle of Coke that he became aware of this young woman. Before anyone else had a chance to move she rushed towards the kitchen to get the bottle. Timothy heard her high heels click as she crossed the room. Her back was outlined by a too-tight uniform and her legs detailed in tight muscles that ran tapering to bright-red, high-heeled shoes.

He stopped eating and leaned back in his chair, taking the time to compliment the cook so that she felt secure enough to lumber off to her defiled kitchen. There was nearly a collision as she approached the swinging door just as the young woman came smashing her way back into the dining room. The cook "tsked" her way out of the room while the young woman swayed towards the table. She placed the bottle of Coke in front of Timothy, keeping her hand around its base as he reached for it. For a moment their hands touched, fingers laced around the ice-cold, green-tinted swell of the glass. The moisture of condensation made his hand slip a little, pressing their fingers closer together.

She stood back and Timothy noticed that the top button of her uniform was undone, and when she leaned over just before she returned to her position next to the sideboard he could see down the front of her green smock. Her nipples were dark and raised in gentle, brown bulges at the edge of the dress. Timothy felt such desire that he reached up and touched her breast. The guard didn't notice and the young woman let his hand remain for a moment. She reached down and pressed her nails into the back of his hand. She pressed so hard that they cut into the flesh in tiny crescents of blood. Then she stood back.

"My name is Juanita. Tonight I am going dancing. Dancing at Dorado's. It is dark and hot and wet."

And she turned. He called out but she didn't pay any attention even when he swore. He followed her towards the kitchen but when he got there she had gone. He caught the cook smoking a cigarette. She startled to her feet in a great thud. Timothy praised her cooking again and then casually asked about the young woman who had been helping out. The cook said only that Juanita had left early for the night.

When Timothy crossed the living room on his way upstairs, he saw that some of the men had returned. They looked exhausted and the light from the courtyard splashed in through the window onto their faces. All the papers that they had gathered were being fed into a growing bonfire that danced in the restless wind that remained from the day. The bonfire spread orange and black colors across the yard and into the living room.

The men who had come back into the house were watching the VCR while the fire flickered its reflection on the screen, glinting across the image of two women who were kissing each other. The men cheered as one woman's hand moved down the other woman's belly. Timothy walked away from the television set and up the stairs but in his mind he mixed up memories of the small-screen pornography, of the housemaid and of the woman who had looked at him through the afternoon gate.

In his room he paced back and forth, not bothering to close the drapes. He tried to drive away the night thoughts but couldn't, so he turned on more and more lights as he paced and thought about a place called "Dorado's," a place that would be dark and hot and wet.

The courtyard fire had burned through all the papers and only a filigreed pattern of charred paper glowed against the night. Timothy stripped and walked back and forth, back and forth. The idea that someone might be watching, even though he'd checked to make sure no one really was, made him more and more excited. He knew he was going to have to leave the house. To see a woman who, like him, could not stay out of the dark.

## ✻ 63 ✻

Jack was starting to feel a little better. When he'd arrived at the general's villa he paused just to catch his breath. That moment had stretched into an hour before he felt well enough to attack, then another ten minutes had passed while he ran through a checklist of what would happen if he decided to try and reach Timothy directly. Some of the other mercenaries used to laugh at the way Jack would try and plan for everything that could go wrong. A lot of the guys who laughed were dead now, and, even though he might be in piss-poor shape, Jack was still alive. He had the feeling that, much as he'd like to get all this over with, a frontal assault would end up with only one person being dead, and that person might not be Timothy.

So he decided to wait, enjoying the old feeling of power that came with being a hidden observer. He watched the truckloads of newspapers arrive, watched them spin away, watched still more arrive and enjoyed the spectacle of the bonfire. It brought back memories of watching the Protestant boys setting off their bonfires on Guy Fawkes night and memories of how he would join in, rushing around with a fiery torch and laughing a triumphant ecumenical laugh into the childhood night. Jack felt like laughing again as he watched Timothy peering out into the night after the bonfire died down. The blaze of light outlined the good Shepherd peeling off his clothing so he could stride around the room naked and erect. This went on for minutes until suddenly Timothy began to dress himself again, all of a rush and in clumsy moves that lurched him against the window sash as if he'd been drinking. Jack could see him look into the mirror and groom his hair, brushing it again and again as if he was counting the number of strokes. Then the light snapped off.

He glanced down towards the window that showed the staircase, where he assumed Timothy would descend to the front entrance. He waited but there was no sign of him on the stairs. Just when he was getting ready to go closer to the house, he heard a small scuffling sound rush from the outside of the villa. Then there was stillness.

Finally he saw a shadow against shadows, a move in the darkness that told him Timothy was trying to leave without anyone in the house knowing that he was going.

Jack took a chance. He scooted along the low-cut wall that surrounded the general's home, then over to a DeSoto that had been parked just up from the gate. He made a few adjustments to the trunk lock with his knife, and when he heard the lock spring open, he jumped into the trunk, pulling the lid down after him. He tugged a little too much and then realized that he had accidentally locked himself inside. All he could do then was listen

and try to breathe quietly. He also began to sweat
profusely. He didn't think he was wrong about
what Timothy's next move was going to be. Footsteps came round the trunk and stopped by the car
door.

Timothy tried the driver's side and found it
locked. Then he crossed over and tried the passen-
ger's door before he struck it lucky. There was
another silence of some minutes until the V8
throated out at the night and Jack was rolled over
and bounced within the trunk when the DeSoto
squealed its way towards the softbelly nighttime
Panama City.

# 64

Juanita didn't know how she could stand the wait for Timothy.

The moment when he had reached for her breast and she had to stay there pretending to like it had seemed an eternity—but this wait in the club was years longer. Back in the dining room she had tried to keep from thinking of her sister. Azucar must be avenged and if she remembered her even for a second, the look on her own face would scare Timothy away. Red and Magda and the American woman, Karen, had all told her that she must pretend to be attracted to this man. They had also told her to use blood, to use pain, and to slowly bring him where they all wanted him. The last part was easy to remember. She looked around the club.

A Venezuelan hooker was dancing the cha-cha with a Canadian businessman while his friends loosened their ties and winked at each other. The music, which came from a tape recorder older than the hooker, played a watery version of "Strangers in the Night." Totally ignoring the rhythm of the music, the businessman (Roy to his

friends) managed to smash into a nearby table
filled with empty cocktail glasses which clattered
and shivered to the floor while his friends had
themselves a chuckle.

From the back of the room Timothy was watching. He sat in a dark corner and swirled the tepid
remains of a tequila sunrise. A tiny umbrella floated upside down in the liquid. He kept staring towards the bar, looking past the clutter and glass
that had spilled across the floor and watching Juanita. In this light she looked about fifteen, wearing
a low-cut black dress that opened down the front
until it met at her navel. Timothy didn't look away
when she saw him and started. It was obvious she
hadn't seen him slip in and he liked that, he liked
to startle. He stroked the glass as he thought of other ways he might surprise her later.

Juanita left the bar and moved towards him. She
was wearing bright-red lipstick done in a slash
over her lips, making them pout like teardrops.
When she arrived in the center of the dance floor
she stood right in the middle of the saltshake of
broken glass on the dance floor.

Timothy stood up. He was still in his three-piece
suit, but when he moved towards Juanita he caught
the beat of the new tape that had replaced Frank
Sinatra. This music was hot and Latin, steamy
jungle. He pressed close and breathed in Juanita's
perfume. She leaned back for a moment increas-
ing the pressure on his groin just before she
danced away from him.

"How did you get in here?" she shouted over the
music. He just grinned back at her, until she spoke
again.

"I like your eyes."

She kicked off her shoes. Her feet were bare and, as she danced closer and closer to the glass, they looked pale, missing the shards, at first by inches and then by millimeters, until some of the smaller fragments began to nick at the edges of her heels whenever she spun around.

Timothy slipped off his shoes, leaving on his socks and dancing right through the middle of the glass. When he moved back so did Juanita, leaving a trail of bloody footprints behind them on their way to the bar. For a moment they pressed together again and then the music stopped.

They picked up their shoes and walked out into the night. When the music started up again, no one else danced.

The DeSoto moved slowly away from the curb. It was dark, long and loud as it butted its way through the nighttime traffic. The sound from the damaged muffler rolled into the trunk bouncing around with Jack who was busy ricocheting off the spare tire. Finally the car settled down as it reached the main highway. The sounds of cars passing became fewer, and the noisy bellows from huge transports stopped altogether. There were three distinct bumps before the car came to a stop.

Jack leaned towards the airhole that he'd drilled through the edge of the trunk with his knife while Timothy was out getting lucky. He could hear more sound from outside in between the squeaking springs and shocks of the car. Just as it was really beginning to get on his nerves, the squeaking stopped and he heard a door open and then slam shut again as the car lifted while the young woman and Timothy got out. Jack decided to wait a minute for safety before he used the tire iron to break out.

The noise was amazing and he wondered if he should have taken some more time and quietly picked the lock, but when he did open the trunk and peer around, no one was looking back at him.

When he stepped outside his legs bucked and he fell to the ground. Frantically he worked to massage his legs back to life. While he did, he stared around him, trying to see where Timothy had gone and what had happened to the woman with him.

He was in the old part of Panama, where Morgan had his fort, and where the ocean salted the air. The sky was clear, making the moon strain through the ruins to powder the ground. Suddenly he heard Juanita scream.

## 65

Moonlight had stripped the wall where Juanita was tied. She bled starkly from the first cuts that Timothy had inflicted, but she had obviously kicked out in rage or fear, because he was lying on the ground clutching his groin. He was coughing and retching, and in the middle of his agony managed to pull out a revolver. At first he could hardly raise the barrel, but as his strength returned the gun shifted and leveled towards Juanita. By now Karen, Red and Magda—all her friends— should be here, but they weren't. She decided this was simply the way of the world so she crossed herself and closed her eyes. That meant she only heard the shot and felt the bullet whiz by to ping and dust away from the old stone wall.

Juanita opened her eyes and saw that Timothy was now on his feet, but trying to shake something from his hand. It glinted in the moonlight, catching the flare in between the trickle of blood that ran down the knife that was pinning the gun, locked into the grip of his pierced fingers. With his other hand he reached over and pulled out the knife, letting the firearm fall to the ground.

Jack stepped from behind a crumbled arch into
the moonlight while Timothy scrabbled after the
gun. Just as Jack was about to make a swift move
and finish off Timothy, he was amazed to see Red
appear from behind the other end of the wall. Red
motioned him away from Timothy's line of sight
and slid back himself.

As he did, dozens of whores moved into the center of Morgantown, led by Magda who stepped,
with her long black boots, firmly on the gun. She
let her pointed heel go through the trigger guard
and then kicked it away. Timothy, blood now
leaking down his fingers, held his hand up to
shield his eyes from the moon while he stared at
the circle of women shifting closer and closer to
him. Many of the women had cameras: Polaroids,
Instamatics, every kind of camera that he'd ever
seen, and, as they all began to blaze flashbulbs at
him, he raised his hand higher and higher while
trying to back towards a dark corner. But when he
retreated there was a wall of naked legs to make
him stop.

His hand bled over his shirt front and as he entwined his fingers to plead for mercy the blood
welled and dripped. Juanita watched him plead
and thought of Azucar. She screamed at him. The
camera flashes continued again and again until
they strobed in great pulses against his closed eyelids, red and dark, red and dark. He opened his
eyes, and when he did he saw all around him the
women holding photographs of Azucar.

There were small snaps, and some enormous
blownup photos where the grain swam like stars
when the moon is new. Juanita held a huge photo
that showed a group of whores. In the photo she

had her arm around her sister. Timothy turned his head to one side. Everywhere he looked he could see flashing lights and the naked body of Azucar. He was naked in all the shots, sometimes with Azucar alone, other times joined by another woman and sometimes another man, sometimes with a young girl, and all now blown up and caught by moonlight.

He sprang to his feet and ripped at the nearest enlarged photo, tearing it so the white edge of the paper looked like flesh. But even as he tore it, the whores tore at him, ripping away his jacket, his white, bloodstained shirt, his trousers and underwear until, naked and bleeding, he was spun around in the moonlight.

Then he slithered back as he saw Karen and Red. She was shouting questions at him, and Red stepped in to hit him so cleanly and clearly that he bounced back against the wall of legs.

The questions never stopped.

"When did you get the pictures?"

"When did you find Azucar?"

"Why did you kill?"

"Who knows your secrets?"

"Who knows your thoughts?"

"Who knows your secrets?"

"Who knows your thoughts?"

He closed his ears, he tried to keep out the words, the questions about him and some whore, of words about love from Red for the whore, and he pushed at the wall of women and it would not give. Then suddenly they moved back and there was a tunnel of darkness leading to the shadows spider-webbed into a corner and he spun his way there soft and folded, until the lights all swung his way. He looked up and every voice stopped except two, before he felt a sponge on his face making him so thirsty that he sucked water from it, and there was more water, and people stroked his head, and some soothing balm was poured over his itching, cut fingers, then there was red wine and he drank deeply while the questions continued, but they were loving queries that only wanted to know why he hurt and why he did the things he did, so he found that he was talking about his father, and about death and pain, of how he liked to give pain, and even more receive it, and how he had to pretend but now he didn't, and finally how he had liked killing the whore because she had photos that showed him the way he had to pretend he wasn't, and how much better it felt to take life instead of giving it, and how he was proud and not ashamed, and then he saw that the cameras had stopped flashing, while only one steady light remained on, like a sun above an eye and then he saw the video camera, and saw Red and Karen along with Magda standing around the back of the camera, their faces bathed in the blue-gray light.

He remembered who he was and what he had to hide. And realized that he had been video-taped by them. And that he would not look beaten, but cleaned and refreshed because the tape was made after they'd cleaned him up. That was after the other photos had been made. More photos that no one should ever see. And he lunged towards the camera, but was grabbed. He struggled and struggled but the grip of the old man who was holding him increased beyond the pain that he sought, and he fell back to the ground. Karen took out the video cassette from the machine and the whores turned the photos over to her, while Red and Jack hugged each other.

Timothy retreated into the corner where the stone was rough against his back. The corner was quiet. He looked at the whores and then up to the moon. It seemed that there was only himself and the moon. He let it hold and rock him.

## 66

The jungle sounds were at top volume and lizards wept in the shadows. Homeless insects buzzed back and forth and vampire bats slowed as morning neared. One light shone into the thicket and settled near the charred remains of Jack's hut. As the lantern rested on the stump of the tree that had blown up a few days earlier, dawn creaked into the sky.

While more and more light seeped into the clearing, Karen, Red and Jack looked towards the ruins of the hut. Jack spent an hour or so sifting through the melted hulks of records and pulling out the metal discs of earlier recordings and a couple of cylinders from the late eighteen hundreds. He started to stack them against the remains of the doorposts until he saw that there would be no saving his cherished music.

He stopped when he came to the blackened shell of the trunk. Some of the picture frames had survived in a twisted and rainbowed sheen of dark metal, but no photo had been left intact. Jack crouched in the middle of the ashes and began crying. Red sat beside him.

"Maybe we can talk them back."

"How the hell can you talk a picture back?"

"Easy, I start off telling about the day you bandaged my hand when I was a little boy, or about the time the wedding photos were taken or about the first car—the Pontiac, the blue one. Then you tell me the things you remember about it."

"How do you know about that? You broke into my goddamn trunk? No wonder the place burned down! Did it explode?"

"Not till I needed it to."

Karen came close.

"I got the wedding dress, it's back with Magda at the whorehouse."

Jack got up and walked away from the hut to stand with his back towards them. This meant Red knew that he was his father. And yet he was still talking to him. He felt like weeping again, but this time with relief. Fragments of the door were charred to the burned hinges against one tilted doorpost. Red reached over and closed it. He walked towards Jack who started off on his own into the jungle. Red and Karen followed in his steps. A parrot squawked at them and other birds joined in, flying in great colored pinwheels around the trio. Insects winged in bluebottle-green patterns down the path, while butterflies floated bread-and-buttered against the sunlight.

While they walked, Karen talked to Jack about the ocean and Gloucester, of Em and the summer in her paintings, of spring coming to New England, while Red sang the praises of whorehouse pianos, and how they could make a special trip to Boston, buy one and bring it back to play beside the ocean.

They reached the slippery log that would take them across the stream towards Panama City, towards the world's newspapers ending the career of Timothy Shepherd, towards Gloucester where they could find out more about being the same family.

Jack paused, about to stare back at the place that had been home in the clearing, but he didn't. Instead he took quick and sure strides across the moss-covered log. Red and Karen did so with more care. After they had crossed over, Jack turned back and pushed. The heavy wood slipped off the bank and into the muddy stream. It dipped, sank and then slid back to the surface, bobbing towards the waterfall. A scarlet macaw landed and began pluming its feathers in the droplets that dipped over the moss.

He waited until Karen and Red were beside him and then strode into what seemed to be a solid wall of jungle. The leaves parted and flicked across their faces as they moved towards the city, then closed again. For a moment the foliage shook and there was the sound of birds calling to each other. Then the leaves stopped trembling, the sun grew hotter. Light played across the stream and the macaw, making one quick cry, flew to a nearby tree.

The jungle echoed and then grew quiet.